MY BEST FRIEND'S BROTHER

A FRIENDS TO LOVERS ROMANCE

Hazel Kelly is the author of several romance novels. She was born in the United States and lives in Ireland.

D1736344

MY BEST FRIEND'S BROTHER

A FRIENDS TO LOVERS ROMANCE

Hazel Kelly

First published 2016.

ISBN-13: 978-1539536239

Printed and bound by CreateSpace.

Cover Artwork – © 2016 L.J. Anderson of Mayhem Cover Creations

MY BEST FRIEND'S BROTHER

A FRIENDS TO LOVERS ROMANCE

Hazel Kelly

First published 2016.

ISBN-13: 978-1539536239

Printed and bound by CreateSpace.

Cover Artwork – © 2016 L.J. Anderson of Mayhem Cover Creations

"The greatest thing you'll ever learn is just to love and be loved in return."

- Eden Ahbez

Prologue

We used to call ourselves The Three Musketeers.

I know it's cliché, but we were only kids.

They usually took turns being in charge, which was fine with me. I was just happy to go along with them.

After all, I thought I was the luckiest little girl in the whole world. Most of my classmates only had one best friend, but I had two: my best friend Izzy and her twin brother.

Back then, I hoped things would never change, but that's the problem with more. Once I saw a glimpse of it, it was impossible to stop wanting it.

Especially when it came to Shane.

ONE

- Andi -

I didn't know where else to go.

All I knew was that I had to find someone I could trust, and unfortunately, that's not always as easy as it should be on a college campus.

I could taste the blood on my split lip as I raised my hand to knock on the massive front door. But before my knuckles made contact, some random frat guy threw it open.

If there had been a single drop of adrenaline left in my system, I probably would've jumped, but I spent it all just trying to make it to that side of campus. It was a strange sensation, though, being so sober and wasted at the same time.

The frat guy barely glanced at me- just enough to walk around me- but he left the door wide open I stepped into the doorway and took in the room.

There was a younger guy doing homework on a couch by the back windows. And near the enormous fireplace on the wall to my right, under a huge plaque covered in Greek letters, there was a group of guys playing poker.

One by one they turned to look at me. The last one to glance over his shoulder was Shane.

"Andi." He stood up so fast his wooden chair shot out behind him. "Are you okay?"

As he crossed the sticky floor towards me, I felt some hidden reserves of energy well up in my throat.

"Do you need to sit down or something?" His green eyes searched mine as he set his hands on my shoulders.

I wanted to speak, but I hadn't even considered what I might say, and when all the words I could think of started fighting to be the first out, I burst like a damn.

The tears spilled down my cheeks in uncontrollable surges. Apparently, I did have some feeling left after all.

"Come on," he said, his face full of concern as he linked his arm in mine.

It was only the second time I'd ever seen him make that face.

The first time was in high school when we were in the hospital waiting room after Izzy's car accident.

I remember thinking then that I never wanted to see him make that face again. And now here I was being the cause of it. I tried to stop crying, reminding myself that Izzy had been fine in the end.

If anything, she became even bolder after having her immortality validated. And I would be fine, too. Eventually.

I might even be able to go back there again, to that stairwell where...

"You can't just walk away from the game, Shane," his friend called. "You have to give us a chance to win our money back."

Shane fixed his eyes on me. "Give me one second."

I took a deep breath and rolled my eyes up to see if I could absorb the next round of tears.

He turned around and shouted at the boy hunched over his textbook on the couch. "Pete!"

The kid lifted his eyes towards Shane.

"What are you doing right now?"

"Tyler's chem homework."

"Not anymore," Shane said. "Take my spot at the table."

He glanced back at the workbook in front of him. "But Tyler-"

"Needs to do his own homework," Shane said. "And you can tell him I said so."

Two of the boys at the table groaned. The other looked confident that he'd soon have his money back.

"I'm sorry to barge in on you like this," I said so only Shane could hear.

"Don't be," he said, turning back to me. "You're my knight in shining armor."

My bottom lip started to shake.

His eyes dropped to my mouth. "You're bleeding," he said, tilting my chin up gently so he could take a closer look.

I let my gaze fall to the side. Perhaps I shouldn't have come to him. What if he just said I told you so and made me feel more foolish than I already did?

"What happened?" he asked, leading me up the stairs.

"Mike and I-"

His face dropped.

"-got in a fight."

The muscles in Shane's jaw clenched like a zipper.

"It was just a misunderstanding. It was my fault."

He pushed his bedroom door open.

I stepped inside and took a deep breath. When I turned around, he wrapped his big arms around me, and I buried my head in his chest.

"Are you hurt?" he asked.

I could smell the scent of Zest soap off him as I shook my head. "No. I just got scared."

He leaned back and lowered his head to meet my gaze. "You know that isn't okay, right?"

I nodded.

"And that you have to tell me what happened because seeing that look on your face when you walked in-" He grabbed the back of his head and exhaled.

For a moment I felt like he was judging me, like he was remembering the disappointment he'd expressed when I first told him Mike and I were dating.

He told me I deserved better and that Mike was a worthless piece of shit who wasn't good enough to carry my books, much less hold my hand.

But I let him do a lot more than hold my books anyway. And now I was in deep shit, scared to death of the only person I'd spent any time with in the last six months, with a sore jaw, a busted lip, and a broken heart.

And despite everything, what hurt the most was that I'd disappointed and inconvenienced my best and oldest friend in the whole world.

The black futon in the corner looked broken in at least two places so I leaned against the edge of the bed.

Shane sat beside me. "What exactly happened, Andi?"

"It was a misunderstanding, like I said. Mike saw a picture of me and-"

"Why do you feel compelled to defend this guy when he's clearly scared the shit out of you? I swear to god if you don't tell me why you keep rubbing your jaw, I'm going to take my best guess and leave you out of finding a solution to this problem."

I swallowed.

I could tell he was serious because I recognized his tone of voice. It was one I'd heard him use with Izzy dozens of times, but never with me.

"He saw a picture of me kissing another guy on the cheek at a birthday party and flipped."

"When you say flipped…?"

The scene flashed back in my mind, and while I wasn't reliving the pain of the event, each emotion passed through me again...

The shock of him pushing me against the stairwell's concrete wall.

The fear in my bones as I tried to get away so he'd stop shouting in my face.

The anger that surged through me when I tripped and busted my lip on the handrail.

And the vulnerability I felt when he squeezed my jaw in his hands so hard I thought he was going to break my face.

T W O

- Shane -

My mouth had never been so dry.

And by the time Andi finished telling me what happened, I was so distracted by how red and blurry my vision had gone that I could barely focus on the words tumbling out of her mouth.

Still, my eyes fell on each part of her body as she mentioned them, and as she told me that Mike had squeezed her small, delicate jaw in his hand so hard she feared it would break, I felt a dark knot of anger harden in my guts.

I recognized the dark feeling, too. I'd had it once before. In high school. When Izzy got in that car accident.

If I'd waited for her after her lacrosse game, it never would've happened. I would've gotten her home safely like I did every other day.

Instead, she told me to go ahead because her team was going out for milkshakes… or something else so stupid you'd never think twice about risking your life over it, if you only knew the future.

Fortunately, she got away with a few bruises and a broken collarbone. Her co-captain, the driver, bled out before she reached the hospital.

For me, the gnawing feeling finally went away when I saw Izzy's face and realized she was going to be okay. But I didn't know if Andi was going to be okay yet.

She kept saying she was fine, but she also kept slipping in these pathetic little excuses, as if she were more interested in defending Mike than anything.

And that worried me because it meant the Andi I knew and loved wasn't just broken up on the outside.

And once again, I had the strange and irrational feeling that it was all my fault.

After all, when she started dating that prick, I pulled away. Frankly, I couldn't stand anything about him, and the thought of him putting his hands on her- even romantically- was more than my mind could tolerate.

They actually came to the same bar where I was drinking with my friends once, and I felt so torn. It had been months since I'd seen her smile or heard the sound of her voice, her laugh.

But I went home minutes after I noticed them.

Because I knew that if I spent even ten minutes watching him buy her drinks, touch her lower back, and bury his face in her hair to whisper in her ear, I was going lose it- and maybe her forever as a result.

But obviously I'd abandoned her when she needed me most. And now the strong, confident woman I used to know was scared and hurt and hugging herself at the end of my bed.

"Say something, Shane."

I went to my mini fridge and pulled out a can of Coke. Then I popped the tab, took the first sip, and handed it to her.

She refused it.

"This isn't your fault," I said, fixing my eyes on her big brown ones.

"Thanks."

"I mean it, Andi. Could you even hear yourself when you were talking just now? The guy's abusive, and you're defending him."

"He's not abusi-"

"Just don't. You think that was a fit of passion?"

She pursed her lips and flinched when the dried crack in them stretched.

"Any man who uses his physical strength to hurt or intimidate a woman isn't a man at all."

She scooted back on the bed and crisscrossed her legs.

"You know that, don't you?" I asked. "Even if he's been brain washing you-"

A sharp flash shone in her eyes. "I'm not brainwashed, Shane. Fuck you for saying that."

I was almost relieved to see her express something apart from sadness and exhaustion.

"Sorry. I didn't mean to upset you."

She shrugged. "He just got jealous. A little jealousy is normal, isn't it?"

I dropped my head for a second while I considered how to answer her. "Not if you act on it. Not if you use it as an excuse to hurt someone or take something from someone else."

She swallowed.

"The way he robbed you of feeling safe with him."

She sighed. "I know you're right. I'm just trying to get my head around what happened after being so shaken up."

"It's okay. Take all the time you need. You're safe here."

She nodded.

I rubbed my forehead.

"What?" she asked.

I dropped my hand and looked at her, fearing I'd never be able to let her out of my sight again unless she did as I asked. "Promise me you'll never see him again."

"He'll want to talk this through. I have stuff at his apartment-"

"Promise me, Andi. I'm not fucking around."

She furrowed her brow and shook her head.

"Then why did you even come here?"

"I didn't know where else to go."

"No." I sat back on the bed beside her. "You came here because you know you can trust me, because I want the best for you. And this guy is the worst."

Tears began to pool in her eyes again.

"And if he's capable of doing something like this once, he's capable of doing it again, and next time you might not be so lucky."

She nodded and made a face like I was actually getting through.

"Think about it. If he would do this because he saw a picture of you kissing a friend on the cheek, how would he react if he knew you were sitting on my bed right now?"

A scene played behind her eyes that only she could see.

"Promise me."

She squinted. "What about my stuff?"

"I'll get your stuff," I said without thinking.

Her breath stuttered. "Okay."

"Promise."

"I won't try and see him again."

"There is no try."

She rolled her eyes.

I didn't crack a smile.

"I know you're right, okay?" she said. "I'm just a bit too flustered to be making promises of any kind right now."

"Make this one," I said. "For me."

She cocked her head.

"And I'll do everything I can to keep you safe and help you forget this ever happened."

One corner of her mouth curled up. "That sounds pretty good right now."

I leaned forward and kissed her hairline, holding the back of her head to keep my lips there.

"Thanks," she said, squeezing my leg.

"You'd do it for me."

She laughed.

"What so funny?"

"The thought of some girl throwing you around."

I smiled.

She sat back. "I would kill her though."

"I know," I said, my chest swelling at the fact that she seemed better already.

A moment later, her phone buzzed on the bed behind her.

We both glanced at it.

Mike's face was plastered across the screen.

THREE
- Andi -

I stared at the phone, each ring causing a heartburn like stabbing in my chest.

It was only when the ringing stopped that I realized I'd been holding my breath... and that I had nine missed calls from the same number.

"Call him back."

I looked up at Shane and shook my head. "I have nothing to say to him."

"I couldn't agree more," he said. "But I think you should call him anyway."

I furrowed my brow. "And say what?"

"That you'll meet him at his place in a half hour to talk things over."

I squinted at him. He could be so hard to read with his steely, chiseled features. But he seemed so calm, so rational. I desperately wanted to believe there was a method to his madness.

Unfortunately, I knew exactly what would happen if I went over there. Mike would bury me in excuses, dismissing his behavior by saying he'd only snapped because of his intense feelings for me.

Then he would insist that he never meant to hurt me or scare me or shake my trust in him, and he wouldn't stop insisting until I forgave him.

My phone started to buzz again.

"Tell him you'll come," Shane said. "And you can stay here while I go get your stuff."

My stuff. It was hard to think with Shane sitting so close to me. But I knew it was a bad idea for them to be in the same room, and I knew that such trickery would really piss Mike off.

On the other hand, I was confident that Shane could handle himself, especially in the company of someone he believed was a coward.

What's more, pissing Mike off was a prospect that was becoming more appealing with every passing minute now that I knew I was safe, now that I'd told someone what happened.

I never did that the other times. I just carried the toxic feeling of betrayal around with me and tried to make sense of it in my own head.

But saying out loud what he'd put me through had given me new perspective. I knew his behavior was something I'd never want Izzy, for example, to tolerate.

"Andi."

I pursed my lips.

"Just do it. I'll get your stuff, and this will all be over."

Did he know this wasn't the first time something like this had happened?

I picked up the phone and took a deep breath. I knew I could do it. I lied to Mike all the time about where I was going and who I was with. I had to so he wouldn't flip, so I could see my friends.

Was that some kind of abuse in itself?

Shane reached over and pressed the call button on the screen before I was ready, but I wasn't annoyed with him. If anything, his support was the boost I needed.

"Baby whcre are you?" Mike said, all the vitriol gone from his voice. "I've been trying to call you like crazy."

"Sorry, I know," I said. "I was… at the library." It was ridiculous, but it would have to do. Who goes to the library after their boyfriend attacks them in a stairwell?

"Stay there. I'll come pick you up."

"No," I said, startled by the urgency in my voice.

"We have to talk, Andi. I owe you an apology."

"Yes you do." And I wanted it. I did. But maybe my willingness to hear him out was part of the problem, part of the vicious cycle we'd gotten sucked into. "But I'd rather talk in private."

"Cool. Then-"

"I'll meet you at your apartment in a half hour."

"Sounds good," he said. "I can't wait to make this up to you. I know I overreacted and-"

"I gotta go," I said. "We can talk when I get to yours."

I hung up the phone and double checked that I'd definitely ended the call.

Shane stood up and crossed the room, crushing the empty Coke can before tossing it in the garbage can.

"Are you sure about this?" I asked.

"I'm sure that I don't want you near this guy ever again."

"You know he's going to be angry when you show up instead of me."

He rolled his eyes. "He's always angry."

There was no point in arguing, no point in defending Mike's character. Not anymore. Despite the fact that I was still totally confused about my feelings for him, there was one thing I wasn't confused about.

And that was my feelings for Shane, my trust in him. Our friendship had suffered from my decision to go out with Mike, and I could see now that it hadn't been worth it.

I never wanted to turn my back on him again. He was one of the good guys, and I was lucky to call him a friend.

He sat on the edge of the bed and slipped his feet into his gym shoes. "What do you need me to get from Mike's place?"

I rolled my eyes up to the ceiling as my possessions flashed across my mind. I'd left my favorite blush on the desk in his room, and I had a leftover Club Lulu in the fridge, an extra toothbrush, and a white robe I got for free that time I stayed in the Abbott Hotel.

But none of that was important.

What mattered was that Shane made it back safely, and the less stuff he had to grab, the better.

"My leather jacket is on the hook behind the door," I said. "And my IPod and my leather boots are in the bedroom by the desk." I couldn't be sure, but I think he flinched when I said my leather boots were in the bedroom.

It just happened to be where I took them off. It wasn't anything kinky like that. But the fact that Shane might've imagined that side of me or even pictured me in just my boots made me feel strangely excited for a fleeting moment.

"Is that it?"

I thought hard about whether there was anything else I would miss, knowing it was vital to remove any excuse I might have to go back there.

"There's a book on the coffee table. It's all pictures of Bowie, and he signed it for me in New York-"

"I remember," he said. "When you were visiting your cousin."

I nodded. It was nice that I could count on him to remember stuff. It almost validated my existence in some way. "Anyway, if he hasn't already sold it on eBay to spite me, I would really like to have that back."

"Okay," Shane said. "Jacket, Boots, IPod, Bowie. Is that it?"

I nodded. "Those are the things I can't easily replace anyway."

"Right."

"Along with you," I said. "So please be careful."

"Sure thing."

"Oh- I almost forgot. He keeps a bat behind the front door."

Shane furrowed his brows.

"He plays for a club tea-"

He moved his legs shoulder width apart. "When were you going to tell me that?"

"I don't think he'll swing it at you. I just thought I'd mentioned it."

"Thanks," he said, slipping his phone in the back pocket of his jeans. "Did you have dinner already?"

"No."

"I'll add that to my list," he said, walking over and putting his hands on my shoulders. "Stay here."

"I will."

He went to the door, put his hand on the handle, and looked back over his shoulder. "And help yourself to whatever. What's mine is yours."

"I really appreciate you doing this, Shane."

"It's nothing," he said. "All for one, remember?"

I smiled, and the way my face stretched took me by surprise.

He left without another word.

FOUR
- Shane -

Mike threw the door open a few seconds after I knocked, his face twisted in a pained expression- as if he were poised to plead and apologize.

"What the fuck are you doing here?" he asked, his face hardening as his eyes darted down the hallway to see if I was alone.

"I came to deliver a message from Andi."

His jaw clenched as he crossed his arms.

And while it hadn't been my initial plan, I went ahead and punched him in the face.

He stumbled back. "What the fuck, man?!"

I stuck my foot in the doorframe to keep him from shutting me out.

"I think you broke my fucking nose." His eyes grew wide as a trickle of dark blood pooled in his cupped hands.

I shrugged and walked inside. "Yeah, well, shitty stuff happens to cowards who raise their hands to women."

"I didn't raise my hand to- You can't come in here!"

I stood and faced him where he was standing against the wall, thinking this is what it must have been like for him to watch Andi cower before him, afraid of what he might do next.

"The punch was actually just a gift from me." I swung the front door shut with my foot.

His ugly mouth fell open.

"Andi's message is that it's over, and she never wants to see or speak to you again."

He rolled his eyes. "Yeah, right. I'll believe that when I hear it from her."

"You'll believe it now," I said, planting my hand on the wall beside his head as he lifted the bottom of his shirt up under his nose. "Because if you ever so much as look at her or text her again, I'm going to come back here, and next time I won't be alone."

He scoffed. "Is that a threat?"

"Yeah, Mike. It's a threat."

He craned his neck back. "What are you going to do? Sick your lackey frat boys on me?"

I stared down my nose at him. "Why don't you clean yourself up before you make a mess," I said, moving farther into the apartment.

The first thing I saw was the Bowie book. It was on the low coffee table in front of the couch in a stack of other large hardbacks next to a little hair clip.

I thought of the last time I saw Andi with her hair down. It was the same night I saw her and Mike at the bar.

She only took it down for a second, but I remembered how shiny it looked as it fell around her shoulders in loose waves. Everything seemed to move in slow motion as she ran her fingers through it.

She clipped it back again right away, and I remember having this weird feeling that the moment wasn't enough, that I wanted more.

It was a feeling I'd had regularly around her since we were sixteen, and it was always at the strangest times. Like the first day I noticed her collarbone- like really noticed it.

Or the first time I saw what her toned legs looked like in heels. Or that New Year's Eve in high school when a bunch of us squeezed into my buddy's van to go to a different house party and she ended up half sitting in my lap.

I had to think about Jabba the Hut to keep from getting hard. If memory serves me, later that night was the first time I ever…

Mike cursed in the bathroom and turned the tap on, interrupting my train of thought.

I pulled a plastic bag from the back pocket of my jeans and slid the Bowie book and the clip inside. Then I looked to my right and saw his cracked bedroom door.

I pushed it open and tried not to look at the crumpled sheets where he'd probably put his hands on her, where they'd probably had make up sex dozens of times, where he'd probably buried his face in her silky hair and…

I swallowed and tried to focus on the task at hand, finding her boots by the desk a second later. They were tall and black, and regretfully, I'd never seen her in them before.

I folded them in half and shoved them in my bag.

Then I saw her iPod on the desk. The headphones were already wrapped tightly around it, and I didn't waste any time adding it to my haul.

A moment later, the hair on my neck stood up, and I glanced in the mirror beside the desk.

Mike was standing behind me with the metal baseball bat, his knuckles white where he was clenching it. "I told you to get the fuck out."

"My bad," I said in my most cooperative tone. "I didn't catch that, but I was just leaving anyway." *Please let her leather jacket be on the back of the door.*

He angled his body ever so slightly, and I felt the air move in front of me as I jumped back a split second before he planted the bat in his own dry wall.

I raised my eyebrows. "Good luck getting your deposit back after that."

He started to pull it from the crumbling wall, but I stepped up beside it, put a hand over his pulsing wrists, and shook my head. "Don't swing that at me again," I said, fixing my eyes on him.

"Or what?" he asked, keeping his hands on the end of the bat despite the fact that I had it pinned against the wall. "You gonna fuck my girl? Isn't that what you plan to do anyway?"

I didn't dare let my mind explore that possibility. "Look, Mike. I just want Andi to be safe and happy, and she can't be those things with you."

He huffed and let go of the bat.

It bounced on the floor beside my feet.

"Of course she can."

"No. You're going to have to find someone else to pick on."

"Why isn't she here?"

"Because she's afraid of you, Mike," I said, standing tall to make the most of the inches I had on him. "And if I ever suspect she has reason to be again, you're going to need a lot more than a bat to protect yourself."

"You're full of shit, Shane."

"Try me," I growled, pushing past him.

When I turned the corner, I could see the fringed elbow of her leather jacket in the hanging pile on the door.

I slipped it off the hook, replaced the other coats, and draped it over my arm.

"I'm calling Andi. This is fucking bullshit-"

I turned around and spiked the phone from his hand.

When he looked up to protest, I grabbed his throat. "Are you really this thick, Mike? I don't like having to repeat myself."

He pried at my vice grip in vain.

"If you ever contact her again in any way- a wave, a whistle, a text- I will personally see to it that every finger on your hands remains for purely decorative purposes."

He gagged.

"Do we have an understanding?"

"Yeah," he croaked.

"Say it's over."

"It's over," he wheezed, pulling at my wrists.

I released him then and let myself out, eager as hell to start forgetting his face.

FIVE

- Andi -

As I leaned towards the mirror in Shane's room to examine the split in my bottom lip, I realized I was lucky I hadn't chipped a tooth.

How would I have explained that to people? That it happened when I was running from my boyfriend? The person I supposedly loved most?

Not that I ever said it.

Mike did, though. A lot, especially when he was apologizing for his latest outburst, and it was always nice to hear. No one else had ever said it to me before.

But as I turned in front of the mirror to see if his fingertips had left bruises on the back of my arm, I began to think maybe it was meaningless.

Perhaps whatever we had wasn't love at all.

I thought of the people I knew who definitely loved each other. Shane and Izzy came to mind first. They were twins, of course, so it wasn't a romantic kind of love, but they would never do anything to hurt each other.

And while I could recall one time when Shane scared Izzy so bad she peed her pants a little, it was only for the sake of a Halloween prank, and he swore up and down he didn't mean to scare her that bad.

All he did was creep up to the window behind us wearing a scary mask… though it wasn't half as scary as Mike's face was an hour ago when he clamped his hand around my jaw.

I thought he was going to break it, that my bones and teeth were going to crumble in my mouth. I knew then- deep down- that I had to leave him.

Yet at the same time, I doubt I would've been able to completely swear off seeing him again if Shane hadn't made me promise.

I lifted Shane's aftershave off the dresser in front of me, sniffed the spray release on top, and hoped he would be back soon.

It bothered me that I didn't see this coming, that I didn't know Mike was capable of being such a bad guy. But he wasn't as jealous and controlling in the beginning.

Then again, maybe he was, and I'd foolishly believed it was sweet.

I sighed and looked at the framed picture atop the dresser of Shane and Izzy with their parents on Christmas, each of them wearing an ugly sweater and a silly grin. Their whole family had such a great sense of humor, and the photo reminded me that I could probably get through anything as long as they were in my life.

The top drawer of the dresser was full of gym clothes, which made me recall the last time I'd seen Shane all sweaty after a workout.

Why didn't he have a girlfriend?

I knew there were a few girls he fooled around with regularly, and he seemed to choose between them when he needed a date for something- which was all the time for frat guys.

For a while, he was spending a lot of time with a Theta whose shiny hair went all the way to her waist. The only thing longer was her legs and- I suspect- the list of designer handbags she owned.

Then there was the Chi Omega with the blue eyes, blonde hair, and tight gymnast's body. Worst of all, she actually seemed like a nice person, though I remember throwing up in my mouth a little once when I heard her admit to someone in the rec center that she and Shane were more than friends.

Lastly, there was that Indian supermodel who was in all his finance courses. And the fact that she was as intelligent as she was gorgeous- with her pretty brown skin and her obscenely long lashes- probably made her my least favorite.

Not that she wasn't an alright person. They were all alright. They just weren't good enough for Shane. Their senses of humor fell short for one. Most importantly, they didn't know and love him.

Not like I did anyway.

I still remember the day their family moved in down the street. My parents brought over a pie or something just to "welcome them to the neighborhood" (i.e. make a good first impression and let the new blood know they were being watched).

Anyway, when they got back, they told me the new neighbors had a little girl my age that I could be friends with.

This was great news because I was seven and three quarters and quite ready to expand my social girl. Or rather, I felt that I'd outgrown the girl at the bottom of the cul de sac who always seemed to have poison ivy.

But when I met Izzy later that day and realized she had a twin brother, it felt like Christmas morning.

Not only had I never met real twins before- which made them instantly fascinating to me- but when Shane showed me how he could burn a hole in a leaf with nothing but a magnifying glass, I knew he was the one to deliver the excitement that had been missing from my life.

Not that my parents didn't do their best, but I was an only child and the result of several costly rounds of IVF. As a result, they babied me so much that sometimes I felt like I might as well have been properly bubble wrapped to save my mom the extra hand wringing.

Every time I got so much as a scratch, she would act like it was the end of the world. She took me to the doctor for every fever, every sneeze, and every goddamn hiccup.

The worst, though, was if I bumped my head. She'd get so panicked I'd worry I lost brain cells that were crucial to my living up to her academic expectations.

It was so much pressure, and although I understood it, that didn't make it any easier.

But when the Jennings twins showed up on the scene, all that began to change. At first I thought it was the fact that I finally had a little gang looking out for me. But in hindsight, I suspect it was because Shane inspired so much confidence in people.

Not only was he eleven constantly mentioned minutes older than Izzy, but he was a natural born leader and his charm was the gift that kept on giving.

I'd hear a knock at the door and listen as he greeted my mom and made a fuss over whatever smell was billowing out of the kitchen. Then he'd ask if I could come out to play.

But the masterstroke was that- before we even hit the driveway- he'd say, "What time would you like Andi to be home, Mrs. Oliver?"

Every. Time.

And he always got me there, too, though the onus was usually on me to come up with a suitable story for what the hell we'd been doing all day since the truth was often more than my mother could handle.

But to say she was delighted that Shane and I were headed to the same college twelve years later would be the biggest understatement ever.

So I guess I wasn't the only one that thought he was a good influence on me. Even Nervous Nancy felt that he was the cure for her darkest fears.

There was only one problem with him being so great, and that was that I couldn't help but compare everyone to him.

And in fifteen years, no one had ever come close to measuring up.

S I X

- Shane -

I was halfway home when I realized I was clenching my fists so hard they were getting sore.

Sure, I'd scolded Mike and knocked him around enough to get his attention, but as far as I was concerned, he got off too lightly.

On the plus side, I'd managed to successfully suppress how deep my feelings of hatred went for him.

Because it wasn't entirely personal. I never liked any of the guys Andi went out with.

The least offensive was probably Jason De Marco, who took her to prom, and that was only because we played hockey together back then, and I thought he was a decent guy.

Of course, after Izzy told me he'd given Andi a fat purple hickey on her neck and that he tried to push her head down, I avoided him like the plague.

I don't know why exactly. I always thought it was simply because- next to Izzy- she'd always been the person I was most protective of.

What's more, I knew how special she was, and I had this idea in my mind of how I thought she deserved to be treated, an idea no one ever seemed to live up to.

At least Mike was out of the picture now, which was a relief. He was the worst guy to catch her attention yet.

And to be frank, I think the reason I hated him most was that his behavior reminded me of my own jealousy.

I still remember the first time I saw her flirt with someone in high school- like really flirt. Like hair twirling, eyelash batting, cheek blushing flirt. I remember wishing she'd look at me like that, that my attention would reduce her to a sweet, giggling mess.

Maybe I was too familiar for her to see me that way, or perhaps it was the fact that she and my sister were so close.

But that didn't stop me from noticing the curve of her ass or the twinkle in her eye or her shapely lips.

But noticing was one thing.

It would've been quite another to do anything that couldn't be laughed off or denied, anything that might challenge the deep trust she and Izzy had in me.

I pushed the door of Andi's favorite sandwich shop open and listened as the chime rang out under the floor mat. Then I ordered a wreck for me, a spicy turkey for her, and two Oreo milkshakes to go.

"Can you put some extra Oreos in the bag?" I asked.

The young man behind the counter nodded.

I was trying to remember what frat he was in when an elbow brushed against my arm.

"I didn't think you were an extra Oreos kind of guy?"

I turned towards the familiar voice and felt a surge of warmth in my stomach when my eyes found her crimson smile. "Sonia. Hey."

She glanced down at the leather boots sticking out of the bag in my hand.

"Oreos and drag, huh?" Her voice was as smooth as her clear brown skin.

"Not exactly," I said, trying to remember how long it had been since-

"I thought you were going to come out last weekend?"

I shrugged and accepted my change from the cashier. "I was going to, but my sister came to town so I had to change my plans." It wasn't a complete lie. Izzy's art school was only a few hours away, and she did swing by all the time. Last weekend just hadn't been one of them.

Sonia pursed her lips.

The guy across the counter slid the bag of sandwiches towards me and set down a tray with two shakes in it. "Your extra Oreos are in the bag."

"Thanks," I said.

"Well, I won't keep you," Sonia said, eyeing my meal for two. "But don't be a stranger." She put a hand on my shoulder and pressed her cinnamon smelling cheek to mine.

My mind flashed briefly to the last time we hung out. We'd pressed a lot more than our cheeks together.

But a moment later, I thought of Andi waiting anxiously in my bedroom, pining for food and an update on what I can only assume had been one of the worst nights of her life.

"See you around," I said, heading for the door and picking up my pace.

When I got back to the house, I climbed the stairs, shifted the bags to my left hand, balanced the shakes against my chest, and knocked, since the last thing she needed was someone barging in on her after the day she had, even if it was my room.

She opened the door wearing one of my hoodies a second later, the bottom of it so long it nearly made her frayed jean shorts disappear.

Her eyes lit up when she saw me and stayed bright as they bounced around my full arms.

"A little help?" I handed the shakes to her.

She smiled as she took them.

"I hope you're hungry," I said, setting the sandwiches down on my desk.

"How did it go?" she asked, eyeing the bag with the boots.

I handed it to her so she could see for herself.

She took it and rummaged through the spoils. "You got everything."

I furrowed my brow. "You said that as if you doubted me."

"Never," she said, throwing her arms around me and squeezing me just tight enough to remind me that she was still shaken up.

I held her head against my chest and didn't let go until I felt her loosen her grip.

"Thanks, Shane," she said, taking a step back and looking at me, her fat lip impossible to ignore. "I owe you one."

"Just stay away from him and we'll call it even," I said, taking the sandwiches out of the brown bag and laying them side by side.

"What did he say?" she asked, taking her sub to the edge of the bed and unwrapping it carefully so the paper became a little placemat.

"Not much." I took a sip of my shake. It was creamy and delicious and tasted like being a carefree kid again.

"Don't be vague," she said. "I've been going crazy here worrying he might hurt you or say nasty things about me to you or-"

"What the hell would that matter?" I asked. "You know I don't give a shit what he thinks about anything."

She shrugged. "Still."

"Well, he didn't say anything nasty about you, and I had no trouble getting your stuff. Convincing him to leave you the hell alone was a bigger job than I anticipated, but it's over now-"

"Did you hurt him?" she asked, her voice as soft as her chocolate eyes were wide.

"Just enough to scare him," I said. "Like he did to you."

She swallowed.

I took my sandwich over to the end of the bed and sat down beside her. "He's fine, though. Trust me. I only hurt him enough to get his attention."

She pursed her lips and looked down at her sandwich.

"I would've done the same for Izzy."

She nodded. "I know."

But by the look on her face, I got the feeling that she had no idea how much I really cared about her.

Then again, how could she?

I'd always kept it to myself.

S E V E N
- Andi -

We didn't talk much as we ate our sandwiches. Instead, we listened to the mild domestic happening in the room next door until Shane put on some music to drown out the sound.

Not that I was really listening anyway. On the contrary, I was trying to process- and guess- what happened between him and Mike.

To be honest, though, I wished I could forget about Mike altogether.

Sure, things were fun in the beginning- and the sex had been energetic in a way that made it easy to ignore our increasingly animated fights- but for the most part, Shane was right.

He was no good for me.

My grades had dropped in two of my classes. I'd spent virtually no time with Shane, and I hadn't gone to visit Izzy once since Mike and I started going out.

But worst of all, I didn't like who I'd become as a result of dating him.

I was more meek lately and unsure of myself. I'd started lying to my parents about serious stuff, like my grades and how my boyfriend was treating me.

It was pathetic that someone could come into my life and overwhelm me like that until I hardly recognized myself.

And when he squeezed my jaw, I felt fragile for the first time in my life, and I hated it.

I wanted to feel strong and confident, and I wanted to be in a relationship where my grades didn't suffer and the guy I was sleeping with didn't do things I couldn't tell my friends about.

So I was grateful for Shane's help, grateful that I could count on him to talk some sense into me and force me to take action… especially when all I felt strong enough to do was curl up in the corner until the whole thing blew over.

But it wouldn't.

The only thing that was ever going to blow was Mike's temper as soon as something else set him off, and even though I felt like a coward for letting Shane do my dirty work for me, the important thing was that it was over and I was safe.

If only Shane didn't see me like a sister.

I swear our closeness was as much a blessing as it was a curse.

Just once I wanted him to look at me the way he looked at those girls I'd seen him with- like my feelings and insecurities were the last thing he was thinking about.

Maybe that's why I kept dating guys who had no real respect for me- because I couldn't figure out how else to get that possessive intensity that I always craved from Shane.

"God I needed that," he said, crumpling the crummy white paper that previously held his sandwich. "Is yours okay?"

"Perfect," I said, covering my full mouth. "I owe you one."

He furrowed his brow. "Stop saying that. You don't owe me anything."

I swallowed. "Sorry."

"And stop saying you're sorry." He raised his hands and threw the wad of paper in a perfect arc so it landed squarely in the small green garbage in the corner. "It doesn't suit you."

I knew he was right. I felt like all I'd done the last two months with Mike was apologize. I'd started to say it even when it didn't make any sense.

"Can I save the rest of this?" I asked, realizing there was really another meal in the half eaten sandwich before me. "Chuck it in your fridge for the moment maybe?"

"Of course," he said, standing at the edge of the bed while I wrapped it up. "Besides, you need to save room for dessert."

I furrowed my brow. "I thought the milkshake was-"

"I got extra Oreos," he said.

I smiled. "Oreos, huh?"

He nodded and took my sandwich over to the fridge.

"Dessert and a distraction then?"

He looked over his shoulder at me. "My thoughts exactly."

My eyes traced the length of his defined jaw. "I didn't even know you could get extra cookies there. Is that another one of the perks of being big man on campus?"

He closed the fridge door with his foot. "More like one of the perks of saying please."

"I see." I propped some pillows up at the head of the bed. When I leaned against them, I was convinced a burst of his cologne released around me. "Do you have any milk?"

He scrunched his face. "There's milk in the kitchen, but I have to warn you. At least thirty of the guys that live here are repeat offenders when it comes to drinking straight from the jug."

"Right," I said, crossing my ankles. "I'll stick with my milkshake then."

Shane laid down beside me and put the bag between us. "You go first."

I rolled onto my side, pulled an Oreo from the bag, and held it up between us.

His fingers brushed mine as he tried to get a good grip on the side of the cookie closest to him.

"Ready?" I asked, raising my eyebrows.

He nodded and began to twist.

The icing came off on my side. A surge of warmth burst in my stomach. "Truth or dare?" I asked.

He narrowed his eyes at me. "Truth."

I pursed my lips, but stopped when I felt the crack stretch across the bottom one.

"Well?"

"How come you've been avoiding me?"

He turned an ear towards me. "I haven't been avoiding you."

"But we haven't hung out in ages-"

"I've been avoiding your ex."

I glanced down at the cookie bag.

"Because you deserve better, Andi. And it breaks my heart to see you happy with such a-"

"I wasn't that happy."

"I know," he said. "But what was I supposed to do after I begged you not to go out with him and you did anyway?"

"For what it's worth, you were right from the beginning," I said, falling back against the pillows.

"I don't care about being right. I care about you being happy and safe."

I rolled my eyes. "Safe. You sound like my mother."

He flinched like he didn't agree.

I took a sip of my shake.

"As far as I'm concerned, the only good thing that came out of your relationship with that wannabe wife beater is those leather boots," he said, nodding towards the bag by the door.

"They are pretty hot boots," I said. "I'll wear them for you sometime."

His cheeks flushed.

"I didn't mean it like that," I added quickly. "I meant-"

"I know," he said, holding up another Oreo.

EIGHT
- Shane -

I didn't want to dwell on the thought of her in those boots.

I don't know why I even mentioned it, especially when she was laying on my bed in my sweatshirt after a day when I'd done enough questioning my motives as it was.

After all, the bottom line was that Andi trusted me, that she always had, and that nothing was worth threatening that trust.

And yet all I could think about was how much I wanted to kiss her cracked lip and make it better.

She grabbed one side of the Oreo I was holding, and we both twisted again.

"Yes!" she said, looking down at her icing covered half. "Truth or dare?"

"Truth."

She tilted her head. "Don't you want a dare?"

"I've had a daring enough day as it is."

"Okay."

"Plus, the truth is more interesting, don't you think?"

She shrugged. "Sometimes."

"Shoot."

"Who are you taking to your barn dance this year?"

"I haven't decided yet."

She craned her neck forward. "But you must've thought about it."

"I guess."

"I thought you were seeing that Indian girl?"

I shook my head. "Seeing is too strong a word."

"What about the Chi O then? The one that thinks you're crazy about her?"

I raised my eyebrows.

"I overheard her talking about you."

"What did she say?"

"She just made it sound like things between you guys were kind of serious."

"Well, they're not."

"With anyone?" she asked.

"Did Izzy put you up to this?"

"Not exactly."

"Tell her to mind her own damn business. I don't try and trick her into telling me which mustached beret model she's watching black and white movies with-"

"Yes you do."

I scooted back against the pillows. "I'm ready for the next Oreo."

She smiled and pulled another out of the bag. "Feeling lucky?"

I twisted the cookie and failed to get the icing again. "These are rigged."

"You picked 'em."

"Truth," I said.

She sighed. "Okay. As a friend, how bad is my lip for real?"

I stared at it.

"Oh god, really? Is it seriously taking you that long to come up with something moderately reassuring to say?"

"It's fine," I said, trying to ignore the drop in my stomach. "It's a perfectly fine lip."

Her face dropped. "More like a perfectly fine busted lip."

I shook my head. "You don't look busted. I promise."

Her lashes cast shadows on her cheeks when she dropped her eyes. "Maybe not, but people aren't exactly going to line up to get a piece of-"

I tilted her chin up with my fingers, leaned forward, and kissed the side of her bottom lip where the crack had formed, holding my lips there just long enough to notice she'd stopped breathing.

Then I pulled back and placed a hand on her cheek. "See-" I said, staring into her shiny eyes. "There's nothing wrong with your lips."

She swallowed and leaned away, staring at me like she recognized me but couldn't place who I was. "Why did you-" She brought the fingertips of one hand to her lips.

"Because you're beautiful, Andi. Unconditionally. And it's time you got that through your thick head."

Her eyes smiled. "You can be really sweet when you want to be."

"Don't tell anyone," I said, leaning back against the pillows and sliding my hands behind my head. "I don't want to ruin my reputation."

"Your secret is safe with me," she said, curling her bare legs up into my oversized sweatshirt.

"Good."

"Will we do one more?" she asked.

I grabbed the edge of the bag and peeked inside. "I swear to god if I don't get the icing this time, I'm going out to buy more and we're doing this all night."

"Choose carefully," she teased.

"There's only one left."

"You still get to choose your side though."

I straightened up and stretched my arms in front of me and then out to both sides, cocking my head like I was preparing for the game winning pitch.

She laughed, and the sound made my heart glow in my chest. How could I have gone so long without that life affirming sound?

"Come on already," she said. "Don't keep the fans waiting."

I exhaled and reached in the bag. Then I pulled out the final Oreo and held it up between us.

"Are you sure that's the side you want?" she asked, raising her eyebrows and looking between me and the cookie in question.

"Don't fuck with me," I said. "Just twist the damn cookie."

"Okay, but only if you're absolutely sure you're ready. I mean, if you need to do some lunges or something-"

"Shut up."

Half her mouth curled into a smile as she took the cookie facing her and gave it a twist.

I fist pumped when I saw that I had the icing covered side.

"Ridiculous." She shook her head. "I can't believe you won after that silly display."

I tapped my temple with two fingers. "It's all about visualizing the win. Maybe I can give you a few pointers next time."

"I won all the other ones!"

"Because I let you," I said. "I threw them so I could get the game winning Oreo."

"The game winning Oreo? I thought every one was a game winner."

"Good point," I said, tired of gloating. "Pick your poison."

She sighed. "Truth."

"Are you sure?" I asked. "Because the dare involves those boots and-"

"I'm definitely sure."

I can't believe I mentioned the boots again. What the hell was wrong with me? "Last chance to change your mind?"

"Truth, please. Final answer."

"Do you want to stay?"

She scrunched her nose. "Stay what?"

"Here. Like stay the night?"

She glanced at the Miller Time clock on the wall and then back at me. "Like on the futon?"

"Actually, the futon is- unlike your lip- genuinely busted."

"Uh-huh."

"I just thought we could watch-"

"Oh god please don't say Netflix and chill."

I laughed. "Come on now. My game is better than that."

Her lips fell apart.

"Not that I'm playing games." *Shit.* "I just meant that I've got this movie I haven't seen, and it's been a long day for both of us- especially you- and I'll sleep better if I know you're safe and-"

"Stop rambling," she said. "What movie?"

I walked across the room and pulled a DVD off the shelf, studying the front as I carried it over to her. "Izzy brought it last time she visited. It's one of those B horror movies about a bunch of sorority girls who accidently kill one of their sisters."

She took the DVD and examined the front and back.

I sat on the edge of the bed and watched her dark eyes dart back and forth as she studied the praise the film had received from a bunch of fake entertainment magazines.

"It looks brilliant," she said.

I raised my eyebrows. "Yeah?"

"Totally. Plus, Izzy has exquisite taste in films."

I laughed.

"And the truth is I'd love to stay," she said. "It's really decent of you to offer, and you're right. I'd rather not be on my own tonight."

NINE
- Andi -

Twenty four hours ago, I thought I'd be waking up next to Mike.

Not that I was terribly disappointed.

To say he was a bed hog would be a huge understatement. Every morning, he'd be sprawled out on his back like he'd been making naked snow angels all night.

Meanwhile, I'd be lying along the edge of the bed, clutching the covers because he always kept his place so cold- him being a human sweater and all.

But he'd always pull me close as soon as he woke up and noticed his morning wood, which isn't to say he wasn't sweet in the mornings, because he was. It was the nights where he'd forget himself like a real life Jekyll and Hyde.

For a while, I really believed I could help him change. I thought my sunny disposition could keep him from giving into his demons, of which he had many. But I was being naive.

He was always going to be skeptical and slow to trust, always going to believe the world was out to get him.

And that fact alone made us incompatible.

After all, I tended to give people the benefit of the doubt and believed deep down that most people were inherently good.

Perhaps that's why so much time in his company made me forget myself.

But it was all over.

I could start again this morning with a clean slate, and as soon as my lip and bruises healed, my relationship with him would be a thing of the past. A mistake, certainly, but one I had every intention of learning from.

And the knowledge that it was over was the most freeing feeling in the world. It felt as if my heart had sprouted little wings and was fluttering weightless in my chest.

And I knew I had Shane to thank for that.

The first time I woke up was around five thirty. It took me a second to remember where I was- probably cause I'd never been horizontal in Shane's room before.

We used to sleep together all the time when we were kids. He and Izzy and I would have sleepovers in their basement on the pullout couch, each with our own blanket curled up around us as we watched movies.

Izzy always took the middle, though, partly because it seemed like the most natural arrangement and partly because she liked holding the popcorn. And even back then, I already knew those were the greatest nights of my life.

How would I ever be able to top the kind of energetic, safe fun we used to have together?

Thank god I appreciated it while it lasted.

Because obviously once we were teenagers, not only did we not fit comfortably on the pullout anymore, but there was no longer a sleeping arrangement that everyone was comfortable with. Not that a discussion was ever required.

Shane just kind of opted out when he realized he preferred the company of boys and video games.

So Izzy and I were left to our own devices, which was fine... except that was when Shane started to intrigue me in a way he never had.

I watched from a distance as his interests changed along with the shape of his jaw and the fit of his clothes. I watched my silly childhood friend become a handsome man and struggled to pretend I was as disinterested in his development as Izzy.

Not that she and I didn't have our own shit to deal with.

I hated getting boobs, hated the way my hips turned out and used to bang into things. Even worse, there were a few years where my emotions felt like they were being controlled by an amateur puppeteer, and there was no telling when I might lose my cool.

What's more, I was convinced that my overprotective mother was out to completely ruin my life at the time, which just proves in hindsight how entirely off my rocker I was.

And the whole time I wished I could be more like Shane, who seemed to be getting cooler by the day while I was just getting crazier in seemingly direct correlation to how frequently I suffered breakouts.

Needless to say, when it came to nostalgia, it was those early years I missed most. Because things were simple. Things made sense. No one ever wanted anything from me.

Best of all, I got to spend every day with Shane and Izzy under the naive pretense that things would never change.

But of course they had.

And nothing was more a reminder of that than the sight I woke up to at five thirty a.m.

Shane was beside me, sleeping on his stomach, with his strong arms bent out to the sides and his hands under the pillow. But that wasn't what most intrigued me about him.

First of all, he was sleeping with his mouth shut-something Mike rarely did. I stared at his lips for a moment and recalled how he'd touched them to mine, recalled the inappropriate way my body felt when he did it.

There was just enough soft light squeezing in through the blinds behind the bed that I could admire how youthful his chiseled face looked at rest.

I kept my breathing steady as my eyes traveled down his body. His back was smooth and bare, and his relaxed muscles caused a rolling landscape that was more gorgeous than any I'd ever seen.

I wondered what it would feel like to sink my fingernails into his back and feel his muscles flexing under my palms as he moved over me, in me, his hot whispers against my ear.

The thought alone made a burning flush travel from my stomach up to my cheeks.

Finally, my eyes settled on the sheets that lay over his ass. They were just high enough that I could see the curve of his butt where it met his lower back but nothing more.

Part of me wanted to lift the sheet so I could see if he was naked, but I knew knowing wouldn't make it any easier to lie there beside him.

Lifting the sheets would only blow my cover.

After all, the fact that I'd been head over heels for him since the day he taught me how to take a bunch of willow tree branches in my hand and swing back and forth like Tarzan was my best kept secret.

Besides, I knew better than to want what I couldn't have.

T E N
- Shane -

I felt like such a jackass leaving her there.

The last thing I wanted was her waking up at the frat house by herself and thinking I'd abandoned her.

Which struck me as funny since I slipped out in the morning without waking girls all the time and never thought twice about it before.

But for some inexplicable reason, I didn't want to miss Andi's sleepy morning face, didn't want to miss the first scratchy word out of her mouth.

And of course I was curious to see how she looked in my t-shirt without a bra on underneath because I'd been thinking about her tits on and off since she started hiding them from me a decade ago.

Not that I could help it.

Frankly, I couldn't see how any man who was ever lucky enough to see the sparkle in her dark eyes or the way her slightly lopsided smile lit up her face wouldn't want to see more of her. Or everything.

Regardless, I didn't have much choice.

I may have been a jackass for leaving her, but I would've been an even bigger jackass if I'd blown off charity duty.

Not only had I not missed a game in the last three years, but I enjoyed it.

Basically, a few of my frat brothers and I played wheelchair basketball with a group of high school aged guys from the surrounding area.

In the beginning, they used to kick our ass all the time because none of us could maneuver our wheelchairs for shit, but we'd improved enough that it was finally competitive.

And while the main reason for showing up every three Sundays was for the kids, it made me grateful.

When I was young, I took my health and athleticism for granted. And sports were everything to me.

It broke my heart to think it was so much harder for these guys- who I'm sure needed sport as much as I did- to find people to play pickup games with.

So it was the least I could do to give back.

What's more, it was humbling, and humility was something I wanted to get better at.

After all, sophomore year I started becoming kind of a dick as a result of so many women throwing themselves at me.

And I didn't want to become a typical fraternity jerk. I wanted to be a good guy with his feet on the ground who just happened to be in a frat.

Fortunately, Izzy and Andi called me out pretty quick, and I got back on track to becoming a well-rounded person whose ego fit comfortably through doorways and in rooms without high ceilings.

Which was good. Because what would be the point of busting my ass to get an education if I became an unbearable prick in the process?

I wiped the sweat off my face with my shirt and said good game to the other guys, matching their appetite for talking smack at the same time. Then I poured some Gatorade down my throat and glanced at the clock.

It was 10:30. Surely Andi had gotten my note by now.

All it said was where I'd gone to and that I'd call her later, but I'd left it right by my pillow so she'd see it in the same breath that she realized I was gone.

I was going to add that I had a great time last night, but it seemed too vague and sleazy considering the situation that had brought her to my doorstep in the first place.

But that didn't mean it wasn't true.

I had enjoyed myself. I knew I shouldn't be surprised at how much since she was one of my oldest friends, but her company was so refreshing.

I was so used to being around women that were dick hungry posers, their every word designed to manipulate, seduce, or fish for compliments.

But Andi wasn't like that.

She didn't throw herself at me or show up in so much makeup I was worried about finding rogue eyelashes in my bed. She breathed normally- without trying to suck in her stomach and stick out her chest- and she treated me like a regular person.

Best of all, she actually had a few brain cells to rub together and could hold a conversation about something other than the life and times of reality TV stars. The only downside was that time always passed by too quickly when I was with her.

And that made me want more of it.

In fact, when the thought crossed my mind that she might want space while she was getting over this whole thing with Mike, I felt my throat close up.

Because if there was anything I'd learned last night- besides the fact that our lips seemed to fit together so perfectly I wished I'd tried them on properly- it was that I'd spent enough time away from her, and I was sick of it.

I wanted her back in my life in a big way. She was good for me. I knew it in my head, and I could feel it in every part of my body when she was around.

She made me laugh. She made me forget myself. She made me horny as fuck.

And I hated the idea that when she was ready to move on, it might not be with me. Yes, it was a problematic, complicated idea, but weren't some of the best ideas like that?

I knew as soon as I'd kissed that sad crack in her lip that I wanted to be the guy to make her forget about him, the guy to show her how she should be treated.

And no matter how hard I tried to convince myself that it was a bad idea to lust after one of my oldest friends- my sister's best friend no less- I knew that there wasn't a jerkoff within two hundred miles of campus that could look after her like I could.

Which meant that maybe- for both our sakes- this was an itch I ought to seriously consider scratching.

Otherwise, I'd always wonder what if...

What if I really kissed her? Would she kiss me back?

74

What if that awkwardness between us as teens was down to something real, something we both felt and had been denying for years?

Then again, there was a chance that if I went for it, she would completely reject me and it would piss her and my sister off to the point that my life would be hell for a while.

Or maybe she'd just laugh it off.

Perhaps I could find some way to come on to her that would make it easy for her make a joke out of it if she wasn't up for it.

It was hard to guess what would happen, especially because I didn't know her as well as I used to.

All I knew was that I wanted a chance to get to know her again.

And I promised myself that if I had even one moment of doubt as to whether I could love her better than anyone else, I'd back off.

But something told me that wasn't going to happen.

E L E V E N
- Andi -

I laid around in Shane's bed a little longer than I should have, letting my eyes scan and memorize the room.

After all, I'd probably never wake up in his bed again, and it was fun to be that girl for a few minutes, that girl that wakes up in an unfamiliar room after an incredible night with a stranger.

Though he was far from it.

Then again, last night had been special, but even if the feeling I had in my gut was only our friendship being rekindled, it was still worth it. Still progress.

Eventually, I heard movement and voices in the house, and the awkward notion of still being there when he got back began to overshadow the comfort I got from laying my head on his pillow, his note clutched in my hand.

I got up and dressed, carefully folding the shorts and t-shirt he'd let me borrow so he'd know I hadn't stolen them.

I considered washing and returning them, but I figured I was as weak as the girls I'd heard him complain about who never returned his stuff after spending the night. And seeing how he'd so selflessly returned my stuff to me yesterday, it only seemed fair to show him the same respect.

Once I'd gathered my things, I poked my head into the hallway. The coast was clear so I pulled the door shut quietly and crossed the landing to the stairs.

There were guys all over the place on the ground floor, but no one seemed phased by my creeping around. I still flinched, though, when the heavy front door squeaked as I opened it out onto the porch.

Before I reached the sidewalk in front of the house, two other girls came out behind me. They were both in tight dresses with their heels in their hands.

I suspect they were still drunk from the night before based on the vacant stares they gave me before turning the other way.

That's when I realized I was so far from the walk of shame stereotype there was no reason to be awkward.

If anything it was a walk of pride I was enjoying, though I suppose I would've been even more proud if something had actually happened considering what an incredible guy Shane was.

Still, that kiss was the most exciting thing I'd been part of in a long time. Sure, I felt pathetic for reading into a "make it better kiss" like that, but I couldn't deny how it made me feel.

It felt- for lack of a better word- loaded.

I mean, no one had ever held a gun to my head, for example, but I like to think I'd be able to tell whether it was loaded or not, whether there was intent behind the threat.

And that kiss felt loaded. Like there was an intent- an energy- behind it. Like the slightest flinch from either of us might've caused an explosion.

But it was probably only wishful thinking.

And I knew I shouldn't allow myself to make wishes like that, wishes that could never come true, wishes that made it hard for me to be a good friend.

Shane and I would never go there. Could never. We'd been frolicking in the friend zone for so long the doors to other possibilities had rusted and grown over with moss.

There was no getting out of this. There was no more to come. This was it, and I'd be a fool to be ungrateful for what we had.

Plus, Izzy would be crushed.

They'd gone to so much trouble to make sure I never felt like the third wheel when we were little. And as teens, she and I had been conscious to never make Shane feel like that either. So even if he liked me like that, I couldn't do that to her.

I turned the corner and crossed to the sunny side of the street, enjoying the warmth on my face as I dodged the occasional curbside evidence of other people's overindulgent Saturday night.

Besides, what if it didn't work out?

I liked to think of myself as an optimist, but the majority of romantic relationships failed.

Therefore, it was too big a risk to even consider.

Up to this point, I'd been very lucky in my life. My birth was a fluke in itself. Then I'd managed to pull through the complications I had after birth.

I walked away without a scratch when I was playing Skip-It in the driveway and a drunk driver ploughed into our mailbox, and I'd only sprained my ankle when I fell off the neighbor's trampoline.

And then there was getting away from Mike last night before he really hurt me and the time that, well, the list went on and on when it came to times I got lucky.

And someday if my luck ran out, I couldn't risk it being related to my relationship with Shane.

He was my rock, the force that kept my compass pointing north.

Without him, I was much more likely to lose my way, or worse, myself.

I probably imagined the energy behind that kiss anyway because I was fragile and confused after all the excitement yesterday.

And I was pretty lame for reading into it so much when all he'd done was show me a bit of compassion when I needed it. A better use of my energy would be toning down my desperation for his attention.

Because that could put our friendship at risk, too, and right now, I needed him.

I'd never say that, of course. It was too needy. But in my heart, I knew that spending time with him was the best way for me to reconnect with the Andi I was before Mike broke me down.

Because no one lifted me like Shane. No one made me feel more myself, more capable. And I needed that right now more than I needed anything else.

I'd just pushed my apartment door open when my phone rang. It was Izzy.

I closed the door behind me before answering. "Hi."

"Did you just wake up?"

"No," I said, clearing my throat. "I just haven't talked to anyone today yet."

"I thought you were going to call me back last night?"

I slumped on the couch, feeling weak as soon as I hit the worn cushions. "Yeah, sorry about that. I was too busy breaking up with Mike."

"Shit, Andi. I'm sorry."

"It's fine. Really."

"Are you okay?"

"I'm better than I'd be if I stayed with him." I didn't want to tell her anything more, didn't want to admit to anyone that last night wasn't the first time he'd scared the shit out of me.

I knew she'd freak and tell me I deserved better. And as nice as that was to hear, the important thing was that I was starting to believe it myself.

"How did he take it?" she asked.

"Like a complete prick."

"Mmm."

"But he's out of the picture now, so I'll be toasting to my fresh start right after I have some breakfast."

"What about Stephanie?"

"She's away this weekend at some kind of religious retreat that God's always wanted her to go on."

"Why didn't you tell me? This would've been the perfect weekend for me to come down."

"She didn't tell me she was going until the last minute."

"Well, I do want to come again soon, especially since we didn't get to hang out much last time cause Mike was a shitty sharer."

"Yeah, sorry. I promise we'll make up for lost time. Any weekend you want. Just give me a heads up."

"Sounds good."

I smiled. It was amazing how my best friend's voice could make the world stop spinning.

"And for the record, I'm glad you're moving on," she said. "You can do so much better."

"I know." I slipped my sandals off and put my feet on the edge of the coffee table.

"Okay, well, I'm glad you're okay. I got The Ink when you didn't call."

I rolled my eyes. The Ink. Short for inklings. It was a pet name Izzy had for her gut feelings and intuition, which were often eerily accurate.

For a long time, she only got inklings when it came to Shane. I figured it was some weird twin thing. But after a few years, she started getting them about me, too-claimed it was all down to frequencies and energy.

So it was no surprise at all to hear her spidey sense was going ape shit last night.

TWELVE
- Shane -

I took a deep breath and knocked on the door.

There was no answer.

I tried once more, a little louder this time. And then the horrible thought she might be out with Mike became a lump in my throat.

I opened my mouth to call her name and then closed it again, turning on my heels towards the stairwell instead.

"Shane?"

I spun back towards the door.

Andi was standing in a towel, and her dark hair was dripping small streams of water that pooled beside her collarbone.

"I didn't realize-" I swallowed, trying to keep my eyes on her face. "I should've called."

She cocked her head. "You gonna come in?"

"If it's not a bad time."

Her eyes smiled. "Not at all. What's up?"

I lifted my left hand. "You forgot your sandwich."

Her eyes dropped to the leftover sub in my hand.

"I didn't know if it was an accident or-"

She narrowed her eyes at me as if she could see right through my pathetic excuse to come see her.

"Thanks," she said, taking a step back to open the door wider.

I stepped past her, the flowery scent off her wet hair filling my nose.

She closed the door behind me and locked it every way she could.

There was a bottle of champagne- or rather, two thirds of a bottle- on the coffee table beside a small mug.

"Have you been drinking?" I asked.

"Would you judge me if I said yes?" She stepped up beside me, gripping the top of the towel where it cut across her chest.

"Of course not," I said, noticing a sparkle in her eye that made my groin twitch.

She took the sandwich from my hand and walked towards the small kitchen nook on the other side of the sitting room. "Stephanie's at a retreat until late, and after yesterday I figured I deserved a sloppy chill day."

"Understandable," I said, my guts clenching when I realized we were alone and separated by nothing but a wet towel. I exhaled through my nose and ran a hand through my hair.

"So what'll it be?" she called from around the corner.

"What do you mean?"

She poked her head out of the kitchen nook. "What can I get you to drink?"

I had a test the next day that I really should've been preparing for, but if I went home, I'd just be fighting off the distraction of a house full of guys. And frankly, the distraction here was far more enticing. "What have you got?"

"Anything you want besides liquor and red wine."

I furrowed my brow. "Does that mean my choices are beer or white wine?"

She nodded. "Or champagne."

"I'll take a beer," I said. "But I can get it myself. You don't have to-"

I heard a beer cap clatter against the kitchen counter. A moment later, she came around the corner with it.

That's when I really got the urge to pinch myself.

Could this really be happening? Andi in a towel? Bringing me a cold beer after I'd been thinking about her like a horny teen all day?

"Bottoms up," she said, handing me the bottle.

"Thanks," I said, taking a swig. "But I really should be going."

Her face dropped. "What? You just got h-"

"I need to go buy a lottery ticket."

She furrowed her brow. "I didn't know you played the lottery?"

"I don't, but I just showed up uninvited to find you soaking wet in nothing but a towel and you invite me in and bring me a beer. Come on. This is obviously my lucky day."

She rolled her eyes and pushed her free hand against my chest. "Shut up."

"Your lip looks better already."

She froze and stared at me, her eyes hard to read in the dim light.

I lifted her chin and looked at it.

Her breath hitched in her throat.

I dragged my thumb across her lip so lightly I barely skimmed it and stopped right before the red crack.

"I should get dressed," she whispered, breaking my trance.

"Of course," I said, dropping my hand and knowing I'd missed a chance to kiss her again. Then again, I didn't know how long she'd been drinking, and she was the last person on Earth I would ever want to take advantage of.

"Make yourself comfortable," she said, nodding towards the couch. "I'll be out in second."

One side of my mouth curled up in a smile. "Let me know if you need any help in there."

She raised her eyebrows. "Let me guess. Undergarments are your specialty?"

"Wouldn't you like to know?" I asked, my eyes flashing.

"Yeah, you got me," she said, waving me away as she started towards her room. "I lie awake wondering about it every night." She shut her bedroom door without looking back at me.

I took a seat on the couch, sinking into the ancient cushions as I let my eyes scan the items near the champagne.

There was an open copy of Aesop's fables face down on the table at the start of a story called "The Lion in Love," which I assumed Andi had been reading since she'd loved stories with animal characters for as long as I'd known her.

Beside it, there was a pamphlet for a religious retreat clipped to a note.

Andi, if you need me for any reason, this is where I'll be this weekend (I'll have my phone). I'm back Sunday night. Have a great weekend, xx Steph

I opened the pamphlet. The subject matter was a bit heavy so I only got a few paragraphs in, but it seemed to reiterate the basic understanding I had of Steph's beliefs, which was that God chose things for her that were fated, and it was up to her to use her free will to stay on track towards her destiny.

And by the number of attendees they claimed they'd have at the gathering, she wasn't alone.

Personally, I was all for people having their own beliefs, but it did strike me as odd that she was so devoted to becoming a doctor when I personally struggled to see how science and religion were compatible.

At the same time, though, part of me wished I had the beliefs she did.

Not because I needed the security blanket of faith to sleep at night, but because being able to use God's will as an excuse for my actions seemed like the kind of crutch that would offer tangible piece of mind when I needed it.

"You thinking of enrolling for the one next month?" Andi asked, her hip cocked at the end of the couch. She was wearing a yellow sundress that went down to the floor.

"Only if you'll go with me."

"No chance in hell," she said, plopping on the couch beside me, her hair dripping less after a good towel dry.

"Not your thing?"

She topped up her mug with champagne and leaned back on the couch. "Not at all. Don't get me wrong. I love Steph to death, and she is hands down one of the smartest, kindest, least judgmental people I've ever met."

"Okay."

"But I hate the idea that everything is fated." She crossed her legs towards me. "I don't know how I'd get up in the morning if I believed everything was already chosen for me, if I believed all I had to do was go through the motions and not ask questions."

"You don't think it would take some pressure off if you thought that?"

She shrugged. "I suppose it might, but isn't pressure what makes life interesting? I mean, what really thrills me isn't the idea of fate. It's the idea that I can change the whole course of my life in an instant if I want to."

I cocked my head.

"I could wake up tomorrow and start over, and I wouldn't need anyone else's approval… especially not the approval of some virgin who's gotten all his life experience from books."

I raised my eyebrows. "Whoa."

"Don't tell Steph I said that."

"Of course not."

"And I don't mean to sound so harsh," she said, angling her body towards me.

"That's okay. I don't disagree with you."

"I just meant that I like the unpredictability of living my life moment to moment."

I stared at her bare, glowing face. She was so naturally beautiful it seemed unfair that other girls had to go to so much trouble.

"I want to believe that I have the power to change things, that I can be whatever I want." Her eyes went wide. "I mean, who I want. Whatever. You know what I'm trying to say."

"I do," I said. "And I get it. To be honest, I think we've always wanted the same things."

She cast her eyes down at the space between us like she didn't quite agree.

But before I could say anything more, there was a knock at the door.

T H I R T E E N
- Andi -

Every hair on my body stood at attention as I tried to convince myself I hadn't heard the familiar knock.

"Andi, it's me. Open up."

Shane's jaw clenched when he heard the voice.

"I came to apologize, baby. Let me in."

I swallowed.

Shane made a move to stand up, but I rose in front of him and laid a hand on his chest.

"You've done enough," I said. "I can handle this."

His eyes pleaded with me. "I made him promise he wouldn't contact you-"

"Sit," I whispered, nodding towards the couch. "I'm not even going to let him in."

He took a deep breath, his eyes on mine as the knock came again, followed by a forceful jiggle of the doorknob.

"C'mon, baby. I'm going crazy out here," Mike said, shaking the whole door in its frame.

"I'll be right here," Shane said, squeezing my hand. "You got this."

Having them so near each other made it really obvious how inappropriate my feelings for Mike were. I mean, every cell in my body was intimidated by him and ill at ease with how unpredictable he could be.

And then there was Shane, who was more like a mountain. A shield. An impenetrable force that made me feel completely safe. Any uneasiness I felt around him was down to my own inappropriate attraction as opposed to his behavior.

"Andi, I-"

Mike stopped speaking when I slid the chain lock off.

Part of me wanted to turn and look at Shane again, to draw strength from his gaze, but I could feel him staring at me so hard it was almost like he was propping me up anyway.

I undid the deadbolt next, followed by the button on the knob. Then I planted my foot behind the door to make sure he didn't try to push his way in and cracked it open.

Mike was standing in the stark hallway with a bouquet of wildflowers… and a thick white bandage over his nose.

"Hi," I said.

His whole chest seemed to deflate when he saw me, as if he'd been holding his breath for two days. "Hi."

I raised my eyebrows. "What are you doing here?"

"I came to apologize," he said. "And I brought you these." He extended the flowers in my direction.

I shook my head. "I don't want flowers from you, Mike. I want you to leave me alone."

He furrowed his brow. "Can I come in?"

"No. You can't."

"But we need to talk."

"There's nothing to talk about. We're through."

He pushed the door and it only opened an inch before it hit the side of my foot. "It's like that, is it?"

"Yeah."

"After everything we've been through?"

I glanced down at the worn carpet between us and then raised my eyes towards his. "What we've been through was hell, Mike, and I'm done."

"You don't mean it," he said. "Give me one more chance to show you how-"

"What?" My eyes narrowed. "How long you can go without hurting me again? How many lies I have to tell to feel safe around you?"

"Lies?"

"How many bullshit excuses you can make up for why it's okay to treat me like you have been lately?"

"No. To show you how many-"

"Save it," I said. "Your words don't mean shit to me anymore, and neither do you."

His face dropped.

"I'm all out of last chances with your name on them so you'll have to find someone else to push around."

"Oh my god he's there isn't he?"

I furrowed my brow. "What? Who?"

He dropped his hand so the flowers hung at his side. "The prick who put you up to this."

"Nobody put me up to this-"

"The prick who broke my nose yesterday."

Lucky for me, I was as horrified as I was amused, which was the only reason I managed to keep from smiling.

He craned his neck forward. "Weren't you even going to ask what happened to my fucking nose?"

I shook my head. "No, I wasn't. Because like I told you, I don't care about you anymore. Your nose, your anger, and your bogus GPA are no longer my concern."

His lips formed a straight line.

"Besides, whatever happened, you probably had it coming to you."

His face began to redden around the white bandage as he flexed and fisted his free hand.

"But for what it's worth, I wish you every happiness and hope you can learn to manage your jealousy so-"

"You know he just wants you for himself, right?"

I turned an ear towards him. "Excuse me?"

"Shane. Your so called friend. He's always wanted me out of the picture and-"

"Well now you are," I said. "And if you ever come to my door again, I'm going to call the police."

"You're not serious."

"I'm as serious as domestic abuse, Mike."

His eyes bounced back and forth between mine.

"Are we clear?"

"Just tell me if he's here," he said, raising up on his toes in an attempt to peek over my head. "I'm dying to know how quickly he weaseled his way into your-"

"Get lost, Mike. My life isn't your business anymore."

"That's what I thought."

I rolled my eyes.

"Watch out for him, Andi. I don't know what he's told you, but he's only after one thing, and it's not being your fucking shoulder to cry on."

"Have a nice life. I hope you get yourself some help."

As soon as I shut the door, I heard the bouquet explode against it.

Then I listened to his steps disappear down the hallway and locked all three locks again, suddenly conscious of how hard my heart was beating in my chest.

"You were great."

I turned around to find Shane standing a foot away with a kind look in his eye. "Yeah?"

He nodded and opened his arms. "Come here."

I stepped into his hug and let him wrap his arms around me while I wished he didn't smell quite so good. Couldn't he turn his sexy down or something so it wasn't so loud all the time?

I squeezed two clumps of his shirt in my fists and pressed my forehead into the crook of his neck. "You didn't tell me you broke his nose."

He shrugged, squeezing me in the process. "I didn't realize I had."

I didn't want to let go, but I knew I was dangerously close to holding on too tight and too long.

"I'm in a bit of a pickle now," he said when I stepped back.

"Why?" I asked, raising my eyebrows. "Cause he outed you for the secret crush you have on me?"

He smiled. "No. Cause I told him that if he ever came anywhere near you again, I was going to beat him to a pulp… or something like that."

I glanced down. "I see."

"And I like to keep my word."

"I know."

"But I'm also aware that you cared for that guy at some point, and I don't want to lose you cause I got violent with some asshole that's no longer relevant."

"Lose me?"

F O U R T E E N
- Shane -

"Disappoint you," I corrected. "Not that I wouldn't find pleasure in taking some of his dignity away." *Or watching the pledges use him for batting practice.*

"It's okay," she said. "He doesn't deserve your attention."

"Your call," I said. "But only cause I've never given him one more chance before."

She pursed her lips.

"If he contacts you again, that's his luck run out," I said. "So I need you to tell me if-"

"I will, Shane. I promise."

I exhaled.

"And thanks again for… being so great about this."

"I just wish you'd come to me the first time this happened."

She rubbed the back of her neck.

"Cause this wasn't it, was it?" I asked, cocking my head.

She raised her face to mine and shook her head. "Not even close, I'm afraid."

My heart felt sore at the thought. "Oh, Andi," I whispered, lifting one hand to her face so she couldn't look away. "Promise me you'll demand better for yourself from now on."

Her eyes started to water. "I promise."

I let my hand fall to her shoulder. "If only to keep me out of prison."

She laughed and stepped back. "Deal."

"Good. Cause I have so much going for me and-"

She rolled her eyes. "Speaking of all the things you have going for you, how about another beer?"

"It seems only right considering how much that little incident seems to have sobered us up."

"I couldn't agree more," she said.

My eyes fell to her ass as she disappeared into the kitchen, and I shook my head like a wet dog. Now was not the time to let my mind go there.

"Now," she said, setting a bottle of Bud down on the coffee table in front of me before taking a seat. "I think it's time we discuss the elephant in the room."

"Go on," I said, assuming she wasn't talking about the hard on I'd been trying to fight off since I arrived.

"Why don't you tell me about the secret passion you've been harboring for me that's just been brought to my attention?"

My whole chest felt like it was going to take flight. "Well, Mike and I had a long heart to heart at his place yesterday, and he just had this way about him that made me want to spill his guts- sorry, my guts."

She smiled.

"And he finally got me to admit the overwhelming desire I've been hiding all these years."

She laughed. "So how long have you been madly in love with me?"

"Easy. Remember when everyone got really into collecting stickers in second grade?"

Little creases sprang up around her eyes. "Of course."

"Well, I knew I was in deep the first time you showed me your sticker collection."

"Go on."

Hazel Kelly

"Everyone else had their stickers all mixed up," I said. "But you had your foamies and your fuzzies and your oilies separated not only by sticker type, but by theme."

"And that's when you knew?"

"Pretty much," I said. "But for a long time I was confused about whether it was you I loved or if it was just your possum family fuzzies."

"And when did you make the distinction?"

"Remember the day Izzy was pulling you on my skateboard behind her bike?"

"Oh god."

"And you tipped forward and scraped half your face on the driveway?"

"And then I had to cover my face with Neosporin before school every day like a slimy sea monster."

"Yep."

"I wish you'd forget that ever happened."

"Are you kidding? When you said you were going as Zombie Miss America for Halloween, I knew it was more than puppy love."

"Shut up." She shook her head and took a swig of champagne. "I was so gross no one could even look at me. And for real, gross. No special effects."

104

"I could look at you."

She narrowed her eyes at me. "Yeah. I guess you could."

"You'll always be Miss America to me."

"Seriously, stop. I'm not that depressed. And I'm no Miss America."

"Only because you're too smart," I said. "But I'll always see you that way."

She cocked her head. "What way? As a zombie head attached to a fourteen year old's body?"

I smiled. "Something like that."

"Wonderful."

"Now it's your turn to tell me you find me similarly irresistible."

"In your dreams, Shane."

She didn't know the half of it.

I watched a half dry wisp of hair fall in her face, and as she pushed it back behind her ear, the thin strap of her dress fell down over her smooth shoulder.

There was no bra strap beneath it, and I felt knots in all the most dangerous places.

She caught me staring as she pulled the strap back on her shoulder. "Don't be gross."

"You don't think I'm gross."

She blushed.

I felt a surge below the belt that made me forget all about our history for a moment.

"Maybe not," she said. "But I'm sure that's only because we've been friends for so long."

Friends. At one point, the label might've been a source of pride, but now it just felt like a curse.

"And if you met me now?" I asked, raising an eyebrow.

She dropped her chin. "Are you fishing for compliments? Is your ego really that delicate?"

"No. I'm just genuinely curious."

"You're not my type."

"It's cause I'm too handsome and clever, isn't it?"

She drained her drink but kept an eye on me.

"Or is it my muscles?" I asked. "Do you think there are too many of them?"

She leaned away to top up her mug of champagne. "All that and more."

"Mmm."

"Why do you ask?"

I shrugged. "I'm trying to figure out if you'll be able to keep your hands off me if I ask you to my barn dance."

"Excuse me?"

"Sorry. What I meant to say was, will you accompany me to my barn dance next weekend?"

She furrowed her brow. "As your date?"

"Only because you can't come as my hat."

"Smart ass."

"What do you say?" I asked, draining my beer and trying to act calmer than I felt.

"I say thanks but no thanks."

My chest tightened.

"I know I've had a trying weekend, but I don't need a pity date. I can pick myself up just fine.

"It's not a pity date."

"What is it then?" She raised her drink to her lips.

"It's a barn dance."

"I get that, but why are you asking me? What about all the girls you usually ask to this stuff?"

"All what girls?"

"I don't know. The Theta with the legs?"

"We're just friends.

"Or that pretty Indian girl? Or the gymnast you used to-"

"For someone that's not your type you certainly know a lot about-"

"What? Things you've told me?"

"Obviously I've said too much, and I apologize for that."

She waved the comment away with her hand. "It's fine."

"No really. Let me make it up to you by taking you to my barn dance."

FIFTEEN
- Andi -

I could tell by the steely look in his eyes that he was serious, but I was afraid to get swept up in the invitation, afraid the night would be all kinds of torturous if I said yes.

I knew he'd be in jeans and a plaid shirt and that was my kryptonite. I could resist a pop star or a pro athlete no problem, but give me a cowboy or a lumberjack any day and-

"I don't know," I said. "Won't it be crawling with sorority girls who'll just give me dirty looks because I'm sisterless and letterless and spent less than a week picking out my outfit?"

"No."

"Yeah, right." Men were so oblivious.

"If anyone's going to be giving you dirty looks, it's me."

My eyes grew wide.

"Isn't that what a good date does?"

God what I wouldn't give to be the girl Shane shot dirty looks at. Even if it was just for one night. "You wouldn't dare."

"I would," he said. "Especially if you wear pigtails for me."

I laughed. "First of all, if I wear pigtails, it will be for myself."

"The motivation isn't what concerns me."

"Second of all, I know you're just trying to cheer me up, but you've already done that brilliantly so you're off the hook. I appreciate the gesture and grant you the freedom to go forth and ask whoever you want."

"I'm flattered that you think I'm being chivalrous, but I'm actually not." His eyes dropped to my lips.

My heart stopped beating.

"But since you're hell bent on backing me into a corner, I guess I'll tell you the truth."

"Which is?"

"That I'm asking you for purely selfish reasons."

I raised my eyebrows. "Oh?"

"Because ever since I picked up that stuff for you yesterday, all I can think about is getting you in some high boots."

I pulled my knees up on the couch and faced him. "You're ridiculous."

"And you're my first choice."

I pursed my lips. Any other girl would say yes in an instant. He wasn't the kind of guy women said no to.

"And it has nothing to do with pity. It's because last night was the most fun I've had in a long time, and I want to spend some time with you before some other asshole sweeps you off your feet and you stop hanging out with me again."

"It didn't happen like that."

"Yeah, it did," he said. "But I was partly responsible because I couldn't bear to-"

I tilted an ear towards him.

"Just let me take you out and remind you how you deserve to be treated before you put yourself back on the market."

I took a deep breath.

"It's been too long since you went out with a gentleman."

I smiled. "And that's you, is it?"

He nodded. "Pigtails are optional."

I rolled my eyes. "And if I say no?"

"You won't."

"How can you be so sure?"

"Cause you love a theme party."

"True."

"And cause you owe me one."

I took a sip of champagne and felt the bubbles tickle my brain. "I thought you helped me out with Mike out of the goodness of your heart."

"Nope."

"So he was right about your ulterior motives?"

"Completely."

I couldn't tell if he was joking. "And you thought he was a useless meathead."

"I did."

"Fine."

He smiled. "You could at least pretend to be excited."

"I am. I'm sure it'll be fun."

He nodded. "It always is."

"Plus, we're seniors. It's kind of my last chance to go to one, isn't it?"

"I'd rather think of it more like there's a first time for everything."

The look in his eye made my heart rattle in my chest.

I desperately wanted to ask if it was a date. Like a walk you home and kiss you at the end of the night kind of date.

But I didn't think I could ask that without sounding hopeful.

I brought my fingers to the cut on my lip. "I hope this heals by then."

"I'm sure it will," he said. "And even if it doesn't, half your face could be scabby and covered in Neosporin and I'd still be honored to have you as my date."

I swallowed. Was there a word for this feeling? When someone else had the power to make you feel pretty even when you felt like you were dragging your feet along rock bottom?

Maybe I wouldn't regret saying yes.

Maybe he would even stay the night if I asked. I mean, I wasn't that worried about Mike coming back. I'd never seen him look so defeated.

But Shane didn't know that. And whether it was an accident or not, he'd hardly left me alone since I asked him for his help, his company.

I should've gone to him a long time ago. The first time this happened. He would've knocked some sense into me the right way, the way Mike never did.

My lips fell apart.

He raised his eyebrows.

"Do you want to-" My tongue swelled in my mouth. Asking him to stay would completely cancel out my nonchalance at his barn dance invitation.

"What?"

The clock on the wall started ticking over everything.

"You probably can't, but-"

"Can't what?"

He was too beautiful, too perfect. Having his attention was too much. It made me feel like Cinderella when the prince can't see anyone but her.

"What are you trying to ask me, Andi?"

The sound of the key in the lock shook me from my trance.

"Andi?" Steph called, opening the door as far as the short chain would allow. "Can you unbarricade the door please?"

I looked at Shane. "Never mind," I said, prying myself off the couch and swerving towards the door. "Hey Steph. One second." I undid the locks and pulled the door open.

Steph had that healthy glow she always had when she came back from one of her Jesus love fests.

"How was it?"

"Great," she said. "Tiring, but well worth it for the-Shane." Her eyes found him across the room. "What a nice surprise."

"Hey Steph," he said.

She looked back and forth between us, doubtlessly noticing the booze on the table. "Am I interrupting something?"

"Nope," Shane said, standing. "I was just leaving, actually." He drained his beer and bent over to grab his empties off the table.

"Don't worry about those," I said. "I'll take care of it."

"You sure?" he asked.

"Yeah."

"Well it was nice to see you, Shane. Sorry if I cut the party short," Steph said, sliding her duffel bag down the hall with her foot.

"Not at all," he said.

Steph picked up her bag, looked at me, and pointed down the hall. "I'll just go drop my stuff and let you guys… yeah."

Shane walked up to the door with his hands in his pockets. "Thanks for the fine drinks and company."

I smiled. "You're very welcome."

"If I fail my econ test tomorrow, I'm going to hold you personally responsible- but otherwise no regrets."

"If it were anyone else, I'd say you were a fool to spend the day drinking instead of studying, but you've never flunked a test in your life."

"True, but like I said-" He stepped into my space in a way I wasn't used to. "There's a first time for everything."

"Don't be a stranger," I said, opening the door.

He gave me one last smile before stepping out. It was full of something mischievous and knowing.

I closed the door and felt my chest loosen like it hadn't since he arrived, and I was about to slide the chain in the first lock when I heard a tap on the door.

I opened it again and let my eyes travel from the wildflowers under his feet up to his face.

"I forgot something," Shane said.

"Oh." I took a step back and opened the door wider so he could walk back in.

But he only took one step. Right up to me. And in the same swift motion, he slid one hand around my lower back and pulled my hair back with the other.

Then he kissed me before I even registered what was happening.

His lips were soft and warm and his tongue pushed slowly in my mouth, surprisingly gently considering the way he'd grabbed me and pulled me to him.

I felt limp in his arms as I bowed against him, my chest crushed against his and the bulge in his pants hardening against my stomach.

After a few swirls of his tongue, I found the strength to raise my hands and grip the sides of his shoulders.

When he set me back down, I felt as incapable of standing as a Barbie doll and fell against the doorframe.

"Okay," he said. "I think that's everything."

I sighed and watched him walk down the hallway.

Maybe there was a first time for everything.

S I X T E E N
- Shane -

My feet barely met the pavement on the walk home, and moving forward required no energy whatsoever.

It was as if I were on thrusters, kicking up a wake of good vibes behind me as I headed back to the house.

Where did little Andi Oliver learn to kiss like that? And why the fuck wasn't I informed?

Not that she was little anymore.

She was a woman now- with curves in all the right places- and no amount of denying that in my head was going to make my body forget it.

Not now. Not after holding her to me like that and feeling the way her breasts felt against my chest.

God help me if I really got her pulse racing, her breath panting against my ear, her hands on my...

I forced the air from my lungs, ran my fingers through my hair, and tried to figure out exactly when she got so damn sexy and why the hell I'd pretended not to see it for so long.

But of course I knew.

Because this whole thing was a recipe for disaster.

We'd been friends for so long- all three of us.

I'd always been the guy she came to when someone else broke her heart. I wasn't supposed to be the one breaking it.

But I didn't want to break it.

Still, I wasn't naive enough to think there was no risk. She was feisty, foolish, and wickedly funny. I didn't normally go out with girls like that.

My dating history read like a list of genuine Miss America wannabes. To say they were as simple as they were pretty wouldn't be unfair.

It's not that I was intimidated by complicated women. Lord knows my sister was the melodramatic queen of dichotomies. Life was just easier that way.

Predictable women didn't cause much trouble. They were easy to manage, easy to satisfy. The majority of them weren't clever enough to hide their feelings, which didn't always make things delightful, but it kept things straightforward.

So I could still have a life and sex.

The closest I'd ever been to dating a complicated woman was with Sonia from my econ class. She was by far the most intelligent woman I'd bedded in years, but she and I would never be serious.

We'd already discussed at length how important her cultural traditions were to her, and she had every intention of marrying a nice Hindu boy that her parents approved of. In fact, I got the sense that she already knew who it was going to be.

So there was no pressure there. Just fun.

What's more, I never stuck with one girl for any kind of celebratory amount of time. I tired of most of them too quickly and then did my best to drift off their radar.

But would I even feel compelled to do that with Andi?

I hadn't tired of her in fifteen years. If anything, I found her more interesting with every year that went by.

I turned down the street and lifted my face towards the last streaks of sunset in the sky.

Maybe I was overthinking this.

After all, we weren't friends anymore. Friends didn't kiss friends like that.

I'd set something in motion, and there was no way in hell I wasn't going to finish what I started.

Because all of a sudden, I felt like I didn't even know her anymore. But it was in the best, most exhilarating way, a way that made me realize how intimately I did want to know her.

And then a funny thought struck me.

Maybe Mike- despite his deep seated ignorance and his anger management issues- had picked up on something in me that I hadn't.

Maybe I'd always wanted more with Andi.

That would explain why the only thing I liked about her having a boyfriend was the fact that it made me feel like I had a bit more free reign to flatter and flirt with her.

Otherwise I hated everything about it, especially if I was unfortunate enough to glimpse another guy's hands on her.

I felt a lurch in my stomach just thinking about it.

And I swear her boyfriends always went out of their way to be extra handsy when I was around. I thought I just had shitty luck, but maybe I was giving off a vibe that they could sense, a vibe that made them question if she'd be better off with me.

Because she would be.

In fact, I believed that so intensely that the obligation I was feeling to see this thing through was growing by the minute, and I was actually relieved that Steph had come home so Andi hadn't had time to change her mind about the dance.

I was halfway up the stairs when my phone rang, which was when I realized how lame I was for thinking about her all the way home. And yet I still wished it had been her calling.

"Yo," I said, unlocking my bedroom door and pushing it open with my shoulder.

"Yo yourself," Izzy said.

"How'd your thing go?"

"My thing?"

"Wasn't the screening for your film class project yesterday?"

"Oh yeah," she said. "It was. I assumed you forgot because you didn't call to wish me good luck."

"And I assumed that you could sense all the good luck I was sending you so it was better not to distract you."

"Nope. Didn't get any inklings that I even crossed your mind."

"Maybe you've lost your powers." I kicked my shoes off and pulled a cold bottle of water out of the fridge, cursing my thirst since it meant I'd have to wash away the taste of Andi's lips on mine. "You should probably see a doctor."

"And maybe you're just an ass," she said.

I laughed.

"What's that thing scientists always say? That the least ridiculous explanation is probably the truth?"

"Sorry, Iz. Something came up and-"

"Save it. I'm not interested in the forced elephant march you had to do with your sycophantic pledges."

"First of all, it's called an Elephant Walk." I held the phone against my ear and unscrewed the bottle.

"You would know-"

"And second of all, we don't really do that. Other frats maybe, but not us."

"I want to know more even less than I believe you."

I shook my head and took a swig of water. "The screening went well anyway?"

"Of course," she said. "And I'm hoping my professor will overlook the editing mistake I made half way through because we're sleeping together."

My eyebrows jumped up my face. "What?"

"Only in my dreams, but-"

"Christ, Izzy."

"Have you talked to Andi?"

"Andi?"

"Yeah."

I squeezed my eyes shut. "Why?"

"I guess she broke up with Mike last night."

I swallowed. "You don't say."

SEVENTEEN
- Andi -

"What the hell was that about?" Steph was standing in the hallway with her head cocked and her hands on her hips.

"What?"

"Oh c'mon, Andi. I just came from a place with zero sexual tension. When I walked in here it was like I'd tripped into the mouth of a volcano."

I raised my eyebrows.

"Mike would've flipped if he'd been here."

I sighed and moved towards the couch, wondering if Shane had somehow sucked the energy from me with that kiss. "Actually, Mike has flipped for the last time."

"What does that mean?" Steph collapsed next to me, pulled her knees up, and tucked her toes between the cushions.

"We broke up."

"When?"

"Officially? A few hours ago." I turned to face her and dropped my head on the back of the couch. "That's why there's a bunch of wildflowers on the doorstep."

"Oh right. I was going to ask about that, but when the suffocating sparks hit me, I forgot."

"He didn't take it very well."

"Good for you."

I turned an ear towards her. "I thought you liked him?"

"Are you kidding?"

"You're always super nice to him and-"

"I did that for you," she said. "And because if I didn't go out of my way to be super nice, I might've given away what I really think about him."

"Which is?"

"That he's a chauvinistic tyrant whose misplaced arrogance makes my stomach ache."

"Why the heck didn't you say something?"

She shrugged. "Would it have mattered?"

I bit the inside of my cheek.

"In my experience, the only opinions that really affect the fate of a relationship are the ones held by the people in it."

"Mmm."

"Unless you're, like, Hindu or something."

I narrowed my eyes at her.

"What?" She pulled her hair thing out and redid her ponytail.

"Are you telling me that if you wanted to marry a Nazi sympathizer or an illegal immigrant or a Muslim guy, your parents' opinion would have no effect on your feelings?"

She craned her neck forwards. "First of all, those seem like really unlikely scenarios considering almost all of my socializing is through the church and-"

"Still."

She rolled her eyes to the ceiling. "I don't think my parents would forbid it or anything."

"Seriously?"

"I think they'd probably talk about it behind my back, but in the end I suspect they would decide it wasn't worth the risk of pushing me away just because they didn't approve of or understand my decision."

"If you say so," I said. "But it's hard for me to imagine having parents that don't feel compelled to interfere."

She lifted a palm between us. "Don't get me wrong. They interfere all the time. I just don't think they would in that instance."

"Right."

"But to be honest, I thank God that I have parents like that."

"I wish I could say the same."

"Think about it. The opposite scenario- disengaged and disinterested parents- isn't better." She lowered her head and stared through the empty champagne bottle.

"There's still some white wine."

She smiled and pushed herself up off the couch. "Guess I might as well have a glass since I'm already tipsy just from sitting next to you."

"You are not."

"Then you can tell me what the hell happened in the last forty eight hours that lead to the situation I just walked in on." She flashed her eyebrows at me before disappearing into the kitchen.

"I wish I knew," I said, my eyes on my feet.

"What does Izzy think of all this?"

"Nothing," I said, lifting my face towards the kitchen. "She doesn't know. Not that there's anything to know." I licked my lips and recalled the warm feeling they had when Shane's mouth was on mine. "Might as well make it two glass-"

Steph walked around the corner with two brimming glasses of white wine.

I smiled. "You're the best."

"Not really," she said. "I just don't really enjoy drinking alone."

"Don't judge me," I said, taking the extra glass. "And I wasn't alone. I was with-"

"Your soulmate?" she asked, sinking into the sofa.

I wanted to laugh but the comment made me freeze.

"Oh please. Like the thought hadn't crossed you mind."

"It obviously crossed yours."

"I've never seen you like that," she said, clinking her glass against mine. "Cheers to you finally ending things with Mike, by the way."

"Thanks," I said, taking a sip and letting the cool sweetness soak my tongue. "And seen me like what exactly?"

She squinted at me. "I guess the best way to describe it is that you looked the way people supposedly feel when they're on ecstasy."

"What the heck is that supposed to mean?"

"It means you looked like you were glowing. Like you were made of light."

I raised my eyebrows.

"Like you could feel a happy beat all the way to your toes and fingertips that no one else could hear."

"Is that so?"

"Yeah," she said. "High as a kite. That's exactly how you looked."

"Are you sure it wasn't just the fact that I've been drinking for a while?" I asked, deciding not to volunteer any specific numbers.

"Pretty sure," she said. "Besides, I've seen you on every notch of the scale between buzzed and tipsy to wasted and comatose, and at no point can I remember you ever looking that happy."

"So happy you had to use a drugs analogy?"

"Only cause I was thinking about them earlier-"

"Whoa whoa wh-"

"Because they came up at the retreat in one of those 'in case you haven't forgotten kids, doing drugs is a sin.'"

"So you aren't thinking of experimenting or anything?"

"No. But some guy told me yesterday that ecstasy was his favorite, and then when I saw your face earlier, I felt like I finally understood his explanation."

I furrowed my brow. "There was a guy at the retreat who's done that?"

"Of course," she said. "Everyone has their own ideas about what it means to get close to God."

"Huh."

"So did you sleep with him?

"What?! No! Nothing else happened."

"Damn."

I craned my neck forward. "Damn what?"

"Just think how sprung you'll be then."

"I'm not sleeping with him, Steph."

"But you would."

"No I wouldn't. We're just friends."

She furrowed her brow. "Andi."

"What?"

She shook her head. "Friends don't say good bye like that."

EIGHTEEN
- Shane -

"I'm glad they broke up," I said, trying to decide how ignorant to play it. "I never cared for the guy myself."

"I know you didn't," Izzy said.

"Did she say it's for good?" I asked. "Because I know she and Mike have had their ups and downs before-"

"Sounded to me like she was well and truly done with him."

I nodded.

"But time will tell."

"Right." I ran a hand through my hair. "When exactly did you talk to her?"

"This morning."

The way Andi looked with her hair strewn across my pillow flashed through my mind.

"So I'll call and check on her soon to see how she's holding up. Ya know, show her some support so she doesn't feel compelled to let that jackass back into her life."

"Good idea," I said, realizing there was still a possibility I could lose her before I ever even had her.

"But if you guys bump into each other-"

I clenched my jaw. I had way more than that planned.

"It might be nice to show her some extra special attention to keep her spirits up."

I smiled. "That sounds like something I could do."

"I thought so," she said in that tone of voice that made it clear I'd provided the correct answer.

"Is that all you called to tell me?"

"Umm…"

I imagined her eyes rolling up to the corner of the room.

"Who are you bringing to your barn dance?"

"My barn dance?"

"Yeah, the one where you wear that checkered shirt and let the bandana hang out of your back pocke-"

"Why do you ask?"

"Curiosity," she said. "It's around this time of year, isn't it?"

"It is."

"So who are you bringing?"

"I don't know yet," I said, only half baffled by why the lie slipped out. "Why?"

"No reason. But don't wait until the last minute to ask someone," she said. "Girls hate that shit."

"Right."

"And if you don't have anyone in mind, you could always take Andi."

I swallowed.

"Just to give her a nice distraction from all this shit she's been through with Mike."

"Uh huh."

"But that's only if you think you can bear bringing someone who isn't dying to get in your Levi's."

I squeezed my eyes shut. Was this just one of those twin coincidences or was she fucking with me and already knew I'd asked her?

I glanced at the clock on the wall.

Enough time had passed that Andi could've called Izzy and told her everything. Yet I had a feeling she didn't, a feeling she wouldn't.

Plus, she was probably too busy catching up with Steph after I left and cleaning up those flowers outside the-

"Please don't have impure thoughts about our oldest friend, Shane."

"I wasn't. I was just-"

"Forget I said anything. I don't think she'd go anyway."

I raised my eyebrows. "What? Why?"

"Well, besides the fact that you won't ask her cause you'd rather get fucked-"

I held my breath.

"She'd probably rather fork her own eyes out than spend an evening surrounded by orange sorority girls falling all over the place in their Daisy Dukes."

"Perhaps."

"Even if that's your idea of Heaven."

"It's not."

Izzy scoffed. "Yeah, right."

"So you don't think she'd have fun?"

"I doubt it's her scene. I mean, I'd rather die myself, but it depends on what's in the keg-"

"I know you think the world would be a more interesting place if we all drank gin and smoked 100's in rooms full of crushed velvet to piano music-"

"Preferably in black and white," she said. "Everyone looks better in black and white."

I sighed. "I hate to break it to you, Iz, but fifties film noir isn't a real place."

"Tell that to Dr. Who."

"Dr. Who?"

"You know, the time traveling-"

"That was a joke."

"You're an idiot."

"Mom doesn't think so."

She groaned. "Just look after Andi, okay? Forget the barn dance idea. It's stupid. But check in on her anyway."

"Will do."

"And check your schedule because I'd like to visit soon, and I know you and Andi would rather I come to you than ask you guys to suffer through a night with my artsy friends."

"They're not so bad," I said. "It's just that we have nothing in common besides you."

"I know. That was more than clear when you guys came for the indie film festival last year."

"I blame you for that," I said. "Andi and I should've just met up with you later-"

"Hindsight is-"

"Instead of letting you subject us to those depressing French films where no one smiles or talks about anything and everything is left unresolved."

"I thought you were both mature enough to appreciate realism."

"Sorry to disappoint you," I said. "But for what it's worth, I did like that movie about the murderous sorority girls you gave me."

"I thought that was more your speed."

"It was hilariously bad," I said. "But worth it for the way their tits were falling out of their tops during the grave digging scene."

"Spare me your detailed review."

I shrugged.

"But do lend it to Andi if you think she'd like it," Izzy said. "She loved that one about the vampire sorority girls I gave her last spring."

"I never saw that one."

"Maybe you guys could swap?"

"Good idea," I said, glancing at the open DVD case on my desk.

"Or have a movie marathon?"

"I'll ask her," I said, grateful for the lead.

"Okay, well, I gotta go."

"Yep."

"Love you, bro."

"You, too," I said, ending the call.

I took my jeans off and pulled on some sweatpants, glancing at the pile of folded clothes that sat where Andi had slept.

I walked around the bed to her side and grabbed the t-shirt in my hands. It smelled sweet and citrusy- like a lemon- and it made me think of how her lips puckered against mine when I pulled her to me.

There was no question that she was surprised, but that hadn't stopped her from kissing me back, from leaning into me, from opening her mouth so I could taste her better.

I tried to throw the t-shirt on my laundry pile in the corner, but even after extending my arm, my hand stayed closed around it.

I threw it back on the bed instead.

Then I walked over to my side, stopping at my desk to grab the practice test for my econ exam the next day.

I spent the next half hour lying on my bed staring at it.

However, despite the fact that my eyes were scanning along the lines of the paper in the right order, nothing was getting through.

All I could think about was Andi.

The whole day kept flashing through my mind- the way she looked in that dress that covered too much of her, the way she stood up to Mike, the way she looked at me when I talked about my memories of her as a kid.

It felt so good to make her smile, to have her laugh in my ears again.

And I knew I was in trouble.

Not only because of how hard it was to shake her from my thoughts, but because I kept it all a secret from the person I was closest to in the world.

And I knew why.

Because Andi may have been our oldest friend, but I didn't want to share her anymore.

N I N E T E E N
- Andi -

I felt my cheeks burn. "You saw that whole thing, huh?"

Steph leaned against the back of the couch. "You mean did I see him kiss you until your whole body hung limp in his arms and your feet practically floated off the ground?"

I scrunched my face.

"Yeah, I did."

I swallowed.

"And I'm sorry. I am. I didn't realize you were about to have a moment like that, but when I saw you, I just froze in the hallway and couldn't look away."

"Perv."

"Not that I blame you."

I turned an ear towards her.

"I can't imagine how you managed to resist him this long."

I raised my eyebrows.

"If he so much as looks at me with those steely eyes, I have to change my underwear."

"Steph!"

"It's true." She shook her head. "He is one fine piece of ass."

"Jesus. He's not a piece of ass."

"Maybe not to you," she said. "But he and I aren't close enough for me to give a rats about his other fine qualities."

I covered my face with my hands.

"You will tell me if he ever puts out a calendar, won't you?"

"Oh my god. I will not." I moved my hands to my cheeks. "And he would never."

"Maybe if you ask him really nice in bed one of these days he'd agree to pose for a few-"

"Let the bed thing go."

"Look who's talking. If you haven't been wondering how deep the feelings behind that kiss go since the moment he left, then you need to see a doctor."

"No I don't. And there's no depth, okay. He just got carried away." I took a gulp of wine. "There's not going to be any sexy photoshoots or any romps in the hay-" Oh god the barn dance...

"How can you be so sure?"

"Because we're just friends."

She furrowed her brow. "Yeah. I'm not convinced that path is going to work out for you guys anymore."

"What? Why?"

"Because when he left here, he looked like he wanted to fuck you yesterday."

I felt my chest contract around my heart, which was beating in some pattern that didn't feel familiar. Hell, ever since that kiss, my whole body felt weird.

"Excuse my language, by the way."

I cocked my head. "Are you sure you weren't simply imagining that look on his face because you just came from a chaste environment that was probably thick with sexual frustration?"

"You do have a point there," she said. "All I know is that if any of the retreat moderators saw Shane look at you like that, he'd get sent straight to confession."

I laughed- partly because I thought she was being funny and partly because the thread of sincerity in her voice made me so nervous I thought I was going to pee my pants.

"Does Izzy really have no idea that this has been going on?"

"Nothing has been going on."

She raised her eyebrows, her clear blue eyes looking right through me.

"But to answer your question, no. I mean, she knows I broke up with Mike, which I thought was the main event this weekend." I sighed. "It was more than enough excitement for me anyway."

"Every cloud, eh?"

I squinted at her. "You really think there was intent there? Like, you think he'd do that again?"

"I think he'd still be doing it if I hadn't come home."

"Shit, Steph."

"Exciting, isn't it?"

I slouched on the couch and stared at the ceiling. "Is it exciting or is it a complete disaster?"

"What could possibly be disastrous about being the object of his attention? He's be far the hottest, kindest, smartest guy who's ever expressed interest in you."

I peered at her out of the corner of my eye.

"I didn't mean for that to come out that way."

"It's fine. I know it's true."

"So what's the problem?" She got up and walked to the kitchen.

I leaned forward and drained my glass so I'd get a healthy top up on her next pass before slouching on the sofa again.

She came in with the frosted green bottle and poured some more white wine for each of us. "Well?"

There was barely a swig left in the bottle as far as I was concerned, but she returned it to the fridge anyway.

"He's my best friend," I said when she came back in the room. "He and Izzy."

"I agree it's not ideal."

"Not ideal?! It could change everything."

She sat down and crossed her legs towards me. "Perhaps, but it could change everything for the better."

"Or it could all go horribly wrong, and I could lose them both."

"Don't you think that's a bit dramatic?" she asked. "I mean, you're all adults now."

"Still. What if something happens-?"

"You mean something more?"

"Yeah." Fuck, was this thing already set in motion? Had everything already changed in the space of one quick kiss? "What if something happens and then it doesn't work out and then he meets who he's really supposed to be with and we can't hang out anymore cause she knows he and I have history?"

"First of all, you should give yourself a little more credit. I think it would be harder to replace you than you think."

A smile broke through my worried face. "That's nice. Thanks."

"You're welcome."

"But what if Izzy can never forgive me for breaking what's always been an unspoken circle of trust between us. I mean, she knows what a head case I am more than anyone on the planet. There's no way she'd be happy if

Shane and I started-" I didn't dare let myself finish the thought.

"Izzy loves you, Andi."

"Yeah, but-"

"And she loves Shane, too." Steph took a sip of her wine and leaned forward to set it back on the table. "I'm sure as long as you guys were happy, she would be, too, regardless of the arrangement."

"They still know too much. Both of them. So what could he possibly want me for? There's no mystery there? He was even reminding me earlier of totally embarrassing stuff he remembers me doing as a kid."

Steph shrugged. "Vulnerability is hot in its own way. Maybe you've been seducing him all these years without knowing it, and it finally got to him."

"That's absurd."

"As absurd as the idea that you've always wanted him, too?"

"I have not," I said, pulling my feet up and leaning against the armrest of the couch.

"Fine," she said. "I know better than to argue with you about your own feelings."

"Good."

"But just so you know, I'm not buying it."

"Fine. Cause it's not for sale."

We were both quiet for a minute, and the only things that troubled the silence were the sound of the ticking kitchen clock and some guys shouting to each other in the street below.

"What am I going to do?" I whispered finally.

"You're going to take it one day at a time," she said. "And not dwell on all the impossible what ifs."

"Easier said than done."

"I don't see what other options you have."

I looked at Steph. Her second glass of wine was visible in her cheeks.

"He asked me to his barn dance."

"That will be fun."

"Among other things." I pushed myself off the couch and picked up my half empty glass. "I'm going to get ready for bed."

"Sounds good," she said. "You should enjoy sleeping alone while you still can."

I smiled and drifted down the hall. Forty eight hours ago I would have bet my life he'd never kiss me. And now Steph seemed so convinced he wanted more.

I pushed my bedroom door open and caught my own eye in the mirror across the room. Could a guy like Shane even go for a girl like me? Wouldn't I look silly on the arm of someone so... so... totally fucking amazing?

Shit.

I needed to rest. All this booze had gone to my head. Surely I was reading too much into all this.

Surely he'd only asked me to his barn dance as a friend.

Too bad I was starting to think I didn't want to be his friend anymore.

F L A S H B A C K
- Shane -

"I can't believe you've never had a Blizzard," I said, scooping a creamy bite of ice cream in my mouth.

Andi shrugged. "I just can't cheat on the chocolate dipped cone. It's never let me down."

I smiled and leaned back against the driver's seat. "I admire your loyalty."

"Thanks," she said. "I admire your sense of adventure."

I glanced at the clock on the dash. "What time did she get out yesterday?"

"I think it was five thirty," Andi said. "But today was the dress rehearsal for the dress rehearsal."

"Does that mean it'll go slower or faster?"

She shrugged. "You're asking the wrong person."

"You going to opening night?"

"Of course," she said. "As if Izzy would ever forgive me if I didn't."

"I know. I just thought it might be fun to pretend we had a choice."

She laughed, the melodic chime bouncing off the car windows. "Don't you think it's great that she already knows what she wants to do with her life, though? Like, I don't really get it myself, but I'm so happy for her-"

I furrowed my brow. "Do you not know?"

"I sort of do. But it changes all the time."

"And if you had to decide now?"

She sighed and dragged her tongue around the base of the cone where some vanilla ice cream had started to escape its chocolate casing. "I guess I'd study psychology. Maybe do social work with high schoolers."

"You'd be great at that."

"Thanks." Her eyes sparkled in my direction. "But I'll probably go in undecided and declare my major later."

I nodded.

"You?" she asked.

"I want to move big piles of money all day."

She laughed. "Like with a forklift?"

"No, like in the stock market," I said. "Unless the online poker keeps going well in which case maybe I'll just retire early."

"I thought your parents made you stop doing that."

"They were going to," I said. "Until I told them how much I'd made."

She raised her eyebrows. "Seriously?"

"And when I said I wanted to use the profits to help pay my college tuition-"

"Let me guess, they shut up about it."

"Pretty much."

"Cool," she said. "So that pays better than my lifeguarding job?"

"I imagine so."

"Because I'll be lucky if I can chip in for books."

"That may be true, but I don't look nearly as good playing poker in my pajamas as you do in your swimsuit."

She swallowed and dropped her eyes.

The sight of her blushing filled my mind with filth.

"You think you could teach me how to do that?" she asked.

"What? Make your best friend blush or play online poker?"

"The latter, jackass."

"Sure, but you have to have a big appetite for risk."

She pursed her lips. "Mmm. I don't think I have that. Maybe you could just really crush it and then look after me?"

"Entourage style?" I asked, watching her push her remaining ice cream down into the cone with her tongue.

"Yeah. What do you think?"

I squinted at her. "I don't know. What do I get in return?"

She shrugged. "You get my company all the time-"

"Priceless."

"And I'll shower you with lots of attention to make sure your ego stays properly inflated in exchange for free room and board."

"Sounds like hard work, but I suppose it beats a nine to five."

"No shit," she said, planning the first bite of her sugar cone with so much concentration I felt my heart swell. "Who are you going to ask to the spring dance?"

I raised my eyebrows. "Who do you think I should ask?"

She kept her focus on her ice cream. "The new girl seems nice."

"I don't know," I said. "The jury's still out on her."

"Who were you thinking?"

"I hadn't really thought about it."

"Well, you should," she said. "Girls hate it when you leave it to the last minute."

"Right. You wanna go then?"

She looked at me with wide eyes. "What?"

"Do you want to go to the dance with me?"

"I-" She scrunched her face.

"What?"

"I can't."

"Because you don't think you can keep your hands off me when I'm all dressed up or-"

"Yeah, that's it."

"Seriously," I said, sticking my empty Blizzard in the cup holder. "It's the last dance before we graduate. It might be fun to go togeth-"

"I already got asked-"

I furrowed my brow. "When?"

"Two days ago."

"By who?"

"Steven."

I straightened an arm against the steering wheel. "Why didn't you tell me?"

"I assumed Izzy already had."

I nodded into the rearview mirror.

"We'll still be in the same group."

"Yeah, of course," I said, surprised at how disappointed I was. "Steven's a good guy anyway."

"Yeah," she said, popping the last bite of cone in her mouth.

I took a deep breath and stared at the auditorium doors, wishing Izzy would come out already… and that Steven fucking Thompson hadn't asked my best girl to the dance.

T W E N T Y
- Shane -

I'd just pulled a red and black checkered shirt over my shoulders when there was a knock at the door.

"Yup," I said, starting on the buttons.

Kevin poked his head in. "Can I get a quick opinion?"

"Of course," I said, tucking the shirt in.

His booted feet kicked the door closed behind him. He was wearing a shirt just like mine and had a hat in each hand. "Should I go traditional country?" he asked, plopping the tan cowboy hat on his head.

"Uh-huh."

"Or-" he swapped the hats he was wearing. "Give this baby a night out?"

I laughed.

His face drooped. "What?"

"Who do you think you are? Fucking Pharrell?"

"No. I just thought-"

"That one looks ridiculous," I said, raising my palms towards him. "In my opinion."

He sighed.

"Then again, I'm probably a lot less interested in current trends than your date is." I turned towards the mirror. "Who are you taking again?"

"Brittney."

I furrowed my brow at my shirt. "The Tri Delt or the G-Phi?"

"The Tri Delt."

I nodded. "Nice."

"As long as I can keep her away from the jungle juice."

I raised my eyebrows and turned around. "What makes you say that?"

Kevin shrugged and pulled his Pharrell hat off. "Apparently it doesn't agree with her."

"I didn't know there was anyone it did agree with," I said, unbuttoning my shirt.

"Yeah," he said. "Good point."

"Plus, she's probably a hundred and ten pounds soaking wet-"

"And a sophomore."

"Yeah," I said, pulling my shirt off and throwing it on the bed. "I'd keep an eye on her alright."

"One of the Beta guys told me if I keep her on vodka, I'm guaranteed a great night."

I walked to my closet and let my fingers tip toe across the hangers. "Is he the kinda guy you can trust or the kinda guy that would laugh if he heard you got your dick yacked on?"

"Oh fuck," Kevin said. "Probably both."

When I found the black and green shirt I was looking for- the one Izzy always said brought out the green flecks in my eyes- I pulled it off the hanger and turned around. "You want my advice?"

"Always," he said.

I pulled the shirt over my shoulders and started buttoning it up. "I'd play it safe and keep her on the beer. It's going to be a long night, and it'll be a whole lot longer if your date gets sick or messy."

He nodded and ran his fingers along the brim of his spare hat. "I suppose you have a point."

"I do," I said. "Trust me on this."

"Plus, she can't suck my dick if she passes the fuck out."

"No," I said, disturbed by the fact that such comments were so commonplace in the sex obsessed shithole I lived in. "And you don't want to give the girls in her house any reason to distrust you cause that shit spreads faster than the clap around here."

"Got it," he said.

I tucked my shirt in and walked to the dresser drawer that had my modest collection of belt buckles in it.

"Damn, Shane. Where did you get those?"

"Salvation Army," I said, throwing them around until I found the one with the galloping stallion.

"Can I borrow one?"

"Sure."

Kevin set his hats on the dresser and compared the one with the crossed pistols to the mean looking eagle. "Hmm."

I slung my belt through the loops, fastened it, and unbuttoned an extra button at the top of my shirt.

"I think I'll go with the pistols if that's okay with you."

"Cool," I said, sitting on the bed next to where I'd set out my black cowboy boots. "I hope they bring you lots of luck."

"Thanks," Kevin said, moving towards the door. "Who are you taking by the way?"

"Andi," I said, reaching for the black cowboy hat in the middle of my unmade bed.

He furrowed his brow. "Andi Andi?"

"The one and only."

"I didn't think she was into this stuff?"

"I think it's Greek life she's not keen on," I said. "But she can't resist a costume party."

"I guess I could see that," he said. "Especially considering your sister is her best friend."

I swallowed.

"Are you guys-"

I raised my eyebrows. "What?"

"Hooking up or-?"

"How about you let me worry about that and you focus on Brittney."

"That's a yes if I ever heard one."

"We're not actually." Yet. But it's not like I was going to tell Kevin I'd been obsessed by the idea all week.

"So is she fair game then or-?"

"No. She's definitely not fucking fair game-"

"Whoa, chill out. I'm only asking because Tyler's taking his younger cousin who's visiting this weekend, and he's always got an inappropriate word to say about Andi."

"What are you taking about?"

"You know, stupid stuff," he said. "I'd keep an eye on him is all."

"Always do," I said. "I wouldn't trust that guy to cook a Hot Pocket, much less leave him alone with my date."

"He is the slimiest. How did he even get in the house?"

"Legacy bullshit. His dad was the president his senior year."

"Ah. That explains it." Kevin pulled the door open.

"Hey- who won the poker tournament yesterday?" I asked.

"Tyler," he said, stepping into the hall. "Because you weren't there."

"Right."

"I thought you were gonna show?"

"There was one online I couldn't miss-"

"How'd it go?" he asked.

"Came out four ahead."

Kevin's eyebrows jumped. "Four thousand?"

"You know it," I said, putting my hat on.

"How do you do it?"

"Patience," I said. "And timing."

"Fuck me," he said, shaking his head.

"The bus is here!" A voice called from downstairs. "Get your asses outside or get left behind."

"See you on the bus," Kevin said.

I nodded and watched him shut the door.

Then I walked over to the window and pulled the curtain to the side.

The yellow school bus was parked in the fire lane outside the house, and the sidewalk was crawling with sorority girls who looked like they were headed to a Dukes of Hazzard casting call.

My stomach felt like a mouth full of pop rocks as I eagerly anticipated Andi's arrival.

After all, I hadn't seen her all week, and tonight was important.

It was vital that I get my head straight so I could make her feel at ease so far outside her comfort zone and, most importantly, so I didn't miss my chance to pick things up where we'd left off.

And I knew she would look beautiful when she showed up. She always did. But I underestimated the feeling I'd have in my guts when I first saw her come around the corner in her barn dance get up.

She was walking down the street on her own, the only girl who wasn't linked arm in arm with a bunch of others as she made her way towards the house.

Her tan cowboy boots showed off the toned legs that stuck out from the bottom of her short jean skirt, and she was in low braided pigtails that hung down over the front of her shoulders.

And I felt the strangest sensation sweep over me.

Because even though everyone was dressed up like country cowgirls and boys, I could've sworn it felt like Christmas morning.

TWENTY ONE
- Andi -

I should've let Steph walk with me.

She offered, but I was too proud to admit how nervous I was about having to wheedle my way into a throng of close knit sorority girls.

I wasn't worried about the guys. I'd spent enough time freshman and sophomore year with Shane that most of them at least recognized me.

But the girls were another thing entirely, and while I hoped Shane wouldn't be able to sense my anxiety, I hoped even more that he wouldn't leave me alone with them for too long.

And just as I was crossing the street towards the school bus, he stepped out of the mob onto the grass along the curb, his gaze fixed right on me, as if he'd seen me coming from a mile away.

He was in black boots and a black hat and his shirt had ribbons of forest green running through it, just like his eyes. I swear if he'd asked me right then to run away and live on a ranch in Montana with him, I would've said yes.

It was a ridiculous idea, of course, but we certainly looked the part.

"You look handsome," I said, smiling as he stepped up to me.

"And you look like the sexiest cowgirl I've ever seen."

"I'd take that as a compliment if I thought you'd ever actually seen one."

One corner of his mouth curled up. "You'd be surprised."

I raised my eyebrows.

"Nice pigtails, by the way."

"I did it to fit in," I said. "Not so you would get the wrong idea."

"Too late," he said, his eyes flashing. Then he leaned forward to whisper in my ear. "But don't worry. I'll only pull them if you want me to."

"I should think so," I said, my voice full of false calm and my nose full of his intoxicating cologne.

Fuck. Maybe I shouldn't have agreed to this.

"Come on," he said. "Let's get a seat on the bus."

He grabbed my hand in his and led the way, my feelings of awkwardness pulverized by the confidence his touch gave me.

I followed him towards the back of the bus, past countless seats that were already occupied by people in their giddy up and go gear.

When he stopped at a seat towards the back, I happily scooted in.

He sat down and faced forward, his gorgeous jean covered thighs like a wall between me and the alien culture around me.

"So," I said. "Where exactly does this barn dance go down?"

"Some dude's farm. About forty five minutes from campus."

"Cool."

"Thanks again for coming," he said. "I've really been looking forward to tonight."

I stuck my hands under my thighs and pressed my knees together before looking at him. "Thanks. Me, too."

"I'm glad you trust me to show you a good time."

"Of course."

"Did you tell Izzy you were coming or-?"

I shook my head. "No. You?"

"No," he said. "I thought we might just-"

I raised my eyebrows. "Just what?"

"Shane!" a voice called from the front of the bus.

He lifted his head up to shout back at the guy. "What?"

"Your help is needed in the keg transportation department."

Shane turned to me. "I'll be right back." Then he gripped the seat in front of us to pull himself up and raised his eyebrows at me. "Save my seat?"

"Unless I get a better offer."

He nodded and took off, knowing as well as I did that a better seatmate was unlikely to present itself.

I turned to look out the window. Across the street, a small group of frolfers were frisbeeing their way around an open green space.

And I didn't mean to start eavesdropping on the girls behind me, but their conversation was just too juicy.

Plus, it seemed a safer bet than dwelling on the inexplicable magnetism of Shane's ridiculous belt buckle… and where it might lead.

"So this is, like, so messed up you're going to die," the girl behind me said to her seatmate in a strong Chicago accent.

"Go on," the other girl said.

"So the older girls told our pledge class that they were going to take us away to some lake house to celebrate the fact that we got picked to be in the house."

"Cool."

"Right? But the night we got there, they gave us this big speech about how- if we wanted to be Thetas- we had big shoes to fill and a good reputation to maintain."

"Sure," her seatmate said.

"So get this. One of the prettiest girls in the house takes off her shirt, and another girl takes a marker to her and starts circling parts of her body that the girl needs to work on. You know, like the back of her arms and where her love handles would be if she even had any."

"Oh. My god."

"And then they tell us that we're all going to be subjected to the same treatment."

Her seatmate gasped. "No!"

"Yeah. For real."

"So did you get your fat circled, too? In front of everyone?"

"Just listen. So when the first pledge is about to take her shirt off, the doorbell rings, and all the upperclassmen go, 'Just kidding! Pizza party!'"

"Fuck me."

"Isn't that hilarious?" Chicago asked.

"I feel sick," the other girl said.

"They got us good."

Her seatmate laughed nervously. "They got you alright."

"I thought it was fucked up at the time," Chicago said. "But we all laugh about it now."

Her friend scoffed. "Except for the girls that still think about that night every time they puke up their pizza."

Chicago went quiet.

I was so relieved they were behind me because there was no way I would've been able to hide the shock on my face.

And I couldn't wait to tell Izzy. Or could I?

Would I have to lie about the setting? And what was Shane about to say? I mean, he obviously hadn't told her either.

I pushed a stray wisp of hair out of my eyes.

His failure to mention this to her could only mean one thing- that he knew this was wrong.

After all, there was no way he hadn't talked to Izzy since last weekend. And I had, too.

But neither of us said a word.

Because we knew the truth.

We shouldn't have kissed, shouldn't have liked it, and we certainly shouldn't have been going on what- for all intents and purposes- was basically a secret date.

And yet, if letting him kiss me again like he had last weekend was wrong, I didn't want to be right.

He was so tender, so strong, and he made me feel so bright and safe and treasured.

If only he were someone else, someone it would be okay to feel that way about.

But I wasn't disciplined enough to make myself stay away.

The feelings I had for him just had to be investigated, like the first time a child sees a candle and can't help but put their finger near the flame.

Because even a kid knows getting burned is more interesting than playing it safe.

TWENTY TWO
- Shane -

Andi had never looked so good, and I was having a hard time remembering that we were friends.

But there was a strange feeling in the air between us that made me think she wasn't struggling the same way.

I could tell she was a little out of her comfort zone- just as Izzy warned me she would be. But I wished she could see herself the way I did- as the coolest, smartest, sexiest girl on the bus.

I couldn't just say that, though. When it came to such matters, words were insufficient. Only actions could get the message across.

And that was fine by me because I was ready to show her the time of her life.

I watched her admire the sunset out her window, the curve of her cheekbone against the yellow and pink

173

swirls in the sky. I noticed how she squeezed her hands between her thighs and wished they were my hands…

Would she let me touch her there? Would she let me see that side of her? The side I always ignored for my own sanity?

I hoped so.

Because sanity didn't interest me anymore.

I was much more interested in watching her face as she let go. I wanted to see her lips fall apart and her eyes go dark with pleasure.

"So what were you going to say before we left?" she asked, turning towards me as the bus hit a pothole. "About why you didn't tell Izzy you asked me?"

Fuck. Well that answered the question about where her head was at.

She raised her eyebrows. "Well?"

"I didn't tell her for the same reason you didn't."

"And what reason do you suppose that is?" she asked, cocking her head.

"Because-" I stole a glance at her lips and felt a streak of heat travel up the back of my neck. "This is between us."

She narrowed her eyes at me. "What is?"

"Whatever is going on here."

"You mean the fact that you're getting ideas?"

I smiled. "What makes you say that?"

"Oh please, Shane. It's written all over your face."

"What is?"

She let her head fall back against the tall bus seat behind her.

I let my eyes linger on the bare flesh of her delicate neck before looking back at her face. "Well?"

"You want to make trouble for us," she said. "Or you wouldn't be looking at me like that."

"Like what?"

She crossed her arms and legs. "Like you want something from me."

I laughed.

"Is it the pigtails? Are they really that powerful? Cause I can take them out if they're making you stupid." She reached for the elastic on the one hanging between us.

"Don't you dare," I said, wrapping a hand around hers and pulling it away. "They didn't do anything wrong." I angled my body towards her, the muffled sounds on the loud bus making me feel like we were in our own little bubble. "Besides, they have nothing to do with this."

"With what?"

"The fact that you want to make trouble, too," I said. "Not that I would've personally chosen the word trouble."

"Oh? What would you have said?"

I let my eyes roll up until a word came to me. "Fun would've been better."

She pursed her glossy lips. "Mmm."

"And as far as me wanting something from you-"

She raised her eyebrows.

"You're absolutely right."

"I thought so."

I let my head fall back against the seat and rolled it towards her. "But I don't want anything from you that you don't want from me."

"Is that so?"

I fixed my eyes on hers. "Yeah. It is."

She broke our eye contact.

"And I haven't had any ideas that you haven't already had."

She glanced at me out of the corner of her eye.

"Am I right?"

"Would you believe me if I said no?"

I lifted my head. "Would you lie to my face?"

She swallowed.

"Good," I said. "So it's settled. We'll leave Izzy out of this for the moment and just have a good time."

She nodded, her eyes on me like I was an unpredictable animal.

"Besides," I said, hearing the bus crunch onto a gravel driveway. "If I get my way, there won't be any room between us for an extra person."

She pushed my arm. "Don't be ridiculous."

I craned my neck back. "What?"

"Don't try to put me in some kind of sexual trance with your steely eyes and your chiseled jaw and your-"

"Please go on."

"You wish."

"No really," I said. "It's nice to hear that you're as attracted to me as I am to you."

She rolled her eyes. "You're not attracted to me, Shane. You just can't help yourself from wanting what you think you can't have."

"That doesn't make any sense."

"Doesn't it?"

"Not at all," I said, shaking my head as the bus pulled to a stop. "Because I think I can have you."

Her lashes fluttered.

"And I think I will."

"I'm really flattered, Shane, but-"

"Good."

"Get off the bus."

I smiled. "Sounds like somebody needs a drink?"

"Yeah," she said, standing up and smoothing her skirt down. "A beer for me and an animal tranquilizer for you."

I backed into the aisle and made some space so she could step in front of me.

"Thanks," she said, sidestepping out of the seat.

"And it would be my pleasure to get you a drink as soon as we get off the bus."

"Glad to hear it," she said.

"But as far as the animal tranquilizers, this isn't that kind of party."

"Shame."

"Besides," I said, leaning down to whisper in her ear as the line scooted towards the front. "It'll take a lot more than that to make me change my mind about having you."

She turned around and stuck a pointed finger right into my chest. "Behave yourself."

"Or what?" I asked, my mouth curling into a smile. "You'll make me behave? Because that would be fine with me, too. In fact, I'd probably love nothing more than-"

"Unbelievable," she said, throwing her hands in the air and shaking her head as she turned back towards the front of the bus.

"Yeah," I mumbled to myself. "You are."

TWENTY THREE
- Andi -

I wished I could put it all out there like he was, wished I could just flirt with him like it was second nature.

But it was hard to flex a muscle that had been deliberately left to deteriorate for so long.

And where was this all coming from anyway?

It seemed unlikely that he'd developed a brain tumor, and I knew better than to think it was because he didn't have other options.

Then again, I suppose it could've been that kiss.

I always thought women were more predisposed to being wooed by a single kiss. But if he was even half as intrigued as I was by the sparks that flew in my doorway- by the way our bodies felt pressed against each other- it might explain his sudden change of feelings.

Unfortunately, despite the desire churning in my stomach, my mind was obsessed by all the reasons we were betraying ourselves, betraying Izzy.

Our three way Musketeer loyalty had been the one thing I could always count on. Was it really worth risking it just to see what was behind Shane's heavy belt buckle?

I sighed and leaned against the wall of the barn.

At least I knew where he stood. Sort of.

I watched him oversee the grill being fired up and the tapping of the kegs before delegating pumping duties to a few younger guys. Even from a distance, it was obvious that he wasn't just the alpha male in my life.

The younger boys hung on his every word, and his peers seemed to have endless back slaps and bursts of laughter that they were eager to spend in exchange for even his fleeting attention.

And not surprisingly, there wasn't a single sorority girl that hadn't checked him out.

Did he know how they all looked at him? Like he was head of the pride and they were all just female lions, blinking and posing and trying to catch his eye?

Or was he so used to being checked out that he didn't even notice the special attention his presence attracted?

Either way, even if he hadn't been all those things to all those other people, I still would've been proud to be at the dance with him.

It was a dream come true really, a dream I gave up on long before he surprised me by asking if I'd accompany him to our last high school dance. I lost a lot of sleep over the fact that I said no.

But back then it seemed like a date was all he wanted, whereas this time he obviously wanted more.

And the fact that I trusted him more than I trusted myself put me in a difficult position.

Because I didn't know how to behave.

All I knew was that if he tried to kiss me again

"Funny meeting you here," Tyler said when he came around the corner. His eyes looked me up and down as he planted one hand over my shoulder against the barn.

"Hi Tyler."

He craned his neck back without giving me anymore space. "You remember my name?"

"Yeah," I said, wondering how many of his drunken introductions I'd been subjected to over the years. "We've met a few times."

"In my dreams?" he asked, staring at my mouth so intensely I feared my lip gloss was smeared. "Or in yours?"

"Good one."

He kept staring at me like an idiot, and if his breath was anything to go by, he was already shitfaced.

"So who did you bring to the dance tonight?" I asked, hoping he'd take a hint.

"My cousin," he said. "She's thinking about going here next year."

I raised my eyebrows. "So she's only eighteen?"

He shrugged.

"Don't you think you should keep an eye on her?"

"She's a big girl," he said, shifting his feet so I completely lost my view of Shane. "She can take care of herself."

"I have to disagree," I said, fixing my eyes on him. "And I think it's your responsibility to make sure some creep doesn't get up in her face."

He narrowed his blue eyes at me. "She's fine. She's sucking up to some Thetas over there." He tilted his head in a random direction. "And personally, I'm more interested in what you're doing all by yourself over here."

I swallowed.

"Seems a shame that Shane would abandon you when you don't have any friends here."

"This is all pretty gallant of you, Tyler," Shane said, stepping up with two beers and a wrapped hot dog. "Except I didn't abandon anyone."

I felt my chest loosen.

Tyler kept his hand planted on the wall behind me as he turned his head towards Shane's voice.

"This is the part where you back the fuck away from my date," Shane said, his stance wide.

"Why?" Tyler asked. "So you can piss all around her?"

Shane took a step closer. "No. So you don't get your unwelcome ass kicked."

Tyler dropped his arm and took a step back.

Shane watched him like an aggravated pit bull before turning to me. "That's for you," he said, nodding towards the hot dog. "Ketchup no mustard, right?"

I smiled gratefully and took the hot dog and one beer from him.

"You can go now," Shane said, nodding at Tyler.

Tyler tipped his cowboy hat before turning on his heeled boots and strutting towards the smoking grill.

"He really creeps me out," I said, biting into my hot dog.

"Sorry." Shane drank his beer and kept an eye on the rowdy crowd near the grill. "To be honest, I kind of wish he'd behaved worse just now so I would've had an excuse to punch him in the face."

I swallowed my bite. "Is that something you do a lot?"

"Seasonally, I'd say."

"Why? That seems like such a waste of energy."

"Oh lots of reasons," he said. "Last time was during pledge week. I caught him fireman carrying some catatonic freshman upstairs."

My eyes grew wide.

"When he objected to handing her over, I jacked him in the nose and caught her when he went down."

"Then what?"

"I called some of the girls in her house and sat with her until they came to pick her up."

"That was good of you."

He smiled. "I'm actually a decent guy when you get to know me."

"I'll keep that in mind," I said, licking some ketchup from the corner of my mouth. "Shit- was I supposed to save some of this for you?" I looked back and forth between Shane and my last bite of hot dog.

"No, you're good. I scarfed one when I was over there. She's all yours."

I popped the last bite in my mouth.

"Sorry I let him get anywhere near you. It won't happen again."

"I'm over it," I said. "Besides, he only likes to get in my face because he knows I'm here with you, and he gets off on getting a rise out of you."

Shane shook his head. "That's not it."

"No?"

"He likes to get in your face because you're beautiful and charming, and he's deluded enough to think he has a chance."

"Well, he doesn't."

"And what about me?" he asked, leaning against the barn beside me. "Would you say I have a chance?"

"Jury's still out."

He narrowed his eyes on me. "Give a guy some odds."

I sighed. "You and your gambling addiction."

"Well?"

"I'd say fifty/fifty."

He laughed. "Are those really my odds or are those the odds that you're full of shit?"

I took a sip of my beer and tilted my face towards him. "What do you mean full of shit?"

"I'd say eighty/twenty that you're secretly dying to get me alone and can't wait to put your hands on me."

"That's presumptuous," I said. "And what's with the twenty percent? You having doubts?"

"No. I just know better than to think you're a sure thing."

I rolled my eyes. "I suppose I should be flattered by that."

"By the fact that you're not like all the other girls? Yeah, you should. I love that about you."

I cast my eyes down into my plastic cup.

"Frankly, I always have."

T W E N T Y F O U R
- Shane -

"And I've always admired your confidence," she said. "Though it's a bit full on being the target of it."

"Are you asking me to tone it down?"

She raised her eyebrows. "Yeah. Like way down."

I nodded.

"I don't know how to be like this with you."

I furrowed my brow. "Be like what?"

"Fawning and flirtatious."

"So don't be," I said. "Just be yourself."

"It's kind of hard to do that when you're being fawning and flirtatious."

I drained the rest of my beer. "Why do you suppose that is?"

"Seriously?"

"Yeah."

"Because things have never been like that with us. Things have always been friendly."

"And you're not sure you can handle them getting a little friendlier?"

"Even if I could, what then?" she asked. "Have you thought about the big mess we're going to make if we… go there."

"Obviously you have."

"I can't help it. Our friendship is important to me and-"

"Hey." I stepped between her and the party and tilted her chin up. "It's important to me, too."

Her plump lips fell apart. "Yeah?"

I dropped my fingers from under her chin. "Of course."

She cast her eyes down for a moment.

"And I wouldn't do anything to jeopardize it. Okay?"

"Okay."

"I promise," I said. "You can trust me."

"I know. If anything, that's what scares me most about this whole thing."

"Trusting me?"

She shook her head. "No. How much I already do."

"Truth or dare?"

She furrowed her brow. "Right now?"

I nodded.

"You don't even have an Oreo."

"Truth or dare?"

She sighed. "Dare."

"I dare you to stop overthinking things like such a woman and go on a hay ride with me."

"Is that a euphemism?"

"No."

She narrowed her eyes at me. "Even so, that sounds like two things."

"It's a double dare."

"What about the barn dance?"

I turned away from her to look at the scene before us, reminding myself that while it was nothing novel for me, Andi had never been to one. "If you want to stay here and get your Cotton Eyed Joe on, that's obviously fine, too."

"Can we bring beer on the hay ride?"

"Obviously."

"Fine," she said, draining her cup. "I'm in."

"Great. Let's go."

I glanced over my shoulder after a few steps to make sure she was following me, my eyes drawn to the buttons of her red and white checkered shirt.

"Hey, Barry," I said, summoning a pledge with an armful of firewood.

"It's Bobby," he said, sweat dripping off his brow.

"You've been promoted. Come with me."

He set the wood down where he stood and fell in line behind Andi.

Our first stop was the cooler. "Arms out, Bobby."

He did as I asked, and I loaded his outstretched arms with enough 40's to make a small pyramid.

"Can I help?" Andi asked.

"You're good," I said, leading them behind the barn to where a tractor with an open trailer full of hay was parked in a shadowy laneway that divided two fields of corn.

I stopped at the back of the trailer first and flipped the step down, extending a hand to Andi.

She took it and stepped up into the bed of hay.

"Here," I said, handing the first two beers up.

She grabbed them, set them down, and reached back for three more.

When she disappeared from view, Bobby put his foot on the step.

I laid a hand on his chest. "Actually, you're driving."

The redness drained from his face.

"Make yourself comfortable, Andi," I called. "I'll be right back."

"I can't drive a tractor," Bobby objected as he followed me around the trailer.

"Sure you can," I said. "It's easy. And there won't be any traffic for you to worry about. The only rule is don't flatten any corn and don't go too fast."

"That's two rules."

"Whatever." I stopped beside the tractor and pointed towards the wide driver's seat. "Up you go."

He shook his head as he climbed the steps.

I followed him up and made him scoot over so I could explain the controls.

He paid close attention and recited all my instructions back to me.

"Good," I said, patting him on the back. "You got this." I lowered my first foot back onto the ladder. "Now put the key in, count to ten Mississippi, and then follow that line towards the horizon."

He swallowed. "What if I have to piss?"

"Stop the tractor first and then piss. What the hell kind of question is that?"

"Sorry. I understand."

I climbed down, walked around back, and stepped up onto the wide truck bed.

When Andi came into view, I felt my whole chest swell.

"Well, howdy partner," she said, taking a sip from the big bottle in her hand.

She'd spread a blue blanket across the bed of hay and was leaning back against the stacked bales behind her.

Her legs were extended out in front of her and crossed at the ankles, and the braids hanging over her shoulders caught small flecks of light that made them sparkle as if they were harboring small fireflies.

"Aren't you a vision," I said, sitting down beside her as the engine sputtered to life.

The tractor jolted into motion a moment later, and we watched as the distance between us and the barn slowly grew.

"So," Andi said, breaking the comfortable silence. "Do you always bring your barn dance dates on a hay ride?"

"Pretty much. But you're the first I've gone out with alone."

She cocked her head. "Really?"

"Yeah," I said, reaching for the forty in her hand. "Usually a bunch of us go out together."

"Sounds like fun."

"It is. But I figured since I have a date tonight who's actually decent company on her own, I could make do without the extra people."

She smiled. "No pressure."

"Plus, it's nice to get away from all the drama for a while." I took a swig from the forty and handed it back to her.

"I can imagine."

"It gets a bit stressful living in close quarters with sixty jackasses whose mistakes have a direct impact on your personal reputation."

"I couldn't handle that."

I shrugged. "I don't know why anyone thinks they can."

"Do you regret it? Joining the house?"

I shook my head. "No. A lot of those jackasses are my best friends, and they'd do anything for me."

She nodded.

"But I have a lot of respect for you that you didn't get into the whole scene, especially at this school where the Greek system is such an overwhelming presence."

"It's not like it was a difficult decision," she said. "The thought of going from being an only child to having sixty sisters seemed way more stressful than it seemed exciting."

"Understandable."

"Plus, I don't like being told what to do, who I can and can't be friends with, where I have to be all the time, and what to wear." She shook her head. "That sounds like a nightmare."

"Yeah, it's not for everybody, though I feel confident saying frats are a little more lax."

She laughed. "Lax isn't the word I'd use, but okay."

I knew what she meant. And while part of me felt like I should be offended, I knew I didn't have to defend myself to her.

She wasn't judging me and my choices. She was just being honest, being Andi.

And it was refreshing to be around someone who wasn't prepared to suck up to me just to get a notch on their bedpost.

Being with her was fun, but it meant something, too, and meaningful wasn't how I would describe most of the relationships I'd had with women recently.

And once again the thought crossed my mind that I actually owed that dickrag Mike a favor.

Because if it weren't for him, I might not have realized how special she was, how special she'd always been.

It was like I was finally seeing her properly for the first time.

And wild horses couldn't have made me look away.

TWENTY FIVE
- Andi -

The glowing barn just looked like another star on the horizon after a while, and the hum of the tractor engine became hypnotic in its monotony.

To be honest, I probably could've taken a nap if Shane didn't have his arm over my shoulder.

And as guilty as it made me feel, I didn't want to push him away and pretend I thought he was gross. Because I didn't.

I thought he was funny and handsome and kind, and I didn't want to overthink things and deny myself a moment that any other woman would just enjoy.

And to think I'd spent the whole afternoon convinced I'd made a mistake saying I would come to this thing.

I worried that he'd leave me alone in pits of sorority girls and that I'd be forced to make superficial small talk with people while everyone around me did choreographed dances that I couldn't pick up the steps to.

But he hadn't abandoned me at all.

On the contrary, he'd stolen me away, and he seemed as happy as I was about it.

After all, having him all to myself was such a rare treat, and I was finally getting a chance to know what it felt like to be the center of his attention, which was akin to drinking sweet tea- warming and energizing and good for my soul.

I took a deep breath, letting the earthy scent of the hay fill my chest without lifting my head off his shoulder.

Shane shifted the arm that was around me and turned his face so his lips spoke against the part in my hair. "You fading on me?"

"No," I said. "Just enjoying the moment."

"Care to drag it out or do you want to head back?"

I lifted my head and looked at him.

His face was so close to mine and so handsome in the way it caught the moonlight.

"Is dragging it out an option?" I asked.

"Of course."

"Well, as long as you don't think I'm lame for keeping you from the party…"

He pushed against the hay bales behind us and rose to his feet, causing his cowboy hat to fall from his lap down beside me. "Trust me. We're not missing anything that doesn't happen every night of the week on campus."

"It's your big senior dance," I said. "I'm just along for the ride so it's your call."

He nodded and climbed over the bales at the front of the trailer. "Bobby! Bobby!"

I shamelessly stared at the panty wetting view I had of his butt.

"Turn off the engine!" Shane called.

The tractor engine clicked to a stop.

"Did I do something wrong?" Bobby asked.

"No. Just put the parking break on and come around to the back of the trailer." Shane climbed down off the stacked bales, picked up one of the unopened 40's, and went to meet him by the stairs.

"Everything okay?" Bobby asked, barely tall enough to see me over the truck bed.

"Everything is great, thanks." Shane took a knee and handed him the beer. "You're relieved for the night."

"You driving back then?" Bobby asked.

"I am."

I heard Bobby screw the cap off his beer.

"But you're walking," Shane said.

"What?"

"And in exchange for you not whining like a pussy, you get a beer for the walk and your choice between fifty bucks or a free poker lesson."

"I guess I could use the lesson."

"Good choice," Shane said.

"Is it true that you won a grand at the tournament on Wednesday?"

"Yeah, but keep that to yourself."

"Wow."

Shane held a hand out, and Bobby tossed him the keys.

"Now take a hike," he said. "And if anyone asks where I am, you haven't seen me."

Bobby took off down the dirt road, and Shane rose to his feet.

"A grand huh?" I asked when he turned around. "No wonder he chose the lesson."

He shook his head. "For just one second, I'd like to feel like not everyone knows my business."

"Maybe you should conduct all your business in cornfields?"

He laughed. "Based on how things go tonight, I might consider it."

"And how would you say they're going so far?" I asked, watching him take a seat beside me again.

"Mmm." He held his chin in thought. "Are you looking for a letter grade or a score out of ten?"

"If you even think about ranking me on any type of scale, I will kill you."

"That's what I thought," he said. "But to answer your question, I think they're going great."

"Because my pigtails are adorable?"

He smiled. "Among other things."

I wanted to ask what things, but I would've only been digging for compliments, and the fact that he chose to spend the whole evening with me alone was compliment enough.

"I noticed your lip is better," he said.

I touched the place where the cut used to be. "Yeah. I Neosporined the shit out of it all week."

"That is your signature move."

"God I hope not. Talk about the least cool signature move ever."

"I think it's a pretty good signature move for someone so accident prone."

I cocked my head. "Am I really that accident prone?"

He raised his eyebrows. "Is that a joke?"

"I mean, like, more than other people?"

"Let's see," he said. "Your mom sent you to school with a bagel cutter and enough ShamWows to open a warehouse."

"Hey- you've benefitted from those, too."

"Your dad put extra locks on your door to increase the likelihood that you'd remember to actually use one of them."

I shrugged. "He's always been overprotective."

"And you're the only person I know that has a loyalty card for the dry cleaners."

I craned my neck back. "Is that not normal?"

"In college? Are you serious?"

"Fine. Maybe I'm a little clumsy sometimes."

"It doesn't matter," he said. "I only mention it because sometimes it's hard to tell whether something is an accident with you or-"

"Like what?" I asked, leaning against the hay behind us.

"Like kissing me back last weekend."

I glanced down at my lap. "Oh, that."

"Yeah, that."

"That was-" My eyes searched his face. How could he look so calm when my whole body felt so squirmy? "Unexpected."

He raised his eyebrows.

"I think Steph had to take a cold shower after that."

"So did I," he said.

I swallowed.

"To be honest, part of me felt guilty for getting carried away like that after the weekend you had-"

"Don't feel that way," I said. "It was nice."

"Well, fuck, Andi. I wasn't going for nice."

I smiled.

"If I was only going for nice, I wouldn't have even bothered."

I raised my eyebrows. "You thought it was better than that, did you?"

He fixed his eyes on mine. "Didn't you?"

My lips fell apart.

"I was hard all week just thinking about it. About you."

The shock of his words made my throat close up.

"Sorry. You didn't need to know that."

I angled my body towards him. "Maybe it was better than nice." I laid a hand on his cheek and dropped my eyes to his lips. "Remind me."

He kissed me with an urgency that flooded my body with warmth. And as he sucked the breath from me, I lost my mind in his mouth.

He was right. It was better than nice.

It was the kind of kiss that needed its own backing track, the kind of kiss that could save your life.

He reached over and pulled my hips towards him.

It was only after I straddled his lap and felt his thick fingertips sink into my thighs that I realized my skirt was up around my waist.

I hung my arms on his shoulders and settled in, letting the kisses I'd wanted to give him for fifteen years pour out of me.

But it wasn't a friendly exchange.

He kissed me like he was two seconds away from pulling my hair and stretching me open, and when he pulled my ass towards him so my thin white underwear was right against his hard shaft, I knew it wasn't in my head.

He wanted me, too, and there was no one around to stop us from having each other, from going too far, from making the biggest, most glorious mistake of our lives.

I tilted my hips just enough to feel the length of him against my clit.

He moved his mouth to my neck, pushing my pigtail out of the way so he could kiss the delicate flesh behind it.

I tried to catch my breath then, but my whole body was flickering like a flame. "Shane," I whispered when his fingers found the buttons of my shirt.

I let my head fall back and looked at the sky.

And as I rocked against him, I lost myself in how solid he was and how free I felt in his arms.

TWENTY SIX
- Shane -

I shouldn't have been so surprised at how much I liked hearing her whisper my name.

I'd always loved her voice, her laugh.

But this sound spurred me on and filled me with a singular focus.

I wanted to make Andi come.

She was always so stubborn and independent. I wanted to make her surrender. I wanted to see the look on her face when she gave in to all the good feelings she deserved to enjoy.

And I wanted to make her say my name again and again and again.

I pushed her shirt off her shoulders and cradled the base of her neck as I kissed my way down to her collarbone.

When I unhooked her bra, she inhaled sharply, and I reached under it to cup her breasts.

"Shane- I-"

"Shhh," I said, grazing my thumbs across her nipples until they puckered for me.

She wiggled her arms from her shirt and dropped her bra to one side.

"You're so beautiful," I whispered, pushing a stray wisp of hair out of her face.

Her eyes were shiny, and I could see by her expression that she trusted me. It was a trust I knew I wouldn't dare betray, no matter how much I wanted from her.

I lowered my face to one of her breasts and pulled her tight nipple into my mouth, listening as a soft groan escaped her throat.

With every flick of my tongue, I ached and swelled more for her.

She put a hand on the back of my head and pulled it to her chest, arching her back towards me and letting herself go.

I laid a hand across her lower back and felt her delicate muscles flicker against my palm as she writhed. She felt so good in my hands, tasted so good all over.

I rolled her over, laid her on her back across the blanket, and propped myself up alongside her.

She stared at me through half closed eyes. "You're right," she said. "That was better than nice."

I laid a hand against her inner thigh and slid it up towards her center. I could feel the heat coming off her before I even made contact with her underwear.

A growl escaped my throat. "You're already wet for me."

She swallowed and watched me pull her underwear down to her knees.

I lowered my lips to hers again, dragging my fingertips along her wet slit until she moaned into my mouth.

Then I spread her open, working my thick fingers inside her as she tensed around me.

"Shane," she whispered again, her voice so soft I might've thought she was dreaming if her pleading eyes hadn't been on me.

My fingers were drenched after a few twists of my wrist, and when I found the spot that made her breath stutter, I hit it again and again, burying my fingers knuckle deep inside her.

"You're going to make me come," she said, rolling her head to the side.

I lowered my mouth to her nipple and sucked it between my teeth, churning her insides even faster.

A few moments later, her whole body curled up and melted over my hand.

I pinched her nipple in my mouth as she came, relishing the way she tightened around my fingers.

It was the most fun I'd ever had making a woman come.

I lifted my head to look at her, keeping my fingers where they were so I could feel every surge of her pleasure, every drip of her tension relieved.

Her face looked open and happy and tired.

I slipped my fingers from her and trailed them down her inner thigh.

She lifted her head. "I'm sorry I used the word nice."

I smiled.

"I promise it won't happen again."

I slid my hand over her waist and laid it between her breasts. I could feel her heart beating.

"I feel like a mess," she said.

"In a good way?" I asked, plucking some stray pieces of hay from the top of her head.

She smiled. "In the best way ever."

My balls ached from wanting her and my cock was still bursting against my fly, but I was reluctant to cut short her blissful reverie.

Unfortunately, my phone rang in my pocket and cut it short anyway.

She pushed her skirt down. "Are you going to get that?"

"Absolutely not."

It rang again.

This time I looked at it. "It's Kevin. He's probably just bored of holding Brittney's hair back or something."

"Who's Brittney?"

"No one."

A text came through from him a moment later. *"Where the hell are you? The last bus is coming soon."*

"Fuck."

Andi raised her eyebrows. "What is it?"

"We have to head back. I lost track of time."

"That's funny. I just stopped caring about it."

I reached for her bra and handed to her. "Get dressed," I said, downing the rest of the forty in the hope that it might take the ache out of my blue balls.

I watched her wiggle her underwear back up and put her bra on. It was a brutal low after such a glorious high.

"You want to stay back here or would you rather ride up front with me?" I asked.

"Is there room up front?"

I nodded.

"I'll ride with you then."

I set my hat on her head. "Sounds good."

She kept her eyes on me as she buttoned her shirt.

If only I'd made a move earlier.

There would've been more time to hold her, more time for her to get used to the idea of us.

But the moment had passed.

And while all I had to remember it by was her sweetness on my fingers and an aching sack, I still couldn't believe my luck.

TWENTY SEVEN
- Andi -

It would be understating it to say I was disappointed that our private party got cut short.

And I had to imagine Shane was, too, though he was doing a better job of hiding it.

I should've reached for him instead of just lying there and letting the waves of pleasure wash over me.

If I'd only undone his belt- or laid my hand on his thigh. He would've ignored his phone and given me his full attention.

But it would've been a long walk back to campus.

Still, I felt like a selfish tease.

I let him have his way with me, let him make me feel good, and I still wanted more.

It was as if having my hands on his body was some kind of high I couldn't stop craving.

Plus, there had been no release for him, and I desperately wanted to make him feel as amazing as I did.

So as much as I was trying to respect what he said about heading back, I couldn't help but notice that his arousal had become the elephant in the room- or rather, the tractor.

And there was no telling when we might have another chance like this, a chance to be far away in funny clothes that gave us permission to behave strangely. It was a chance I didn't want to regret missing.

"Shane." I put my hand on his thigh. "I know you wanted-"

"What?" he asked, dropping one hand from the wide wheel.

"More."

He shook his head. "All I wanted was to make you feel good and show you a good time."

I pursed my lips. "Well, you certainly did that."

"Mission accomplished then."

"And yet I've never seen you so tense." I glanced towards his belt buckle.

"Oh, that," he said. "I'm working on that."

I raised my eyebrows. "It doesn't look like you're doing a very good job."

"Yeah, well, you have that effect on me," he said. "And now that I've got a picture of your perfect tits in my mind-"

I slid my hand over the bulge between his legs, barely applying any pressure as I let myself get used to the idea of taking things further. "Do you mind if-" I couldn't say it, but the way his jaw clenched was permission enough.

I undid his belt buckle.

"Andi."

"What?" I asked, sliding his zipper down so I could feel the heat coming off him.

"Don't start something you can't finish-"

"Shhh," I said, sliding my hand down his happy trail into the last place I ever thought it would be.

I held my breath as I wrapped my hand around his girth, torn between the knowledge that what I was doing was serious while the startling size of him made me want to break out in nervous giggles.

I squeezed the base of his shaft, testing how hard he could take it, and when he swelled even more in my hand, I gushed in my already soaked panties.

"Can you make this any easier for me?" I asked, nodding towards the place where my wrist had disappeared.

He nodded towards the wheel, and I grabbed it with my free hand.

When he was convinced that I could keep us on the worn dirt track, he raised himself up, pulled his pants and boxers down around his thighs, and then sat back down on the cushioned seat.

"How's that?" he asked, taking the wheel again.

I lifted my eyes from his swollen cock in my hand. "Better," I said, stroking it.

He looked back at me and his lips fell apart.

"Eyes on the road," I said, picking up the pace.

He tried to respect my wishes, but I could tell by the pained expression on his face that the road was the last thing on his mind.

I scooted closer to him and fondled his balls with my free hand, watching as the anticipation grew in his eyes.

"Jesus, Andi, that feels too good."

I looked down and saw a bead of liquid at the end of his dick. I swiped it with my thumb on an upstroke and spread it around the tip of his head.

His far hand made a fist around the wheel.

I gripped him harder, running my hand up and down him as if he were made of steel, as if I couldn't hurt him.

Suddenly, his free hand swiped the hat off my head.

I stared into his stormy eyes and knew what he couldn't say.

It was good. Too good. And he was close.

I swallowed and looked back at his thick shaft, trying to guess whether he would shoot all over the wheel or erupt in my hand.

But my mind didn't even let me finish the thought.

Instead, I bent over and took him in my mouth, swirling my warm tongue around his head as I kept on stroking.

And when I sank all the way down on him, he let out a deep groan that vibrated through me.

A moment later, he exploded against the back of my throat and I drank him down, flattered at the amount of desire that had built up inside him.

He wrapped a hand around the back of my neck while I swallowed every last drop.

Then I slid my mouth up his cock, licked my lips, and pulled my hand away.

He looked at me with such a mixture of shock and affectionate approval that I couldn't help but be proud of myself.

When I reached for the wheel, he pulled his pants up and tucked himself back in.

As soon as he started steering again, I set his cowboy hat back on his head.

He adjusted it and glanced at me.

"What?"

He raised his eyebrows. "I wasn't expecting that."

I smiled. "Maybe you don't know me as well as you think you do."

He laughed. "No. I'm pretty sure I do. But if I've learned anything tonight it's that I'd like to get to know you even better."

"I think I'd like to know you better, too," I said, my cheeks suddenly warm as I registered what I'd just done.

"Is that a sexual reference?" he asked.

"Maybe. If you play your cards right."

"Well that's great news," he said with a sly smile. "Cause I always play my cards right."

TWENTY EIGHT
- Shane -

We were quiet on the bus ride back to campus, unlike everybody else... Except for a few wasted girls who were curled up in their seats, leaning against their windows while their concerned seatmates patted their backs.

But Andi wasn't drunk.

She seemed wide awake.

And I desperately wanted to know what she was thinking, wanted to know if she was cool with everything that went down earlier out in the cornfield.

But there was no reading to be done on her lips, and her eyes were dark.

When we finally pulled up in front of the house, it was clear who was in a hurry to get to the after party by how quickly they spilled down the steps of the bus.

The other dozen passengers- mostly females- were a bit slower to get to their feet.

"Come in for a drink," I said.

Andi turned in her boots and stepped backwards away from the house. "I think I'm going to call it a night."

"But it's only-" I pulled my phone out of my pocket.

She raised her eyebrows. "A totally acceptable hour to do that?"

"Yeah." I took my cowboy hat off and slid the brim between my fingers. "You're welcome to crash here."

She shook her head. "I'm beat, Shane. This was all-" She looked around at the sloppy cowfolk around us. "Great. But I've had enough excitement for one night."

"I understand. Let's get you home then-"

"I'd rather walk on my own, if that's okay. I'm too tired to be good company."

"I don't believe it."

One side of her mouth curled up. "Thanks for tonight, though. I had a great time."

"Me too," I said, checking her hair for hay.

"Be safe at the after party."

"I think I'm going to skip it."

She cocked her head.

"This night isn't going to get any better." I hooked my thumbs in my pockets. "Especially if you leave."

She rocked up on her toes and held my shoulders so she could kiss me on the cheek.

My body ached for more, and my mind pictured her clothes falling away, revealing all the places I hadn't yet had a chance to kiss her. "Text me when you get home."

"Sure."

"Promise me," I said. "I know everybody says that, but I fucking mean it."

"I know."

I nodded.

She looked at me one more time, as if there were so many unsaid words inside her that she didn't know which to let out first. Then she turned her pointed boots towards her apartment and crossed the street.

And as soon as she disappeared around the corner, I headed in the same direction.

My feet made the decision before my head did, but I wasn't about to let anything happen to her on what was hands down my best day of college yet.

Besides, the fresh air wouldn't kill me, and if I hung around, I'd just have to answer a hundred belligerent questions about why I didn't feel like going to the after party before making sure all the other girls got home safe.

And there was only one girl I cared about.

Unfortunately, I had to keep a farther distance than I would've liked due to the noisy heels on my boots, but I couldn't just let her walk off into the night at this hour.

When I saw her cross the street towards her apartment building up ahead, I stopped in my tracks, watching as her shadow entered the brightly lit stairway.

After I took a deep breath, I turned back towards my place, but something stopped me. It was such a strong feeling there might as well have been an invisible hand on my chest.

I looked back towards the glowing staircase, letting my eyes follow the tiny windows up to her floor.

She should've texted me by now.

My mind was listing a million reasons why she wouldn't have texted just yet, but my body was already taking long strides down the street.

And when I got to the base of her staircase, I could hear voices above me. Distressed, drunken voices.

I took the stairs two at a time, and when I rounded the corner towards the landing for the third floor, my fists clamped shut.

Mike had Andi up against the wall, and he was lifting her by the neck so her feet barely touched the ground.

When she saw me, there was nothing but fear in her eyes as her hands pulled at where he was choking her.

Mike must've noticed her glancing past him because he turned to look over his shoulder as soon as I reached the landing.

I hit him a second later, hit him so hard I felt the echo of the punch in my hand as he stumbled back against the concrete wall.

"Fuck, Shane!"

I glanced at Andi and pointed at the floor above us.

"Why can't you mind your own fucking business?" he asked, shaking his head and stepping in my direction.

"I was going to ask you the same question," I said, ducking as he swung a punch over me before sending an uppercut straight into his gut. "You been drinking tonight, Mike? You're usually a better shot than that."

Mike backed up, holding his stomach and looking for the wind I'd knocked out of him.

Out of the corner of my eye, I saw Andi pull out her phone.

"Why can't you get it through your thick skull that she doesn't want you anymore?" I asked.

"She doesn't know what she wants," he growled, putting his hand up on the wall.

I stepped between him and the stairs that led to Andi. "You know if I killed you right now, we'd both say it was self-defense, and nobody would fucking miss you."

"You and your empty threats," he said, straightening up again. "What's that?" he asked, pointing at the ground between us.

I fell for it like an idiot and he punched me square in the jaw.

It pissed me off so much that I grabbed the shoulders of his shirt and kneed him in the ribs as hard as I could.

He stumbled to the ground clutching his side.

I bent down and pulled his hair between my fingers. "Listen to me carefully, Mike. I've got all kinds of ideas for how I could ruin your life."

A trickle of blood seeped from the corner of his mouth.

"My favorite so far is I tell the cops I caught you trying to rape her-"

"But I wasn't- you wouldn't-"

"I would," I said, pulling his hair harder. "And then I'd make it my business to tell everyone on this campus about you, and I'd take great pleasure in watching you fail to shed that reputation."

"What the fuck is your problem?"

"You being near her, Mike." I scoffed. "Don't you get it? I'll do anything to protect her. And that certainly extends to fucking over a piece of shit like you."

He stuck his tongue out and tasted his own blood.

"So I'm going to give you one last chance to do the right thing and disappear before I make you disappear." I let his head go a little too hard against the ground and stood up, deciding he didn't require any more physical attention.

But as soon as I took a step back, Andi swung her pointed boot straight into his crotch.

Mike cried out and curled towards the wall in the fetal position.

I raised my eyebrows at her.

"The cops are on their way," she said, turning up the stairs. "Let's go."

"Remind me to never piss you off," I said, falling in line behind her.

She turned at the top of the stairs. "Hey Shane."

"What?"

"Don't piss me off."

TWENTY NINE
- Andi -

"What the hell happened?" Shane asked as soon as I'd locked the door behind us.

"You saw what happened," I said. "Mike went apeshit again."

He furrowed his brow. "Did he ambush you on the stairs?"

"Yeah," I said. "Right before you did, stalker."

He put his hands up. "Hey. I was just out for a walk and minding my own business when I realized you probably should've texted me already."

"Bullshit," I said, heading to the kitchen. "You followed me home."

"More like supervised."

I pulled two bottles of beer from the fridge and popped the caps off, letting them roll along the counter. "Well, thanks," I said, handing him one. "I'd really like to be pissed, but under the circumstances, I suppose you saved my ass."

He rubbed his jaw.

I grabbed some frozen vegetables from the freezer. "Here," I said. "To keep the swelling down."

"It's nothing."

I raised my eyebrows. "Don't piss me off."

He shoved the bag of veg against his jaw.

"I'm sorry, by the way."

He furrowed his brow. "You have nothing to be sorry about."

"If I hadn't-"

"Andi. None of this is your fault."

I walked over to the couch, sat down, and pulled my boots off.

Shane followed and took a seat beside me. "What exactly set him off?"

I shrugged. "Who knows? The first thing he commented on was how late it was, and then when he grabbed my phone and saw that I was texting you, he lost it."

He smiled. "So you were going to text me?"

"Of course. I promised, didn't I?"

"It was probably easy to remember after thinking about me all the way home."

One corner of my mouth curled up. "You might've crossed my mind once or twice."

He took a swig of beer and sank back against the pillows.

The clock in the kitchen ticked loudly, reminding me of how late it was. I knew I should ask him to stay, especially after he came to my rescue. "Did you mean what you said back there?"

He raised his eyebrows.

"When you said you'd do anything to protect me?"

"Of course," he said. "I don't say stuff I don't mean."

I folded my legs underneath me and angled my body towards him. "Would you bury a body for me?"

"Can I finish my beer first?"

I rolled my eyes. "It's a hypothetical question."

"Which I believe I answered."

"Would you jump in front of a train for me?"

"No question."

I squinted at him. "Lie under oath?"

"No."

I cocked my head.

"I'm joking. I was trying to convey how easy it would be for me to do that."

"So you would lie under oath?"

He nodded. "Like I said. I would do anything to protect you."

"Hmmm." I rolled my eyes up to the ceiling. "Would you get your body reinforced with metal like Wolverine?"

His face dropped. "I did that last summer. Jeez. You could at least pretend you noticed."

I laughed. "Oh right, sorry. I forgot."

He smiled at me, causing his cheek to crush against the veg.

I took a sip of beer and felt a warm wave of affection wash over me.

A second later, we both turned our heads towards the sound of a key in the door and watched Steph step inside quietly.

Her whole body relaxed when she saw us. "Oh. You're up. Back." She closed the door. "How was the barn dance?"

Shane looked at me.

"It was great. Really fun," I said. "What's with the backpack?"

She let it slide down one arm to the floor. "I was at the library."

I furrowed my brow. "Since when?"

"Since after dinner," she said, leaning against the wall.

"It's almost three."

"Which explains why I woke up face down in my book twenty minutes ago."

I craned my neck forward. "It's Friday night."

"More like Saturday morning," she said. "Which means in twenty four hours I have to dissect a dead pig, and I really don't want to desecrate it any more than I have to."

Shane and I nodded.

"Anyway, enough about me and my semi-conscious state of anxiety. I'll leave you guys to it."

"Not at all," Shane said, dropping his hand full of veg. "I was just-"

"What happened to you?" Steph asked, as if she hadn't noticed the vegetables until they moved.

"Andi can tell you all about it," he said, making his way towards the kitchen. "But you should see the other guy."

"Mike," I mouthed after Shane disappeared around the corner.

"You're kidding me," Steph said.

I shook my head and set my beer on the nearest coaster. "I wish I were." I stood up as Shane was coming out of the kitchen. "Are you sure you don't want to stay?" I blurted.

"I'll just be- uhh-" Steph's footsteps fell down the hallway.

I kept my eyes on Shane.

He stepped up to me. "No, thanks. I shouldn't be here anyway."

I rolled up on my toes. "Have I mentioned how glad I am that you are? That you were?"

He tilted my chin up and looked back and forth between my eyes. "Goodnight, Andi."

My lips parted just before his pressed against mine, and my insides twisted as he pulled my lower back against him.

When I needed to catch my breath, I held his neck and pressed my forehead against his. "That just gets better and better," I whispered, his warm breath still on my lips.

"Promise me something," he said.

I looked at him and slid my hand down his chest. "What?"

"Promise me you'll never give me a kiss on the cheek again."

"You didn't like that?"

"It's not that," he said. "It's just that I can think of a few places I like better."

"Don't be a hornball."

"Don't get me so hard right before you send me home alone."

"I'm not. I said you could-"

He kissed me again- this time with an urgency that perfectly explained why he couldn't stay.

I leaned my whole body against him, as if I could make an imprint of my shape against his chest.

"Trust me," he said. "If I thought I could behave myself, I'd take you up on your offer. But if I don't leave right now, no one in this apartment is going to get any sleep tonight."

I sank down on my heels. "So this isn't over?"

"Far from it, shorty," he said, pulling one of my pigtails.

I raised my eyebrows. "Text me when you get home?"

"Anything in particular you want? Maybe a photo of-"

"Words will be sufficient, thanks."

"Will do."

I walked him to the door and watched him make his way to the stairwell. "Shane."

He looked back over his shoulder.

"You know I want to follow you home, right?"

He smiled. "Get some sleep."

I closed the door and sighed as I dropped my forehead against it.

"You need to wash your mind out with soap, young lady."

I rolled my head towards Steph, who was standing in the hallway in her pink kitty pajamas.

"More like bleach," I said. "I am so fucked."

FLASHBACK
- Andi -

During the three weeks of budget gift giving, it was hard to tell who had me for Secret Santa.

At the end of the first week, I got movie ticket vouchers. That made me think Izzy had me because there were four movies out at the time that we wanted to see.

At the end of the second week, I got a Santa snow scraper. That made me think it was probably Steven because he was practical that way. Plus, he'd caught me scraping ice off my windshield with my history book a few days earlier.

The third week, though, I got a book of coupons for Dairy Queen chocolate dipped cones. That was when it first occurred to me that Shane might be my Secret Santa since he knew my ice cream preferences better than anyone.

However, he could've just been helping someone try to throw me off the scent.

But on the last day of gift giving, I figured out that he had me by process of elimination.

"Oooh," Izzy squealed. "Only one present left! I wonder who it could be from?"

"Yeah, I wonder," I said, shooting Shane a look as I pulled my flashing reindeer sweater down over my red velvet leggings and walked over to the tree.

I bent down and picked up the two attached boxes.

Shane patted the ottoman he was sitting on.

I sat down beside him and undid the ribbon. "Please tell your mom she did a really nice job with the wrapping paper."

He knocked his shoulder into mine. "Will do, smart ass."

I opened the smaller box first, and I could feel everyone's eyes on me as they looked over their warm mugs of Mrs. Jennings' weak ass mulled wine.

When I pulled the lid off, my face fell.

"If you don't like them," he said. "I kept the gift receip-"

"I love them," I said, pulling one of the sparkling snowflake earrings from the box. "But you weren't supposed to spend more than-"

"That rule only exists so you don't have to break the bank if you get someone boring like Steven."

"What the hell, man?!" Steven said.

"Besides, my only other idea was a Bath and Body Works gift set, and you smell good enough as it is."

I felt my cheeks blush and hoped people would think it was the wine. "Well, thank you. You shouldn't have, but I really like them." It was only then that I noticed the little sticker that said they were 14 carat white gold. My eyes grew wide and bounced back to him.

"You're welcome," he said, as if he could read my mind.

"Open the other one already!" Izzy said.

I sighed and looked at him with disapproval, trying to hide the sheer joy I felt that he would pick out something so pretty and delicate for me, that he would break the rules for me.

He shrugged. "Okay, so I had more than one idea."

I tore through the paper, revealing a framed photo that was taken the previous summer.

I remembered the day vividly.

Izzy had spent the afternoon reading a stack of People magazines on a blanket in the grass at the top of the driveway while Shane tried to teach me how to do a proper layup. Finally, after two hours of laughing until my sides hurt and chasing the ball around, I managed one.

Shane was even more pumped about it than I was, and he scooped me up on his back and ran around the driveway saying all this crazy made up stuff about the crowd going wild and my game winning shot.

And at one point, we must've been charging right at Izzy cause the photo completely captured the moment. We looked sweaty and young and our smiles were splitting our faces.

"You okay?" Shane asked.

"Yeah," I said, blinking away the tears that might give away how much it meant to me. "Thanks. I love it."

"Don't get mushy now before you see what's taped on the back," he said, lifting his chin at the photo.

"There's more?" I flipped the picture over, revealing an envelope with my name on it. I glanced at him. "What is it?"

He nodded, urging me to continue.

I pulled out a thick piece of paper. "Season tickets to Six Flags?"

"What do you say?" he asked.

The blood drained from my face. "I say I'm terrified of roller coasters and you know that."

"That's why I got season tickets. So we can take all the time we need getting you used to the idea."

"But-"

"It'll be just like the layup," he said. "You'll surprise yourself."

I pursed my lips, not wanting to ruin the moment for everyone by giving away how horrified I was.

"There's a first time for everything," he said, putting a hand on my knee. "You'll thank me. I promise."

And he was right.

I had five months to wrap my head around the idea, to research the odds of me puking on myself or falling to an early death.

And it took that same five months to convince my parents that roller coasters were actually less dangerous than trampolines and go carts (both of which they did everything to keep out of my sight and mind).

Then, when summer rolled around, Shane kept his word.

The first time we went, we didn't even go on any rides.

We just ate funnel cakes and watched the other smiling customers wander from one coaster to another, including a lot of kids which I found as motivating as I did frustrating.

But by the end of the summer, I'd gone on every ride tons of times, and my favorite turned out to be the Giant Drop- the last one I ever would've dreamed I'd have the guts to try.

And every time I got nervous, he'd hold my hand, look me in the eye, and tell me it was okay to scream.

And I loved him for helping me face my fears, for letting me squeeze his hand so hard, and for never being the first to let go.

THIRTY

- Shane -

My face was still smushed into my pillow when I heard the door swing open and bang against the wall.

Please don't jump on me. Please don't jump on me.

"Who the fuck is she?"

Chloe. I blinked my eyes open and yawned.

"Well?" she asked, ripping the covers on the other side of the bed down.

I groaned and rolled over. "There's no one here."

"That doesn't answer my question?" She was in a short blue jumpsuit with her hands on her hips.

I forced myself to sit up. "Sorry. What was your question again?"

"Who is she?"

"Who is who? What are you doing here?" I rubbed my eyes and looked at the clock. It wasn't even ten.

"The girl you took to the barn dance."

I reached for my boxers on the floor. "She's a friend. Chill out." I turned sideways and pulled them on.

"The kind of friend you disappear for hours with? And then I heard she had hay in her hair when you got back to the-"

"Why do you even know that?"

She picked up a pillow from the other side of the bed and threw it at me. "Because you were supposed to take me, asshole! So obviously all the girls in my house noticed when you showed up with some nobody-"

"That's enough," I said, getting up. I walked over to grab the jeans hanging over my desk chair. "Do you have any idea how crazy you sound? I never told you I'd take you to the dance."

She stomped one strappy sandaled foot on the ground. "But we have a thing!"

I shook my head and pulled my jeans on. I thought Chi O's were supposed to be more chilled out than this. So much for judging someone based on their collective reputation.

"Do you have any idea how embarrassing that is?"

I could see all the white around her blue eyes.

"For all the girls in my house to be getting ready and making sad eyes at me cause you blew me off?!"

"I told you straight up that I wasn't looking for anything serious-"

"Sounds like whatever you had going on last night was pretty serious."

"Sorry. What are you hoping to accomplish by repeatedly reminding me that you have a team of conspicuous blonde spies running lose on campus? Because it's not making me feel closer to you." I bent down to open my mini fridge and pulled out a half empty blue Gatorade.

"I didn't come here to listen to you be a jackass."

I furrowed my brow and swallowed a huge gulp of the cold drink. "Why did you come here then? To catch me with her?"

She looked down at her entwined fingers and swallowed. "I was hoping you might apologize. Or at least explain."

I raised my eyebrows and set the open Gatorade on the desk. "Explain what?"

"Why you didn't ask me?"

I sighed. "Look, you're a great girl, Chloe, and we've had a lot of fun together, but I have feelings for someone else."

She ran her hand through her thick blonde hair and swept it to the other side of her head. "Hold the fuck up. Now you have feelings?"

I walked over and closed the door behind her. If she was going to yell, I didn't see why she should disturb a bunch of other innocent guys.

"Let me get this straight. You just wanted to have sex with me- no strings. And then some other girl comes along and you've got the audacity to have feelings for her?"

I leaned against the door. "Actually, I think I've always had feelings for her."

Her eyes flashed. "What?!"

"I didn't know it when you and I were together, but-"

"You are so much more of an ass than I thought." She shook her head. "Everyone told me to give you a chance to explain, but you're obviously just a commitment-phobe with no respect for women."

I squinted and scratched one side of my bed head.

"I thought we were going to get a place together when we graduated. I thought we were going to give this a real go when-"

I raised a palm between us. "Hold on a second. I never promised you any of that stuff. I think you have me confused with someone else."

Her whole face took on a red flush. "Are you accusing me of something now? Because I'm not the one sleeping around."

I craned my neck back. "So you don't hook up with that Sig anymore?"

Her lips fell apart.

"And your ex from high school? The one who still comes to visit you? You expect me to believe you never give him a little something to keep him sweet?"

"How dare you insinuate-"

"What? That there's a reason we always got along so well? Because there was." I crossed my arms. "But it's not because we want the same things in the long run."

"So you don't even feel bad?"

"For what?"

"For not asking me to the dance when everyone thought you were going to."

"No. I don't," I said. "And I don't know who counts as everyone to you, but based on this fit you're throwing, I actually feel pretty good about the decision I made."

"You're going to regret this, Shane."

I bit my tongue.

"I thought you were smarter than this, but if you're one of those guys that needs to lose something before he recognizes the value it holds for him, then fine." Her eyes were like blue ice. "We'll see who comes crawling back."

"Fine by me, but don't hold your breath."

"Prick," she said, huffing towards the door.

I stepped away from it so she could let herself out.

"Good luck finding someone who can deep throat like I can," she said, yanking the door so hard I thought it might come off its hinges.

"I already did!" I yelled, leaning into the hallway so she'd hear me as she fled down the stairs.

I felt bad as soon as I said it, but whatever. She always got a rise out of me. That's why the sex was so good.

But long term it was a recipe for disaster. After all, she was obviously more unhinged than I realized.

I walked back over to my Gatorade and finished it.

I'd heard rumors of women imagining whole relationships that didn't exist, but it was even more terrifying to witness it firsthand.

Still, I was kind of grateful for Chloe's surprise visit. Because it reinforced the idea that I was ready for something different.

Something real.

THIRTY ONE
- Andi -

I woke up just before noon, and my mind immediately began racing with flashbacks.

Shane's hands on me, pulling me against him, his fingers churning my insides…

His dick in my hand, pulsing against my palm until I put my mouth around him…

Mike's hands around my neck, my heart beat in my bulging eyes. Shane's face when he saw me.

Anything to protect her.

I reached for the glass of water on my nightstand so I could free my tongue from the place where it had dried in my mouth.

Could this really be happening? Me and Shane? After all this time? After all this convincing myself it would never happen?

There's a first time for everything.

I set the water on my nightstand, opened the drawer below it, and pulled out the photo he gave me for Secret Santa.

I didn't usually keep it in the drawer, but I put it in there after the first time he kissed me, as if not seeing him every day might make it easier to shut all the "what ifs" out of my head.

Its regular place was on a thin shelf above my desk next to a picture of me and Izzy dressed as pirates and a photo of my parents on the Fourth of July. It was taken two days after they found out my mom was pregnant.

She once told me she wouldn't have been any happier if she'd won the lottery, and my dad said, as far as he was concerned, they had. Because I was their greatest treasure.

No fucking pressure.

I wondered what they'd think if they knew I was fooling around with the only guy they ever seemed to like. Scratch that- they'd probably been hoping this would happen the whole time, and I couldn't blame them.

After all, he was everything I never thought I could get. He was smart, handsome, funny, and kind. I figured I'd be doing well to score two out of four, though lately I'd been settling for one.

I dragged two fingers along the outside of the frame and looked at the expression on our faces.

We looked deliriously happy. But that could've been down to youth, not chemistry, right?

All I knew for sure was that being with Shane made me feel empowered, made me feel like I, too, had lots of lovely qualities.

And that boost couldn't have come at a better time.

I'd been letting myself be victimized for too long, and that wasn't me. I didn't recognize myself in the scared and self-doubting role I'd assumed in my last relationship.

And I didn't want to either.

I wanted to go back to being that girl that felt brave enough to try new things, brave enough to live in a way that didn't require me to lie regularly to myself and others.

And I could have that with Shane.

Sure, Shane could only pick me up so far. It was my responsibility to find myself again in the noise.

But I was determined to do it.

I pulled the covers off, went to my overflowing dresser, and pulled some gym clothes out of the bottom drawer.

I wasn't exactly disciplined about hitting the gym, but when I did, I hit it hard, often punishing myself on the rowing machine.

I liked that I couldn't watch TV or read while I rowed. Every single part of my body was occupied by the activity.

It was kind of like being around Shane.

Anyway, I always felt strong when I was done, and that's what I wanted to feel now.

Plus, I knew if I let myself wake up slowly, have a coffee, and chat to Steph, I'd never make it, and I desperately needed to do something besides think about the fact that I had my best friend's penis in my mouth last night.

I was halfway to the gym when my phone rang, and my heart fluttered at the thought that it might be him.

"Hi Izzy!" I said too cheerfully.

"You sound like you just woke up."

"No. I just haven't really talked to anyone yet today. I'm on my way to the gym."

"Time for your seasonal fall workout?"

"Shut up. Last fall I went at least twice."

She laughed. "My sincere apologies."

"So what's up? Did you sleep with your professor yet?"

"No," she said. "But you know me. I'm all about the chase. I'll probably lose interest as soon as he actually learns my name."

I furrowed my brow, my feet keeping a good pace below me. "What does he call you?"

"Isssabelle."

"Italian?"

"Yeah."

"Mmm. I can see why him calling you Izzy would suck."

"Speaking of sucking, I'm calling to check on you."

My heart froze in my chest. "Excuse me?"

"I wanted to make sure you're properly on the rebound and not pining over Mike?"

Did she know about last night? "Why do you ask?"

"Because it's my job," she said. "Besides, I can't rely on Steph to encourage you to fuck someone else as soon as possible."

"No. I suppose not."

"Well?"

I sighed and turned the corner, raising my eyes to make sure the gym was still at the end of the street. "I'm definitely not pining."

"Promise?"

"Would I lie to you?" Why the fuck did I say that?

"Right. Well, good. That makes me really happy."

"Good."

"And project rebound?"

I scrunched my face. "I wouldn't say I'm making a project out of it."

"You should," she said. "It's important to move on quickly in these situations, especially because time is running out."

"What do you mean?"

"I mean when we graduate, it's going to become less socially acceptable to make bad relationship decisions."

"And you think whoever comes next will be a bad decision?"

"Only because your choice in men lately hasn't inspired much confidence."

"Thanks for your honestly."

"Of course," she said. "So?"

"So what?"

"So tell me something good."

I stepped into the street to make way for a cluster of joggers. "About project rebound?"

"Yeah. Who've you got your sights on?"

Oh god she fucking knew. "Umm." I squeezed my eyes shut. "How do you know if you're on the rebound or if you just genuinely like someone?"

"Theoretically, I suppose both conditions could be met by the same person."

I hopped back on the sidewalk. "Interesting."

"Why? Who do you like?"

"No one."

"Seriously, Andi. If you don't at least find someone to crush on, I'm going to come over there and pick someone for you."

"That won't be necessary."

"Who's the hottest guy you have class with so I can creep him on Facebook?"

"You're nuts."

"Do you realize how difficult it is for me to micromanage your dating life remotely?"

"Is it more difficult than if you stopped caring?"

"I'll never stop caring," she said. "And I don't mean to be obnoxious. I just think even something casual might help distract you from the bullshit relationship you just survived."

She didn't even know the half of it.

"There must be someone-"

"There's a guy in one of my classes."

"Uh-huh."

"But I don't know his name. He's... shy."

"Okay, normally I would say the shy dope at the back of the class is a lousy target for some slate clearing rebound action, but I'll let it slide since you threw me a bone."

"Thanks."

"But promise me you'll work on having sex with someone as soon as possible."

"Okay," I said, swiping my ID at the gym's front door. "I'll see what I can do."

THIRTY TWO

- Shane -

I lifted my shirt and dragged it down my face. "Okay," I said. "Ready when you are."

Kevin pressed his blonde head into the weight bench. "Ready."

I watched him pick up the bench press bar and reach it over his head, letting my fingers hover just below it at all times so he wouldn't accidentally drop it and knock all his teeth out.

"Yep," he groaned, five reps later.

"One more or I walk away."

"Fuck you, Jennings," he said, his eyes on the bar as it shook over his face.

"Oh look. Britney's here."

He lowered and lifted the bar one last time.

I helped guide it onto the rack.

"I know you were fucking with me," he said, staying on his back for a second before sitting up.

"It worked though, didn't it?"

"Are you kidding? I'd move the Earth if I thought it would impress that girl."

I knew the feeling. "I take it things went well at the dance?"

Kevin made a sheepish face. "You could say that."

"You going to see her again?"

"Yeah." He stretched his neck. "I'm taking her to dinner this week."

"Nice."

He smiled. "She's not at all like I thought she would be. She's sweet and…"

"Stop stalling," I said, gesturing for him to get up.

"Then again." He rose to his feet and swapped places with me, wiping his forehead on his shoulder. "I always thought Chloe was a nice girl so-"

"You heard that, huh?"

He laughed. "Everyone in the fucking house heard it, Shane. She came in like a swarm of angry bees. I thought she was going to murder you in cold blood."

"How exactly? By choking me out? Her hand is hardly big enough to fit around my-"

"You bitches here to talk or lift?" Tyler said, walking past us with some large dumbbells.

Kevin rolled his eyes.

I glared at Tyler's scrawny back and laid down on the bench. "This is the last set, right?"

He nodded. "Yep. So don't leave anything in the tank."

"Deal." I raised the bar over my head and straightened my spine against the mat, pressing my feet into the floor to make sure I was stable enough to pump out some reps.

"So," Kevin said, his fingers hovering below the bar. "Chloe's out and Andi's in?"

"First of all," I said, lowering the bar to my chest. "Chloe was never in."

"Oh right. It was all in her head." He kept his eyes on me as I raised the bar. "I think I overheard that bit."

"Yeah. She's delusional. We've both been hooking up with other people ever since we first got together. I assumed we were on the same page."

"You can't assume anything with women."

"No shit."

"And Andi?"

"What about her?" I asked, a bead of sweat trickling over my temple.

"You disappeared for quite some time at the dance."

"What's your point?"

"Is it serious?"

"I don't know," I lied. "She's hard to read."

"Haven't you known her since you were in diapers or some shit?"

"No." I held the bar with straight arms and took a deep breath. "We were both sufficiently potty trained by the time we met."

"But you never hooked up before?"

"No."

"What took you so long to make a move then? That's not like you."

I lowered the bar, trying to buy myself some time. "You know how sometimes you can't focus on something or even recognize it when it's too close."

"Sure."

I forced the bar up. "That's all I got."

"Couple more, buddy."

"One," I said, my arms burning.

"Oh gosh," Kevin looked across the room. "Speak of the devil."

"Don't fuck with me."

He laughed. "No really. She's here. I was going to fuck with you anyway- don't get me wrong- but she's genuinely here."

"Damnit," I muttered under my breath.

"Make it three for good luck," he said.

I squeezed my eyes shut and lowered the bar. One for the way Andi looks in boots. I took a breath. Two for the way her ass feels in my hands.

"One more," Kevin urged.

I exhaled sharply and brought the bar down. Three for the look in her eyes right before she took me in her mouth. God that was fucking priceless.

I lifted the bar, dropped it into the rack, and sat up to catch my breath.

"Nice set," Kevin said.

I shook my head. "She better be here after that stunt you just pulled."

"Rowing machines, two o'clock," he said, smacking my sweaty back. "You can thank me later."

I lifted my eyes across the brightly lit room. Sure enough, she was there.

"You guys done here or what?" Tyler asked, stepping right in front of me.

I stood up and stared down my nose at him. "Not really. But I suppose you need it more than we do."

He stepped around me, and as soon as he'd unblocked my view, I found Andi again.

I watched the muscles in her legs flex with every stroke, watched the rhythm of her movements as she moved through the imaginary river beneath her.

God what I wouldn't do to be beneath her.

"Oh man," Kevin said, putting his hand on my shoulder. "You're in deeper shit than I thought."

I ran a hand through my sweaty hair and turned to him. "And yet she's the only cure."

He furrowed his brow. "What does Izzy think of you guys getting together?"

"She doesn't know."

He raised his eyebrows. "Oh fuck. Am I, like, obligated to tell her? She gives me a goddamn speech every time she's in town about how I need to let her know what you're up to."

I tilted my head. "And have you ever once told her what I'm up to?"

"Of course not," he said. "But mostly to protect her."

"In that case, do us all a favor and don't start tattling on me now."

He folded his arms. "You think she'd freak?"

"I don't know," I said. "But it's confusing enough without getting her unsolicited two cents."

"Got it."

"You heading back to the house now?" I asked.

"I'm going to hit the showers first, but I won't wait for you," he said, glancing across the gym at Andi. "I know better than to think my company can compete with that."

T H I R T Y   T H R E E
- Andi -

The sweat was really pouring off me after thirty minutes.

I had a few more songs to push through, though, to make it through the album I was listening to. Then I'd call it a day. Or a season. Whatever.

I still believed that one of these days- if I just kept at it- I was bound to fall in love with exercise enough to make it a real priority.

Today could be the day. It was possible. Maybe I would consider it over a big dirty brunch.

Suddenly, I saw a man out of the corner of my eye sit down at the rowing machine beside me.

Normally, I tried to keep my eyes on my monitor and not get distracted by what other people at the gym were doing.

That was one of the reasons I liked the rowing machines in the first place. They faced the windows and were off to the side, unlike the treadmills- which were always full of swinging ponytails and girls wearing just sports bras.

As if I would ever subject strangers to that kind of jiggling. If I wanted to show the whole world my bouncing ass, I wouldn't do it at the gym. And I sure as hell wouldn't do it sober.

Anyway, despite my attempt at disciplined focus, I knew it was a man who sat down beside me because I could see the toned muscles in his lower legs as he rowed. They were so strong I think my mouth might have watered a little.

But after a few strokes, he leaned forward as I pushed back, and I realized he was staring right at me, smiling.

Damn.

I paused the music on my Nano and pulled one of my earbuds out.

"Hey there," Shane said, his arms flexing as rowed along with me. "Come here often?"

I could see his abs rippling on each stroke through his tank top's oversized armholes, and for the first time since I arrived at the gym, my panties felt wet with something other than sweat.

"Hi," I said, wondering what I did to deserve him seeing me like this.

"Your face is a little red."

"And your face is a little-" Hot? Smoldering? "Unexpected."

"I didn't know you used this gym?"

"I didn't know you were into stalking other people while they worked out."

"I'm not," he said. "Just you."

"Aren't I special?" I faced my monitor again and tried to get back down to my goal pace.

"My thoughts exactly," he said.

"Are you just going to keep watching me?"

"Every goddamn stroke," he said. "Until I can't take it anymore."

"Don't be juvenile."

"Don't stroke so hard."

I wanted to be annoyed, but a smile broke through my face. "You're a real pest, you know that?"

"I've heard you haven't made it until you have critics," he said.

I shook my head.

"Not that I'd consider you a critic."

"So what does that make me?" I asked. "A fan, I presume?"

"As if you could deny it."

"What do you want, Shane?"

"I want to know how much longer you need."

I furrowed my brow and struggled to speak normally. "How much longer I need to what?"

"Finish your workout."

"Why?"

"Cause I want to take you for a big dirty-"

I shot a look at him.

"Brunch."

I narrowed my eyes. "You want to take me for brunch?"

"Yeah. At Mama Cita's cause I know it's your favorite."

I pursed my lips.

"And because it's half price cheesy hash day."

"Fuck."

"You know you want it."

I hung my head. "I do want it."

"That's supposed to urge you on. Not give you an excuse to slack off."

"What the hell?" I said, picking up my pace again. "You're the one that interfered with my workout in the first place."

"You looked like you needed some encouragement. I was worried you were fading and that you might crash your boat."

I rolled my eyes. "I don't believe that. I think you just wanted to come see how disgusting I am up close."

"You don't look disgusting," he said. "If anything, you have a borderline sexual glow."

"Oh please."

"Seriously. It's going to be awkward for me to stand up and walk away."

I dropped my eyes to see if he was really-

"You totally looked," he said. "You're insatiable."

"Walk away right now, and I'll go to brunch with you."

"How long do you need?"

"Why?" I panted. "You got something better to do than wait for me?"

He stopped rowing and sat sideways on his machine. "Andi."

"What?"

"Look at me."

I dropped my hands, stopped moving, and cocked my head at him.

He fixed his eyes on me. "Waiting for you is the best thing I've ever done."

I groaned. "Fuck off, and give me ten minutes."

"Take fifteen," he said, standing up. "I'm hitting the showers."

I swallowed.

"I'll meet you out front, shorty." Then he squatted down next to me and lowered his voice. "And don't worry about showering. I like you dirty."

"And I like you farther away," I said. "And I am so showering."

It took everything I had not to turn and watch him walk away, especially knowing full well how his ass looked in gym shorts.

Instead, I exhaled and picked up the pace again, which was easy to do. Between the thought of him sudsing himself up in the shower and the promise of cheesy hash, I really had no excuse to slack off.

I popped my earbud back in and pressed play, letting the beat of my workout mix drive the rhythm of my legs.

And just when I was ready to let my mind wander back to Shane in the shower, Izzy popped into my head.

I could imagine the expression on her face as she encouraged me to sleep with someone asap.

And there's no way it ever would've occurred to her that Shane occurred to me.

We'd kept our hands to ourselves for so long, and I'd mastered pretending I was resistant to his charms.

But everything was different now- the way he looked at me, the way he made me feel, the way he made me crave.

It was all too real too ignore.

Besides, Izzy was right. I did need to get laid. Hell, I wanted to get laid.

And there was nothing that frightened and exhilarated me more than the prospect of sleeping with Shane.

Which meant I had to consider it.

After all, despite my dearest friendships being at risk, my fear of losing him had morphed into something else: the fear of never having him in the first place.

And I knew there was only one thing strong enough to kill fear.

Action.

T H I R T Y F O U R
- Shane -

She was glowing when she walked out of the gym swinging her little drawstring bag.

"Well if it isn't Sporty Spice," I said, checking out her toned legs before she got too close.

"And if it isn't that one boyband member who can't dance."

I laughed. "I can dance."

"My bad," she said. "Did I confuse you with the one who can't sing?"

"Does it matter if I can make you sing?"

She narrowed her eyes at me. "I'd like to see you try."

"I know you would," I said, stepping off the sidewalk to cross the street. "But let's eat first."

We took the shortcut across the quad to Mama Cita's like we had a hundred times, but this time was different. This time there was a distracting mutual attraction that made our fleeting moments of eye contact nerve wracking.

We were about to walk through the doors when she stopped so abruptly in front of me, I nearly ran her over in my urgent quest to follow the cooked bacon smell.

"What?" I asked, staring down at her twisted face.

"I forgot my wallet," she said. "I deliberately didn't bring it to the gym so I wouldn't be compelled to do this exact thing so-"

"I can spot you."

"I know, but I don't want you to think I'm that girl who pretends to reach for her wallet at the end of the meal but who really has no intention of paying her way."

"I don't think you're that girl."

She exhaled, her chest falling an inch.

"And I can think of lots of ways you can pay me back so don't even worry about it."

She poked a finger into my right pec. "No."

"No, what?"

"Just no," she said, a mock glare in her eyes.

I followed her to the corner table she always went for.

"What is it about this table that you like so much?" I asked.

She shrugged. "It's my table," she said, sitting down. "It's a good distance from the bathroom. I can face everyone or face no one if I want. Plus, it's close to the pie display so I can feast my eyes."

"But you never get the pie."

"Sure I do."

I furrowed my brow. "Which is your favorite?"

"Would top seven be sufficient?"

"Okay," I said. "I believe you."

She opened her menu and leaned back in her chair as the chorus of cutlery on plates and weekend joviality swirled around us.

I watched her focused concentration. It was the same every time. She read each item as carefully as if she might be quizzed on it later and then- without fail- ordered the exact same thing she always did.

I found it amusing that she believed she had an open mind every time when her mind was obviously made up before she ever even walked through the doors.

"So what are you thinking?" I asked, playing along.

"Mmm." Her eyes bounced around the menu. "I'm torn between the Supreme Omelette and the Chocolate Chip Pancakes."

"Two good choices."

"Either way, we'll get a large cheesy hash to share."

"Of course," I said, watching her scrunch her face in deliberation. "And for what it's worth, I think you should go for the omelette."

She raised her eyes at me. "Yeah?"

"The protein will be good for you after your workout."

"That's what I was thinking," she said, nodding for a moment before closing her menu. "The Supreme it is."

It took everything I had not to laugh.

"What?" She fixed her brown eyes on me.

"Nothing."

"Why are you making that face at me?"

I craned my neck back. "What face? I wasn't making any face."

"Yes you were," she said. "Don't look at me like that."

"Like what?"

"Like I'm adorable or something." She poured some water into her glass and then mine, the half melted ice cubes causing her to splash all over the table. "It's freaking me out."

"I'm sorry. How should I look at you?"

"Normally."

I shook my head. "I don't know what that means."

"Please don't make this weird, Shane. It's already hard enough making eye contact with you after-"

I raised my eyebrows. "After what?"

"After what happened."

One corner of my mouth curled up. "Is that because you'd rather be eyeing something else or-"

"What can I get you folks?" A middle aged woman with an apron cutting her stomach in two appeared at the table.

"One Supreme Omelette, a large order of cheesy hash to share, and I'll take the Meat Lover's Omelette," I said.

"And to drink?" the woman's eyes flitted up for half a second while she scribbled on her notepad.

"Two glasses of orange juice, please," I said, smiling as she turned on her heels.

Andi cocked her head. "You're ordering for me now?"

I groaned. "I order for you all the time. It's not like I didn't get what you wanted."

"I know, but-"

"Just stop," I said. "Seriously."

"Stop what?"

"Looking for things to freak out about. Everything is fine. Nothing has changed-"

"Everything has changed."

"No it hasn't. It's in your head."

She crossed her arms. "How have things not changed?"

I sighed. "Because you're still my favorite person in the world- besides Izzy, obviously."

She pursed her lips.

"So don't be weird just because last night was the best night of your life and you don't know how to handle it."

"You don't know that."

"Well, it was the best night of mine anyway."

She swallowed. "Really?"

"Of course." I took a sip of water. "To be honest, the only thing I feel bad or weird about right now is the fact that I ever shared you with anyone else."

She cast her eyes down and her glowing cheeks flushed. "Don't be," she said, lifting her eyes back to mine. "Because if you hadn't, I wouldn't understand how good last night was."

I smiled. "I knew it. You're fucking in love with me."

"Don't flatter yourself."

"Fine. As long as you agree that there's no reason to stop enjoying each other's company just because we allowed ourselves to enjoy it a little more than usual."

"I suppose not," she said. "But don't pretend last night doesn't change things."

I shrugged. "So what if it does? I thought David Bowie was your idol."

"So?"

"So he was the ultimate chameleon, the poster boy who made change cool."

Her eyes lit up. "Are you suggesting that Bowie would think it was a great idea for us to fool around?"

"Are you kidding?" I asked. "He would be like, 'Good for those kooks! So glad they embraced the ch-ch-ch-ch-change-'"

"Shh! You've made your point."

"Good," I said. "In that case, have you decided yet?"

She pushed some half dried hair out of her face and leaned an ear towards me. "Decided what?"

I smiled. "How you're going to pay me back for breakfast?"

THIRTY FIVE
- Andi -

I folded my arms and leaned against the frame of Steph's open door.

She was studying a pack of notecards, absorbed in a way I'd never been in anything. Well, almost anything.

And I admired her for it. Not for her devotion to keeping index card companies in business, but for her commitment to achieving her goals.

I liked to think I would've been just as devoted if I had a calling. Unfortunately, nothing had grabbed me as intensely as to warrant that kind of time and attention.

"You just going to stand there watching me or what?" she asked, keeping her eyes on the cards.

"Yeah," I said. "Until I'm done stewing in my pit of jealousy. Then I'm going to offer to make you some tea."

"Jealousy?" she asked, checking the back of the card at hand and looking over her shoulder at me. "Why jealousy?"

"Oh you know. The usual. Knowing what you want to do with your life."

"Trust me," she said, laying the stack on her desk between two other perfectly aligned stacks. "Knowing what you want to do with your life is totally overrated."

I laughed. "Yeah, people are always telling me they wish they had my complete lack of direction."

She slung an elbow over the back of her chair. "I wouldn't worry about it. The important thing is that your grades are good and you have options."

"A lot of options I'm not particularly drawn to."

"It's okay to not know the future."

"I know. I just feel like I was sold something different, ya know? Like I thought I would know what I wanted by the time I had to declare a major- at the latest. And instead, I feel increasingly less certain about what I'm going to do when I graduate all the time."

She smiled. "Too much time in the psych department would make anyone overthink things."

"So it's not me?"

She shook her head. "No. Your problem is a good one."

"And what exactly is my problem, Dr. Stone?"

She smiled. "You're interested in too many things."

"It doesn't sound like a curse when you say it like that."

"It's not," she said. "Besides, I know what you're going to do after you graduate."

"Oh? What's that?"

"Shane Jennings."

I let my head fall against the doorframe. "I don't think I can put that on my resume."

"Which is a shame, really, considering it's about the best experience a girl could hope for."

I smiled. "Is that your prescription for what ails me, then?"

She nodded. "Along with a few Hail Marys."

I leaned away from the door. "So how about that tea break since you haven't emerged from your room in twenty four hours?"

"Got anything stronger?"

"Will French press do?"

"Oh god yes," she said, rising to her feet.

I decided not to call her attention to her lazy use of God's name, but I made a mental note that she must've been totally exhausted. "How black do you want it?" I asked, walking into the kitchen.

"What are my choices?" she asked, groaning as she plopped on the couch.

"Will Smith black or Denzel black," I said, filling the kettle.

"How about Tyrese with no shirt on in the rain black?"

I laughed. "I'll do my best."

"I think I need to take a nap."

I flicked the kettle on and spooned some coffee into the French press. "I don't know," I said, coming around the corner. "I like the shit that comes out of your mouth when you're sleep deprived."

"Does that mean you forgive me for eating your leftover cheesy hash last night?" she asked, propping her head up on the back of the couch.

"I didn't know you did that," I said, bending over the TV console and searching through the junk drawer for some eye drops. "But if they helped you push through the wee hours, then I'm glad I could help."

"Who did you go to Mama's with?"

I found the eye drops and tossed them beside her on the couch.

"Thanks," she said. "I guess they look as bad as they feel."

"This is the most stoned you've ever looked for sure," I said, checking the clock when I heard the kettle click off.

"It's the most stoned I've ever felt," she said, leaning back to water her eyes.

I sat on the arm of the couch. "Better?"

She nodded. "So? It was Shane, wasn't it?"

"Yeah."

"Was it a date?"

"Who the hell knows? I just ran into him."

She raised her eyebrows. "Are you guys official yet or-"

"Yeah. As in officially not labeling it."

"Oh, okay." She popped the cap back on the eye drops. "Can I officially be a bridesmaid, though?"

"It's not that serious."

"How dare you lie to me in my condition," she said, pointing a straight arm towards the kitchen. "Go make coffee for your sins."

"I don't think we even have that much coffee," I mumbled, returning to the kitchen. I poured some hot water in the French press and checked the clock again.

"Give it at least five minutes so it's nice and Tyresey."

"Sure," I said.

"And please explain how this isn't serious."

I came back around the corner. "Nothing has even happened yet."

"Look," she said, waving a hand in the air. "I may be a sleep deprived virgin obsessed with medical terminology and coloring books, but I am not an idiot."

"I wasn't implying-"

"I know something happened at that barn dance."

My lips fell apart.

"And you don't have to tell me every last detail because I can't handle that kind of excitement right now, but just tell me did you or didn't you do it?"

"Do what?" I asked, sitting on the arm of the couch.

"It."

"No." I shook my head. "Not yet."

She clapped her hands together. "So you're going to?!"

"Maybe. I don't know." I rubbed my face with my hands. "It's complicated."

"I'm not convinced," she said. "I mean, yeah, normally I think sex complicates things, but in this case, I think it might simplify things."

I dropped my head back. "How? How could it possibly?"

"Because then you can stop making yourself crazy."

"I'm not-"

"Yes you are. All this tension and wondering and will he or won't he and does he want to or am I just imagining it and- it's all too much."

I scrunched my face.

"Just fuck him already and find out."

I raised my eyebrows. "Sorry?"

"At least then you'll know if you guys are wasting your time or if you actually have something that's worth being this worked up over."

"And what about Izzy?"

She shrugged. "Worst case scenario, there's no future for you and Shane, and you never speak of it again."

"That is so not worst case scenario."

She raised her eyebrows.

"What if we sleep together and only one of us feels differently? Or what if Izzy feels betrayed and freaks out? What if I lose them both?"

"You'll still be able to put 'I slept with Shane Jennings' on your resume."

I scoffed. "Oh, well, that's definitely worth the risk."

"Equally, this could turn into Shane and Andi sitting in a tree, k-i-s-s-i-n-"

"Don't," I said, heading back to the kitchen. "Or Tyrese goes down the drain."

"You wouldn't dare," she said. "Besides, I don't need to rhyme to make my point."

"Which is?" I asked, cocking a hip in the kitchen doorway.

"That the wheels are in motion, and you'd be crazy to want to get off this ride."

I stepped out of sight and exhaled. Could Steph be right? I'd been so worried about what Shane might do next that the thought of him being my happily ever after hadn't even occurred to me.

"Andi?"

"What?" I asked, sliding the French press down as slowly as I could while trying not to think about how it would feel to slide down Shane at the same torturous speed.

"Have you seen Mike's Facebook page?"

I froze. "No. Why?"

"He's transferring."

THIRTY SIX
- Shane -

It was after nine when the online tournament finally ended. I could've kept playing, but I was happy with the two thousand dollar profit I'd made.

Plus, I was new to the site. If I won too much money too early, I risked getting blocked from higher grossing games.

I logged out, hoping my winnings would clear my account before the weekend rolled around.

Which reminded me.

I picked up my phone and leaned back, tapping through to my most recent text thread with Andi.

"Fancy coming to a stoplight party this weekend?" I typed before hitting send. Then I set the phone down and flipped my econ book open to where a half finished practice test was holding my page.

"Is that like a Tupperware party because I don't think I'm in the market for any traffic lights?"

I tapped the keys. "There will also be orange cones and racing flags available."

"You trying to piss me off?"

I sighed. "You've never heard of a stoplight party?"

"Have you never heard of picking up the phone?"

I rolled my eyes and hit dial.

"Shane. Why, hello? To what do I owe the pleasure of your call?" she asked.

"I didn't want to bother you in case it was past your bedtime."

"For your information," she said. "I haven't been in bed before ten since I was a teenager."

"Maybe you haven't had a good enough reason to be."

"Perhaps."

"You at home?"

"Yeah," she said. "Having a sexy night in with Freud."

"Sounds creepy."

"Sometimes it can be."

"I could come over and tell you what I've been dreaming about lately if you'd like a chance to practice your psychobabble."

"It's called psychoanalysis, actually, and I'm pretty sure I can guess what you've been dreaming about."

I smiled.

"What are you up to?" she asked.

"Econ."

"Someday we'll wish homework was our biggest problem."

"So I've heard." I leaned back in my chair and twirled a pencil between my fingers. "So you want to come to the party or what?"

"Do I have to dress like a traffic signal?"

"Not unless you want to."

"Go on."

"The stoplight refers to the color cup you drink out of," I said. "Red if you're unavailable, yellow if it's complicated, and green if you're single and looking."

"And you think Freud is creepy?"

I raised my eyebrows. "Interested?"

"I'm interested in what color cup you plan to drink out of."

"Come to the party and find out."

Silence.

"It's not until Friday," I said. "In case that silence was you putting your shoes on to come right over."

She laughed. "You'd like that, wouldn't you?"

"You know me so well."

"I thought I did."

I furrowed my brows. "And now you're not so sure?"

"No. It's not that."

"What is it?"

"It's just- being the object of your attention is hard work."

"You ought to be used to it by now."

"Why do you say that?"

"Because you've always held my attention, Andi. You just didn't realize it."

"Do I get to choose my own cup color?"

"Of course."

"And if I chose green?" she asked.

"I'll be first in line to chat you up."

"That's sweet."

"I have my moments."

"You didn't happen to see Mike's Facebook did you?" she asked.

"No. Why?"

"Looks like he's transferring to Southern."

I clenched my fist around the pencil. "Have you heard from him?"

"No."

"Then his actions aren't my concern." Did she creep him? Does she still care?

"I didn't see it myself. I blocked him after that night I stayed at yours. Anyway, I just mentioned it because-"

I leaned forward.

"I wanted to thank you."

I pursed my lips.

"For looking out for me."

"I'm always going to look out for you."

"I know."

"And not just cause of how hot you are."

"I'm being serious, Shane."

"So am I," I said. "Does that mean you'll come?"

"Will my attendance suffice as cheesy hash payback?"

"It will."

"I'll see you Friday then."

"Wear something slutty."

"The party sounds slutty enough as it is without-"

My phone came to life in my hands. Izzy. "Fine. Surprise me. I gotta go." I hung up when she was halfway done saying goodbye. Fuck.

"Hey," I said, feigning a casualty I didn't feel.

"Are you with a woman right now?" Izzy asked.

"What? No?"

"You sound breathless."

"You're so dramatic."

"Were you just on the phone with her? Is that why you didn't answer my Facebook message?"

"No. I didn't answer your message because I forgot I was online-" Did Andi know that? Is that why she asked if I knew about Mike? "And because I'm studying for a quiz."

"Who is she?"

"There is no she."

"Oh please. You haven't bitched about a sorority girl in weeks, which means somebody is keeping you pleasantly distracted."

"Her name is Econ."

"Are you telling me I'm wrong?"

"I know better than to use those words," I said, leaning an elbow on my desk.

"Especially if it's a lie. Why won't you tell me?"

I squeezed the bridge of my nose. "You're like a goddamn pit bull."

"Is she blonde?"

"No."

"Is she in a house?"

I dropped my hand. "No."

"See? Was that so hard? I like her already."

"Good, I'm glad. Speaking of women you like, did you think of anything clever yet for Mom and Dad's Anniversary-?"

"Oh no you don't. I want to know more about this girl you like so much that you've been screening my calls."

I sighed.

"Or should I keep calling until I catch you drunk and trick you into saying too much."

"That happened one time."

"I'm aware," she said. "And I assure you that I'm in no hurry to repeat the tactic since your attention to detail was a nightmare for us both."

"Have I mentioned that your relentlessness is what I most hate about you?"

"People say I get that from my big brother."

I groaned. "What do you want to know?"

"Her name would be a good start."

"Why? So you can creep the shit out of her social media accounts? Try again."

She sighed. "Fine. What is your favorite thing about her and don't be gross."

I pursed my lips. There were so many things to choose from, but I knew my sister the drama queen would never settle for anything vague.

"I don't have all day."

"I like the way my chest feels when she laughs."

"Oh god. You're farther gone than I thought. How did you hide this from me for so long?"

"I assumed you knew since your inkling muscle is always twitching away."

"That's understandable," she said. "So I forgive your negligence. Now what's her name?"

"I'd like to wait until I know whether or not it's serious before I fill you in."

"Where's the fun in that? I live for angst and drama! Please don't deny me the play by play."

"Sorry to disappoint you."

"Would I like her?"

I scratched the back of my head. "I'm sure you would."

"Are her tits real?"

I squeezed my eyes shut, my mind drawn back to the image of Andi laying in the back of the hay filled trailer, the night sky reflected in her eyes, my hands on her-

"Well?"

"I'm hanging up now."

"Tell me one more thing about her," she said. "And I'll let you go."

I leaned back in my chair.

"It doesn't have to be about her tits."

"She's perfect," I said. "And I'd be lucky to have her."

"Gag me, Shane."

"So I'm not going to jinx the whole thing by gossiping about it with you."

"You're no fun."

"I know a woman who would disagree."

She laughed. "I'll believe it when I see it."

"Fair enough," I said.

Just as long as it's not anytime soon.

FLASHBACK
- Shane -

I was about to knock on the door when I heard the lawn mower fire up in the back yard. So I walked around the house and waited patiently for Mr. Oliver to notice me.

As soon as he did, he powered the mower off and raised a hand in my direction.

"Shane," he said, wiping his palms on his jeans. "Great to see you, buddy. What's up?"

"Nothing much, Mr. O. I was just wondering if Andi was around. Thought she might want to-"

"Shane, honey-" Mrs. Oliver's voice spilled out the screened back door. "Come on in."

Mr. Oliver lowered his face and voice. "Just to give you a heads up, Andi's sulking. Won't eat. Won't talk to us. Won't come out of her room."

I furrowed my brow. "Since when?"

"Since this morning. She found a half dead baby bird. It was World War Three."

I nodded.

A moment later, Mrs. Oliver's hand was on my shoulder. "Can I get you a lemonade or something?"

"Sure," I said. "That would be great."

She nodded and led me inside, blowing me away once again with her warmth and capacity for making people feel welcome.

Then she gave me the scoop on what Andi was so upset about while I drank my lemonade.

Apparently she found a fallen baby robin on the front porch and went to a lot of trouble putting it back in its nest with its sibling. She even went so far as to scoop it up with some newspaper so she wouldn't transfer her scent to it.

According to her mom, she was elated afterwards that she'd been able to give the baby a fighting chance. That didn't surprise me at all since Andi had been a sucker for underdogs as long as I'd known her.

If we played kickball in gym, she always picked the handicapped kids for her team first. If a new kid showed up one day, she'd always risk detention helping them figure out where their classes were. She was the kind of person who literally helped old ladies cross the road.

It was sweet, and despite the fact that her patience often tested my own, I wouldn't have changed it.

She often joked that she was "debilitating helpful," but I knew she appreciated the trait because it proved that she was, in fact, her mother's daughter and that her fertilized egg hadn't accidentally been misplaced at the lab during her complicated birth.

Anyway, an hour later, the baby bird had been chucked out of its nest again, except this time- although it was still breathing- its neck had snapped.

"That's when she got hysterical," Mrs. Oliver said, pushing some warm chocolate chip cookies onto the plate in front of me.

I reached for one right away. "And she's been in her room ever since?"

"She had a funeral first."

I nodded.

"But I think the fact that she buried the bird alive sent her further over the edge."

My eyes grew wide as I chewed.

"Rick offered to bash it with something and put it out of its misery, you know?" She laid her pink fingernails on the counter and shook her head. "But Andi couldn't bear the thought."

I swallowed. "Sounds like a mess alright."

"If you can get her to eat a cookie," she said, nodding at the plate. "I would consider that real progress."

I slid off the tall barstool and lifted the plate. "I'll do my best. And thanks for the cookies. Between you and me, they're the best on the block."

Her eyes smiled at me as I rounded the corner and headed upstairs.

"Andi?" I said, tapping lightly on the door. "It's Shane. Can I come in?"

She didn't answer.

I twisted the knob with my free hand and stepped in her room. She was lying face down on her bed, her cheek crushed against the pillow so I could see her bee stung eyes.

She was wearing a thin tank top, and I let my eyes travel first over the smooth skin on her shoulders before letting them linger on her skimpy shorts, which had a lace trim along the bottom that did little to cover her thighs at all.

It wasn't the first time I wondered when she got so... feminine.

"Hi," she said, blinking her bloodshot eyes at me.

I set the cookies down on her nightstand and pulled her desk chair up beside her twin bed, which was wedged into the corner of the small room.

"What's up?" she asked, without any of her usual chirpiness.

"Izzy gets back from her drama camp today." I glanced at the lucky kitty clock on the wall, swinging its paw like it was impatient for me to make progress. "I thought you might want to go to the train station with me to pick her up."

"Oh yeah. I told her I'd be there."

"I'm sure she would understand if you couldn't make it-"

She laughed. "Oh yeah. That sounds like Izzy."

"No I mean it. It sounds like you had a pretty big day already."

"If by pretty big you mean the worst day ever, then yeah. It's been a pretty big day." She rolled onto her side.

I fought the urge to look at the shallow line of cleavage that peeked out from her tank top. "At least you tried to help, Andi. A lot of people wouldn't have even gone to the trouble."

She rolled onto her back and stared at the ceiling. "Yeah, well. A lot of people are just as bad as that murderous, negligent, evil robin living on our front porch."

I raised my eyebrows.

She lifted her head. "And it's still there!"

I bit the inside of my cheek.

"My parents said it's the circle of life and all this crap and that just because she's a shitty mom doesn't mean she deserves to lose her home."

"And you disagree?"

She rolled towards me again and curled herself into a ball. "Yeah. I think she should fuck off with the precious chick she let live, the one she didn't toss out of her nest like a piece of garbage."

I moved to sit on the edge of the bed and laid a hand on her arm.

"I don't want to see her every day and be reminded of the way her baby- who was still hairless with bulging blind eyes, by the way- looked as it took its last breath."

"I know. And I'm sorry about-"

"Major Tom."

I smiled. "Yeah. I'm sorry about Major Tom. Maybe you could show me his grave later."

She sniffled. "I tried to make it nice. I put some rocks and twigs around it and laid a flower over him."

"I'm sure it's lovely."

"I hope so."

"I think you did a good thing, Andi. I know it was awful and that you're upset, but at least Major Tom didn't come and go from this world without making an impression."

She closed her eyes and laid a hand over mine where it was resting on her shoulder. "How soon does Izzy's train get in?"

"Not for a while. Why?"

She looked up at me, her eyes still full of pain. "Would it be weird if I asked you to hold me for a few minutes?"

I shook my head. "Not at all."

I crawled over her and lowered myself between her and the wall.

Then, just as I was about to wrap my arm around her, she rolled towards me and buried her head against the nape of my neck.

"Thank you," she whispered.

And as I hugged her close, I realized it was the first time we'd ever laid in a bed together.

Just the two of us.

THIRTY SEVEN
- Andi -

I doubted Shane was really expecting me to show up in something slutty.

But I figured, why not?

I mean, I got lucky with the barn dance because the dress code was easy to follow, but I didn't want to look out of place at the stoplight party when I knew there would be tons of sorority girls there going for broke. Or rather, dick.

Surprisingly though, the skankiest thing I could get my hands on came straight out of Steph's closet.

Honestly, it's shocking what some of those good Christians will wear... and how many blowjobs they'll give to make sure they save themselves.

Needless to say, it was an educational day.

Anyway, she had a strappy red dress that was tight enough on top to make the girls really stand at attention.

What's more, it flared a bit at the waist so I wouldn't have to worry about beer bloat, and the bottom cut straight across the most toned part of my thighs, which were looking better than ever after my recent trips to the gym.

I paired it with some Louboutin knockoffs to keep the red theme going, painted my nails accordingly, and curled my hair into some soft waves that fell over my shoulders.

Finally, I applied my secret weapon- Eyeko Mascara- so I would look as deliciously fuckable as possible.

Unfortunately, Tyler was working the door when I arrived and tried to hand me a green cup.

"I'd prefer red," I said, looking down at my dress like can't-you-take-a-hint?

His face fell. "Really? That's a shame. Who's the lucky guy that's getting a piece of that later?" he asked, looking me up and down.

"Bite me, Tyler."

"You know I would," he said, handing me a red cup.

Knowing I would feel way less awkward with a drink in my hand, I headed straight for the keg, the music vibrating up through the floorboards into the bones of my already tipsy legs with every step.

I didn't mean to have quite so much to drink before I got there, but it's not every day that Steph's up for a screwdriver. Plus, all it takes is a few top ups when you're getting ready, and you don't even notice the damage you've done until you hit the fresh air.

Still, while I liked to think I was resistant to pathetic human needs like the desire to fit in and be liked by strangers, I wasn't quite confident enough to rock up to a party like this without a little courage.

Fortunately, Kevin- my favorite guy in the house besides Shane- was working the keg.

As soon as I saw him, I felt my chest relax to the point where I actually began to notice the frequent head to toe looks I was getting as I swiveled through the crowd, which did wonders for my confidence.

Kevin's eyes lit up when he saw me, too. And as he lifted his chin in my direction, the girl with her arm draped around his waist looked back and forth between us, clearly trying to decide if I was a threat.

As a result, I tried to look as friendly as possible, realizing a moment later that I recognized her as Kevin's date from the barn dance.

Kevin shouted some greeting to me and introduced us, though her name got lost in the noise as he reached for my cup.

As soon as it was full, I took a step back so the other thirsty students could budge in. Then, once I was sure I could take a sip without spilling all over myself, I lifted the cup to my lips.

That's when I saw him.

He came around the corner in a jet black collared shirt and the faces around me melted into a blur. He looked like he'd shaved with a brand new razor, and I swear to god I could tell he smelled good from across the room.

As his gaze passed over me, I saw the moment where he caught himself and glanced back. It happened so fast, but his eyes zeroed in on me like a hawk on a mouse.

I swallowed.

He walked towards me with the magnetism of Bond himself, and my insides clenched at the sight of his subtle smile. He was so hot I couldn't think.

"Andi," he said, his voice low and yet- somehow- the only thing I could hear.

"Hi."

"You look-" He checked me out so hard I had to lock my knees to keep from wilting.

"What?" I asked, raising my eyebrows.

"Like you don't belong here."

I furrowed my brow.

"I mean that in the best way possible."

I batted my lashes at him.

"I see you went with red."

I lifted my cup and licked my lips. "That's right. Everywhere."

He clenched his jaw and lifted his own cup. It was red, too.

I squinted at him. "Remind me again, will you? Does that mean you're unavailable?"

"Only where everyone else is concerned."

"I see." I shook some loose waves behind my shoulder. "So I didn't need to dress quite so slutty then?"

"You don't look slutty," he said, his dark green eyes locked on mine. "You look beautiful."

"More like overdressed."

His lips twitched. "We'll take care of that later."

"And now?"

"Now I'm going to tap the next two kegs and put someone else in charge of paying the DJ so no one comes looking for me when I disappear."

I pursed my lips.

"You cool to hang out here for a second? I'll only be a minute."

"I suppose," I said, glancing into my cup. "But don't keep me waiting."

He drained his beer.

"Fifteen years is a long time."

"Too long," he said, handing me his empty cup. "But I'll make it up to you."

I nodded and watched his strong back disappear into the crowd. Then I leaned against the wall and passed the time by scanning the faces around me and making up stories about why they chose their particular cup color.

Until I realized one of those faces was headed right for me.

It belonged to a pretty blonde girl about my height. Well, I assume she was pretty most of the time- when she was smiling- which she most certainly was not.

And neither were the two mean girls flanking her sides in matching LBDs.

I was about to turn around to see if they were staring down someone else when I remembered I was against the wall.

The blonde stepped up to me, her long hair in a fishtail braid that went all the way down to her waist. "So you're the bitch who went to the barn dance with Shane."

I rolled my shoulders back, suddenly registering why she looked so familiar.

"The one with the deep throat."

My eyes grew wide.

She looked me up and down.

I felt my stomach drop.

"What are you, mute? Don't you have anything to say for yourself?"

I only had a few inches on her in my heels, but I tried to make the most of it as I looked down at her and cocked my head. "Yeah. I do."

She craned her neck forward, her blue eyes bulging. "Well?"

"Who the fuck are you?"

And that's when I felt a full beer splash across my face and drip down Steph's dress, followed by two more before I'd even opened my eyes.

T H I R T Y E I G H T
- Shane -

All I saw from across the room was Andi's face right before it happened.

I could tell it was Chloe by her hair and the fact that she was flanked on each side by Tweedledee and Tweedledum, and that awareness was enough to make me hurry over.

But like Andi, I never saw the drinks coming.

I made it there by the time she opened her eyes, but it wasn't like in the movies. The music didn't sputter to an awkward stop. The whole room didn't turn to look.

The party just kept on going- as if the most beautiful woman in the room hadn't just been assaulted.

It made me want to throw up almost as bad as it made me want to grab Chloe by the hair and drag her out of the house like a caveman.

"Get out," I said, stepping in front of Andi and staring down at Chloe's smug expression. "Now."

She scoffed. "We have every right to be here, Shane, just like-"

"You had every right," I said. "Until you did that. You are no longer welcome here- all three of you."

Chloe stared me down for a second like she was trying to decide whether I was serious. "Come on girls. This house is overrated anyway."

My body bubbled with the desire to say something mean as they walked away, something that would tear Chloe down and humiliate her the way she'd humiliated Andi, but she didn't deserve my energy.

I turned around.

Andi was wiping a mixture of beer and mascara from under her eyes. The top of her head was wet and still dripping, though a few of her soft curls had escaped unscathed.

My first thought was to take my shirt off and try to mop her up where the sticky beer was shining against her chest.

Instead, I grabbed her hand and led her through the crowd to the bottom of the stairs.

When we got there, I scooped her up in my arms before she could object and carried her beer scented body up to my room.

As soon as I set her down outside my door, I unlocked it so she could step inside.

I followed a second later, flicking on the switch attached to the bedside lamp before handing her the towel hanging over the back of my desk chair.

"Andi."

She ignored me and ran the towel down her arms.

"Andi. Look at me."

She lifted her heavy looking lashes and raised her eyebrows. "What?"

"I'm sorry."

She dropped her head and started patting the front of her dress, a worried look on her face.

"I had no idea she would ever seek you out, much less-"

"Don't worry about it," she said, her voice cold.

"Can I give you some dry clothes?"

"This isn't even my dress," she mumbled, extending the bottom of it out in front of her so she could see the uneven streaks of beer.

"You want me to send it to the dry cleaners? I can send it right now."

She shook her head.

"Are you okay?" I asked, putting my hands on her shoulders and forcing her to meet my eye.

Her lips twitched.

"Talk to me."

"How did she know what happened in that field?"

I furrowed my brow. "What?"

"I sure as hell didn't tell anybody."

"Neither did I."

"Really?"

I dropped my hands. "Of course not."

"Then why would she refer to me as 'the bitch who went to the barn dance with you, the one with the deep throat?'"

I closed my eyes and squeezed my temples with one hand.

"Not cool, Shane," she said, stepping out of her heels. "I thought I could trust you to not treat me like one of your little whores. I thought I could trust you to keep things between us."

"You can. And I did. I swear."

Her eyes looked too angry to cry, but the hurt in them was painfully obvious. She turned towards my closet, but I grabbed her hand and pulled her back towards me.

"I know why she said that."

"I'm listening," she said, shaking my hand off her wrist.

"She came here the day after the dance. Angry."

She folded her arms.

"And I'll tell you what was said, but please give me a chance to explain-"

"I want the exact words."

"She said, 'Good luck finding someone who can deep throat like I can.'"

She shook her head.

"And I yelled after her that I already did."

Her mouth fell open.

"But I wasn't thinking. I was just annoyed that she barged in here and woke every guy in the house with her crazy accusations. I just said it to piss her off. I know that's immature but-"

"Uh-huh."

"You must know by now that I would never say anything like that about you to anyone, and not just because I don't know how to-"

"What?"

I sighed. "I can't even figure out how to tell Izzy how much you mean to me."

She pursed her lips.

"So there's no way I'd ever waste my breath trying to convince Chloe that you're the best thing to happen to me in…"

Andi raised her eyebrows.

I stepped up to her, sliding a hand around the back of her neck as my eyes dropped to her lips. "Maybe ever."

She kissed me then, and I held her as my whole body responded to her warmth, her sweetness.

I heard her drop the towel a second later as she swirled her tongue in my mouth and tilted her hips against mine.

"Stay," I whispered, letting my hand find the small zipper between her shoulder blades.

She slid her hands up my chest. "Are you sure you aren't just saying what you think I want to hear because you've always wanted to hook up with a girl that was covered in beer?"

I laughed, laying my forehead against hers as I pulled her zipper down to her waist. "Actually, I didn't know that was a fantasy of mine until about five minutes ago."

"So you didn't plan this?" she asked, her eyes bouncing between me and her fingers as she fumbled with the buttons on my shirt. "Having your ex throw beer on me so you could get me naked?"

"Only the getting you naked part," I said. "Which I admit I've been plotting for some time."

"If we do this, Shane, there's no going back," she whispered, her brown eyes looking to me for answers.

I slipped a finger under the thin strap of her dress and dragged it over the smooth curve of her shoulder. "Would you even want to?"

T H I R T Y N I N E
- Andi -

My breath caught in my throat as he pulled down the front of my dress, exposing my bare breasts.

I kept my eyes on him and wiggled the bottom part over my hips. I would've let it drop to the floor, but it had been through enough so I tossed it over his desk chair.

When I looked back at him, he was drinking me in, his eyes on the lacy red boy shorts slung low on my hips.

"What?" I asked, looking down to see what the fuss was.

"That underwear. It's criminal."

I flicked my wrist. "Oh these old things?"

"Do a little turn for me," he said, throwing his shirt over the chair without taking his eyes off me.

My eyes fell to the muscles that littered his chest, admiring the shadows they cast in the dim light. Then I did a little turn, taking my time so he could see how killer the boy shorts made my butt look.

He was clenching his jaw by the time I faced him again.

"I'm not going to lie," he said. "That underwear makes me want to lock you in my room and never let you out."

The corner of my mouth twitched. "Let's see how tonight goes first."

His intense gaze sank down to my chest, and the eager anticipation I felt for his touch soaked my underwear.

He laid his hands on my breasts gently at first, as if they were bubbles that might burst. But when they didn't, he increased the pressure, causing my whole body to melt against his hands.

With the little strength I had, I stepped towards the bed, catching the excitement flash across his face as I dropped my hands to the top of his jeans.

When I'd managed all the buttons, I stuck a hand down the front of his pants. The heat coming off his hard on made my mouth water.

"I don't want anyone but you," he said, grabbing my face to kiss me. "And when it comes to you, I want every inch to be mine."

I slung my hands over his shoulders and pressed my breasts against his bare chest.

He pushed his jeans down and stepped out of them, kneeling on the bed a moment later so I was forced off my feet.

I locked my arms around his neck while he walked forward on his knees, his dick against my belly as he dragged me towards the head of the bed.

After he laid me down, he shifted over me so his swollen cock was against my leg and his face was right above mine. "You're so beautiful, Andi," he said, kissing me again before moving his lips below my ear. "And you smell so good right now."

I laughed. "Do I taste like beer?

"A little," he said, kissing his way towards my collarbone and groping my breast with his hand.

My nipples were so hard they ached, and when he took one in his mouth, the pain only got worse as they tightened against his twirling tongue.

"You trying to take a closer look at my panties?" I asked as he kissed down my stomach and around my belly button.

"Shhh," he said, flicking his eyes up to me as he leaned on his side and ran his fingers up my inner thigh.

I exhaled when I felt his fingers press against my heat.

"You're already wet for me," he whispered, dragging his fingertips across the thin fabric.

I stole a quick breath as he curled his fingers around the top of my underwear, lifting my head to watch as he pulled them down my legs and over my feet.

There was no hiding under his gaze. He was staring at me like he planned to draw me from memory.

I was about to beg for his touch again when I felt the tips of his fingers spreading my own silk over me.

A moment later, he slid them inside, looking up at my face as he sank them into my center one inch at a time. "Fuck that's tight," he said, twisting his wrist.

It felt so good to let him have his way with me after wanting him for so long, and I swear I felt my tear ducts twitch at how overwhelmed I was by his touch, his attention.

It was all consuming, and I knew in every part of me that he'd be able to make me come harder than anyone ever had before.

After all, I was as much his in that moment as I'd always been. I just hadn't realized it until we were naked and alone.

He lowered his mouth to me a moment later, replacing his fingers with his tongue as he squeezed my thighs in rhythm with his licks.

The sound of the party below was distant and muffled as my body responded to the forceful lapping of his tongue against me.

Moaning had never felt so natural.

Best of all, it seemed to spur him on.

"Oh god, Shane," I whispered, letting my head fall to the side as I dug my red nails into his comforter. "That feels too good."

"Just like it tastes," he said, his hot breath against me.

The bright ball of heat inside me grew as he found his rhythm, and my eyelids grew heavy.

When his wet fingers squeezed my breast in sync with his tongue, my legs went numb, and I knew I was moments away from the sweet release I craved.

"You're going to make me c-"

He stopped before I'd even got the words out.

I lifted my head, the pain of the suspense more than I could bear.

"Not yet," he said, kissing my stomach and dragging his wet lips across it.

I furrowed my brow, frustrated that he would get me so worked up and then deny me my-

Until I saw his dick in his hand- saw him stroking it beside my wet entrance- and realized I'd never wanted anything more.

"I want you inside me," I said. "Please."

A flicker of amusement lit up his dark eyes, which he kept on me as he fingered me again, scooping out my wetness and coating his dick with it.

I forgot to breathe then- just like I forgot everything that had ever been in my head. I don't know what happened exactly.

Maybe it was seeing my pleasure on his swollen cock- or the aggressive longing in Shane's eyes- but I couldn't look away as I licked my lips and realized how far past the line we'd gone.

"I'm ready," I whispered, looking up at him, his gorgeous body flexed over me like an apparition.

He guided the tip of his dick to my opening and pushed his way in, stretching me wide before stopping halfway so I could brace myself for more.

Then he sank the rest of the way in, and as he forced his last few inches inside me, I let out a groan that was such a shocking mix of pain and pleasure, I was worried he might pull back.

But he didn't.

Instead, he hovered over me, his eyes on mine as the heat of his throbbing cock held me open.

And after what felt like a blissful eternity, he began to thrust.

F O R T Y
- Shane -

I'd never felt so close to her.

It seems obvious to say that, but I didn't think it would be so good, that it would mean so much.

"You feel incredible," I said, moving slowly so I could watch the subtle shifts in her face as she clenched around every inch of me.

"So do you," she whispered, lifting a hand to my cheek and resting her knees against my hips.

And suddenly it was all too much- the pulsing pressure on my dick, the dreamy look in her eyes. I couldn't handle the swell of emotion taking hold of my throat.

It was too much too soon. Too many feelings. Too many kinds of pleasure. Like joy and bliss and other crazy shit I didn't see coming and wasn't fucking ready for.

I swallowed hard, desperate to regain control of myself before I got totally lost in her, determined to tolerate her beauty in a way that wouldn't swallow me up.

I lowered my face and kissed her, allowing myself to revel in the connection between us for one more moment.

Then I rolled onto my back, taking her with me.

But the stars stayed in her eyes.

"Show me how you ride a dick," I said, pulling her ass down on me as I thrust up inside her.

She laid her hands on my chest and pushed herself upright, looking like a goddess the way her breasts hung before me.

"Are you okay?" I asked, suddenly concerned that I'd misread the dizzy look in her eye and that she was actually going to faint.

She cocked her head and smiled at me, her brown hair falling over one side of her face. "I'm waay past okay."

"Come here," I said, pulling her arm so she fell forward. As soon as her breasts crushed against my chest, I pressed my mouth to hers and tilted my pelvis up, forcing myself deep into her core. Then I held the back of her neck and whispered against her fat lips. "Now fuck me, Andi. I've been waiting for this for too long."

"You and me both," she said, lifting her body so her breasts hung in my face.

I grabbed one with my mouth and the other with my hand, squeezing them both while she slid up and down me, working my dick as she crushed her clit against the base of my shaft.

She moaned as she rode me, grinding herself into a frenzy and forgetting everything but her carnal pleasure.

And I relished seeing this sexy side of her, this uninhibited side I never let myself wonder about. It was pure woman doing what women do best- driving men crazy with primal need.

I reached around and dragged a finger through the silk dripping down my balls. Then I spread my hand over the plump, flexing cheek of her ass and laid a finger at the edge of her rim.

She interrupted her rhythm and looked at me. "What are you doing, Shane?"

"Trust me," I said, keeping my eyes on her as I circled the sensitive, puckered flesh.

Her lips fell open.

"I want every part of you to be mine," I repeated, watching her pick up the pace again as she took comfort in my eyes. "Come for me, Andi," I said, watching her body writhe over me.

A moment later, she started grinding her hips in a circular motion, pressing her clit against me as she sank her fingers into my chest. "You're so deep," she whispered, her head falling to the side so I could see the mascara smudged under her eyes.

She was so fucking hot I feared I'd be hard for days, that the physical pain of wanting her might never subside.

I reached a hand for her breast and worked it in time with her hips, watching her relax into her rhythm and pick up the pace.

"I'm going to come," she mouthed so soft I wouldn't have heard it if I hadn't had my eyes on her lips.

A moment later, I slipped my finger in her ass.

She cried out and bucked against me, her body spasming as it squeezed all the places I'd invaded.

And she came harder than I ever imagined, inflicting a force so great on my dick I couldn't stop myself from coming, couldn't stop myself from grabbing her hips and fucking her orgasm, flooding her center as her pussy milked me so hard my eyes watered.

"Fuck," we panted in unison a few seconds later, smiles spilling across our faces.

She rocked her hips a few more times, as if she were wringing me out, and I felt the mess we'd made drip down my balls, which had never felt so good.

Finally, she laid down and buried her face in my neck. "I can't believe you did that," she whispered.

"Did what?" I asked, laying a hand across her delicate back.

"With your finger," she said, still throbbing around me.

"I can't believe how much you liked it," I said, staring up at the ceiling, thinking I could get used to having her draped over me.

She lifted her head and dragged her fingernails over my scalp. "I did like it," she said, her glassy eyes finding mine. "I've never come so hard."

I raised my brows.

"Ever," she said. "That was- wow."

I smiled, trying to memorize the sweet flush of her cheeks. "It was wow for me, too."

"Really?" She pursed her wet lips. "Is that the hardest you've ever come?"

"Yeah." I pushed the hair from her face so I could see her soft features in the dim light. "Except come isn't the right word."

She batted her dark lashes. "What's the right word?"

"Fell," I said. "That's the hardest I ever fell."

FORTY ONE
- Andi -

"Guess who?!" I heard through a thick fog of sleep.

The voice was familiar. So was the knock.

"Shane!" Knockknockknock. "Wake up!"

My body sprang upright before my mind even registered why the voice was so familiar.

Shane was sleeping beside me, looking so handsome and at peace. I felt pretty bad about shaking the shit out of him... but not as bad as I was going to feel if Izzy caught us like this.

"What?" he groaned, his eyes peeling open.

I pointed at the door.

He didn't get it. Instead, he just reached an arm around me and tried to pull my naked body towards his.

It hurt all over to push him away. "It's Izzy," I mouthed.

"Good morning sleepy head!" she called from outside the door.

He raised his eyebrows and cocked an ear towards the voice.

"Goddamn it, Shane. I don't have all day."

He lifted a hand to my cheek, his eyes smiling as they swept over my face. The moment felt slow and drawn out- too slow for the urgent thinking the situation required- but I didn't hurry him.

Instead, I stared right back, letting myself imagine all the mushy stuff he was probably thinking, all the sweet nothings he might've whispered... if he hadn't thrown the covers over my head and trapped me like a wild bat.

"Shane Jennings!" Izzy called.

"I'm coming, Christ. Hold on."

Izzy groaned outside the door.

My heart was pounding so loudly I thought it might give me away. The rest of my senses were heightened, too. I could smell our sex on the sheets. I could hear Shane slipping on a pair of shorts- his sleepy feet wobbling on the creaky floorboards- a car door slamming outside- the bedroom door opening.

"Hey," he said, his voice hoarse.

"Surprise! So great to see you," Izzy said, her voice sounding squished as if she'd pulled him into a hug.

"You, too," he said.

"I assume by the sheet crease on your face that you haven't eaten?"

"No."

"You down for Mama's? I thought we could pick Andi up, too-"

I scrunched my face.

"That sounds great," Shane said. "But before we do any of that, I need to ask you a favor."

"Are you going to let me in or what?"

"Maybe later."

I imagined how Izzy's eyes would widen as she figured out what was going on.

"Oh. I see."

"Yeah."

"Can I meet her?" she asked.

I held my breath.

"Maybe later," Shane said again.

"But-"

"Will you walk down to the corner and get some coffees?" he asked. "I just need ten minutes and then I'm all yours."

She sighed. "Are you really that ashamed of me?"

"No. Just your inclination to ambush people."

"I've heard lovely things about you," she shouted into the room.

I smiled. So he had mentioned me?

"And despite whatever Shane's told you, I'm really not that scary or judgmental!"

I stifled a snort.

"Coffee, Izzy. Please."

She tutted. "This is the worst welcome ever."

"Yeah, well. It was kind of a late night-"

"I figured that out when I saw the state of the downstairs."

"Coffee will fix everything," he said. "And maybe get a few of those almond biscotti things."

"Fine," she said. "But for the record, I'm not impressed."

"I'll make it up to you," he said.

"Ten minutes."

The door closed a second later, and I heard the lock latch back into place.

I stayed where I was and awaited further instruction.

Shane sat on my side of the bed and peeled the blanket down.

I rolled over and faced him.

"Good morning, beautiful," he said. "How did you sleep?"

I smiled. "Great. But I think the parts when I wasn't sleeping were my favorites."

"Me too," he said, dragging his hand down the side of my arm.

My phone started ringing on the nightstand a second later.

"That's probably Izzy," he said.

"Ya think?"

"Did you know she was coming this weekend?"

I shook my head. "She's been saying she was going to come for a while, but I had no idea she'd picked today."

He sighed, his abs rippling as he exhaled. "I was hoping to spend the day with you to be honest."

"I actually have plans this afternoon so-"

His face dropped.

"That's a joke. I was probably just going to lay around naked with you as long as you'd let me." I trailed my fingertips from his belly button to the top of his shorts. "And maybe force myself to eat something if we worked up an appetite."

His eyes flashed. "I can assure you that we certainly would have."

"How are we going to tell her?"

"We aren't going to tell her anything."

"But-"

"I'm going to tell her," he said. "When the time is right."

"And until then?"

"Try and pretend you're not that into me."

"Easier said than done."

He laughed. "You managed for fifteen years."

"Oh please. It's not like I've been in love with you since-"

He raised his eyebrows.

I couldn't believe I said the "L" word. Fuck.

"Admit my game was already pretty good at seven."

"Absolutely not," I said. "You're the one who sent me mixed signals for a decade."

"They weren't mixed," he said. "They were misinterpreted."

"Well, even so. I'm glad you finally grew a set and made a move."

"If you think about or mention my set again, Izzy is going to catch us in the act and cover us both in hot coffee."

"If she's even getting coffee. I'd bet anything she's waiting downstairs to catch whoever's in here leaving the house."

"Of course she is. That's why you're going to use the fire exit."

I furrowed my brow. "The fire exit?"

"It's not as action movie as it sounds. It's just a back staircase."

"Oh."

"It opens up into the parking lot on Second Street so you'll be home free."

"If you're ashamed of-"

"Ashamed? What the hell are you talking about?"

"I just mean if you're rethinking this now that it's about to get real-"

"Andi."

"What?"

"I'm not ashamed of anything," he said. "Even before all this, you were the thing I was most proud of."

I pursed my lips.

"So don't have any doubts," he said. "Because I don't. Okay?"

I nodded.

"And please forgive me for what I'm about to say."

I cocked my head. "Which is?"

"Put on your clothes and get out."

FORTY TWO
- Shane -

After I saw Andi out, I returned to my room, double checked that she hadn't left any of her personal belongings behind, and cracked a window.

Then I straightened the sheets on my bed and grabbed a fresh white t-shirt from the closet, wondering how I was going to make small talk with my sister when I was still reeling from the night I just had.

Seriously, wow. I knew Andi was special the first time I saw her in her Tiger Lily bikini at my ninth birthday party, but I never could've predicted what a delicious woman she would become.

And I do mean delicious.

One of the first things that crossed my mind that morning was how great it felt to have my face between her thighs, her silk on my tongue.

She was so responsive it was incredible, and I loved how much she enjoyed working my dick.

And I'd been missing out on that for how long?!

I couldn't even stomach the thought. All that wasted time. All those bad dates. All that below average sex with women I felt nothing for.

It was sort of tragic.

And yet, if I hadn't experienced those things, I might not have had the wisdom to realize how good last night was.

Frankly, there was nothing I wanted more than to drop everything and think of new ways to make her come.

And the look in her eyes when I spread her open and massaged her from the inside... It was different than the other girls. Perhaps because I really had her- body and mind- and it was a high unlike anything I'd ever experienced.

But I knew my exhilaration was due to more than just the fact that the sex was out of this world.

Because she wasn't just a good fuck. She was my best friend, and I couldn't help but feel that I suddenly had more to lose than ever before.

It was kind of a sickening feeling.

And yet, it was also like seeing in color for the first time.

"I'm back," Izzy said, knocking on the door again. "Ten minutes later, as per your super diva-like request."

I opened the door. "Did you remember to get my Evian face mist?"

"Yeah," she said, pushing her way in and looking around like an amateur detective who's unable to hide their true passion. "And I removed all the green Skittles from your bath as well."

I raised my eyebrows. "But no coffees, I see?"

"No," she said, craning her neck to look in the corners of the closet.

"There's no one here, Izzy."

"And yet no one left."

"Not through the front door, no."

She turned around, her eyes looking extra wide on account of her Amy Winehouse-inspired eyeliner. "You deliberately deceived me?!"

"No," I said, pulling a yellow Gatorade out of my fridge. "I tried to help you do the right thing."

"Which is…?"

"Respecting my privacy and the privacy of my overnight guest."

She rolled her eyes. "Thank you for tricking me into doing what was absolutely never my intention."

"You're welcome."

"It smells like sex in here."

"Yeah, well. You should've called." I took a big swig and extended the bottle towards her.

"No thanks," she said. "I'll hold out."

"So," I said, chucking the Gatorade back in the fridge. "To what do I owe this happy surprise?"

She sat on the edge of the bed and crossed her thin, legging clad legs. "One of my professors is speaking here tonight before the screening of some docu-drama about the refugee crisis."

"Uh-huh."

"And I get extra credit if I go."

"Cool."

"Plus, I wanted to come see your smug face for myself so I'd know how serious it is with this girl who's made you go all weird."

"I haven't gone all weird."

"Yes you have," she said. "Though I haven't decided whether it's a bad thing yet."

"A bad thing?"

"I mean, don't get me wrong. I understand that eventually we'll both settle down and that we've already started living more separate lives, but I sort of assumed you'd at least wait until I had someone chilling in the wings before you got serious about somebody."

"How insensitive of me."

"I forgive you," she said. "Assuming she's actually special enough to justify you getting so sprung and focused on one girl, especially considering the environment you live in."

"And what environment is that?"

"A carnally obsessed drinking hole."

"Mmm."

"Not that my artist friends are any better," she said. "But we do make a far less atrocious mess."

"We had a party last night."

"More like a collective blackout from the looks of it."

I laughed.

"So should we invite your girlfriend to brunch?"

"She's not my girlfriend."

"As in you haven't made it official? Because you're obviously not seeing anybody else."

How could I explain that girlfriend didn't seem like the right word? That whatever we had was way past being labeled? Or would Andi disagree? Did she need a discussion like that to make her confident about my loyalty? Surely not. If there was anyone who never had to question my loyalty, it was her.

"Well?"

I shrugged. "I guess that's probably a conversation we need to have."

"Yeah, obviously. Women like to know where they stand. So you're welcome. See? I've already helped."

"How will I ever thank you?"

"By answering the damn question about brunch." She craned her neck forward. "Do you want to invite her or-?"

"No. She's got some… stuff."

"Well, I'm starving, and Andi's not picking up so maybe we should just go-"

"Really? Maybe she's just at the gym." I glanced at the clock on the wall. "Why don't you try her again?"

Izzy furrowed her brows. "Like the gym gym?"

"Yeah. She's been rowing."

"Weird," she said, pulling out her phone and dragging her thumb across the screen. "Just when you think you know somebody."

FORTY THREE
- Andi -

The red dress stank of stale beer in one hand while I gripped my heels in the other, making my way home barefoot in a mishmash of Shane's gym clothes.

To say it wasn't how I imagined the morning going would be a ridiculous understatement.

After such a huge night of firsts, I thought I could at least count on some pillow talk or another round of wickedly good sex.

I certainly hadn't anticipated following that emotional roller coaster with a walk of shame.

My phone vibrated again, and I rearranged the items in my hands so I could answer it.

"Hi."

"Andi- I've been blowing you up for a half hour," Izzy said.

"Sorry. I was- my phone was on silent. I didn't realize until just now."

"Oh."

"I'm about to hop in the shower, though," I said, crossing the street towards my building. "So maybe I can call you b-"

"I'm in town!"

"Oh really? That's great news!"

"Please tell me you don't have plans today," she said.

"Nope. I'm all yours."

"That's what Shane said."

I flinched. "Funny. Are you with him now?"

"Yeah, but he wasn't alone when I showed up."

"Busted."

"So busted," she said. "I'll give you the scoop at Mama's. We can pick you up in-"

"I'll meet you there," I said, starting up the stairs to my apartment. "I need to shower and drop something off at the dry cleaners."

"Oh. Okay. Well, is it cool if I put the order in since it's always crazy busy on the weekends and I'm starving?"

"Yeah, sure. That's fine. I won't be long."

"Cool. What do you want then?"

"Shane knows."

"Shane knows," she repeated.

"Yeah."

"Okay, great. Can't wait to see your face!"

"You, too," I said, hanging up the phone and taking the rest of the stairs two at a time.

What the hell was I doing? Lying to my best friend?! Sleeping with her brother?! What a mess!

I mean, last night was the best night of my life, and now I couldn't even enjoy the moment.

On the contrary, I had to pretend it never happened.

I was shaking my head as I pushed my apartment door open, marveling at how unprepared I felt to juggle this day and all its unanticipated moving parts.

When I looked up, I saw Steph sitting on the couch with her thick black glasses on and her hair piled on her head. Beside her, several stacks of notecards and a half a dozen empty mugs littered the table.

"No rest for the wicked, eh?" I asked.

She laughed. "Not by the looks of you."

I stared down my front, following the Final Four shirt to my knees and realizing for the first time how silly the oversized shorts looked with only my ankles and bare feet sticking out.

"I thought the dress looked better to be honest," she said, lowering her notecards to her lap.

"So did I, but Shane's ex threw a beer over me about five minutes after I arrived-"

She craned her neck forward. "You're joking."

"I wish."

"What did you do?"

"Stood there dripping like a wet blanket."

"Crap." She pulled her glasses off. "That is so not how it was supposed to go."

"No shit. But my dry cleaner can definitely sort your dress out so don't worry-"

"What about the rest of the night?"

I sighed and dropped my stuff on the table in the hall. "There are no words."

She laughed and put an arm up on the back of the couch. "That good, huh?"

"I can't even get into it with you cause your soul will go straight to Hell."

"Okay. First of all, don't even joke about that. Second of all, I can think of worse ways to go."

"It's not just that," I said. "I literally don't have time to tell you now."

"You're a horrible tease."

I smiled. "I can think of a guy who would disagree."

"Do you not even have time for a quick coffee?" she asked. "My dress can make it a few more hours."

"Izzy's in town."

She raised her eyebrows. "Izzy Izzy?"

I nodded. "The one and only."

"Is she coming here? Should I move my study party to my roo-"

"No, you can stay where you are. I'm the one that has to get out of here five minutes ago."

"To go…?"

"I'm meeting Shane and Izzy at Mama's."

"Whoa."

"Yeah."

"Does she know you guys are swapping spit yet?"

I felt my cheeks burn. "First of all, we're swapping more than spit."

She slapped a hand over her face, hiding one eye behind her palm.

"Second of all, no."

"You have to tell her."

"Shane said he'd do the honors."

She squinted at me. "And you're cool with that?"

I shrugged. "They're twins."

"And she's your best friend."

I scrunched my face. "It might be too much coming from both of us. I don't want to, like, come at her as a united front. It's too weird."

"What if she's not cool with it and you're not there to explain yourself?"

I turned my palms to the ceiling. "Explain what? The detailed play by play of how I've been falling for her brother the last few weeks? The way it feels when he looks at me? When he-" I shook my head like a dog. "I doubt she wants to hear any of that."

"She's going to want to hear it from you eventually," she said, putting her glasses back on.

"I know, but I trust him and-" I held my breath at the thought. "That has to be enough."

"So what are you going to do at brunch? Act like you aren't picturing him naked?"

I nodded. "Among other things."

"Wow." She shook her head. "What I wouldn't give to be a fly on the wall."

"It's going to be fine."

"Yeah, cause Izzy's really chill."

"Hey- that's not fair. She's not that uptight."

"I'm not saying she's uptight. I'm saying she has a flair for the dramatic, and the longer you put off telling her, the worse it's going to be."

"He'll tell her soon. As soon as the time is right."

"Does that mean you guys have a future?"

"I hope so," I said. "I mean, the guy is already the best thing about my past so, yeah, I guess it's hard to imagine a future without him."

"If Izzy flips, can I be your maid of honor?"

"Let's take things one day at a time."

"If you insist," she said. "Now go get a shower. You smell like a nightclub."

"Thanks for your understanding," I said, leaving with a nod.

I went straight to the bathroom and kicked the door shut behind me as I turned the shower on. Then, while I waited for the water to heat up, I looked in the mirror.

And despite my disheveled appearance, I had a sparkle in my eye that I'd never seen before.

And that sparkle was the knowledge that Shane Jennings was worth the wait.

FORTY FOUR
- Shane -

Izzy pretended she was done grilling me about the mystery woman in my room, but I knew she was merely preparing for another attack.

Sure, I might've behaved the same if I'd shown up and found someone in her bed, but that was different. It was my job to protect her.

Whereas she was just being nosy.

"What can I get you folks?" the middle aged waitress said at a volume that was barely audible over the busy brunch crowd.

"Can I have the eggs Benedict?" Izzy asked. "And a black coffee, please?"

The waitress scribbled for a second and then looked at me. "Meat Lover's Omelette, sir?"

"That's right."

She raised her eyebrows. "And a large order of cheesy hash?"

I smiled. "Please."

Izzy kicked me under the table. "Andi said you'd know what she wanted."

"Oh." I pretended to think for a second. "And one-what's the omelette that has all the vegetables in it?"

"The Supreme," the waitress said.

"That's it. And one of those, please."

"Coming right up," she said, turning towards the kitchen.

"She knew just what you wanted," Izzy said. "Is she the mystery woman?"

I laughed. "You got me."

"I didn't know you were into older women."

I shrugged. "What can I say? A retiree has more time to devote to my needs."

She shuddered and pulled her elbows off the table. "You're disgusting."

"A lot of people react that way at first," I said. "But when they see our sex tape, it's really easy to see how much chemistry we have."

She raised a hand between us. "Eww. Shane. Please refrain from spoiling my appetite. I really need to eat. I've done nothing but drink coffee all day and I-"

I stopped listening. In fact, I think all the noise got sucked out of the room when Andi walked in. She was in a thin teal sweater and dark skinny jeans, and her damp hair fell in loose waves around her face.

The first thing she did was lift her eyes towards her regular table. That's when they met mine.

And if there had been any doubt left that this was the real thing, it was gone. I would never get sick of meeting her gaze across a crowded room, of the swelling in my chest I felt when she headed my way.

She was like all the best things about being home, but I could take her anywhere.

Izzy must've seen her catch my eye, too, because she looked over her shoulder and pushed her chair back in one swift motion.

At the same instant, Andi tore her smiling eyes off mine and focused on Izzy, waving as she weaved through the tables.

I redirected my attention to her swaying hips, my mouth watering at the memory of the previous night.

"Hello my love," Andi said, pulling Izzy into a big hug. "It's so good to see you."

"You too," Izzy said, twisting Andi from side to side. "Your timing is perfect." She let go and took a step back. "We just put the order in."

"Oh good," Andi said.

"Here-" Izzy pointed to her pulled out chair. "You sit here, and I'll scoot in next to Shane so I can look at your gorgeous face."

"What about my gorgeous face?" I asked.

Izzy shrugged. "Meh."

Andi took the seat across from me, her face looking slightly more flushed than usual as she smiled back and forth between me and Izzy.

The waitress came by a moment later and poured a round of coffees.

"The waitress knew what Shane wanted to eat," Izzy said after she was out of earshot.

"Weird," Andi said. "Maybe she has a little crush."

"Seems likely," Izzy said. "Speaking of which, do you have any idea who was hiding out in Shane's room this morning?"

"I know he was seeing a blonde sorority girl a while back."

I fixed my eyes on Andi. "She's dead to me."

Andi shrugged. "Sorry, Iz. That was my best guess."

I sighed. "It was just some girl. Let it go so we can enjoy our breakfast."

"Normally I would," she said. "But after what you said-"

Andi raised her eyebrows. "Which was?"

Izzy leaned back in her chair and folded her arms. "He doesn't want to tell me yet because he thinks he's falling in love with her."

Andi's eyes grew wide. "What?"

Izzy shook her head. "I know. Shane and true love, right? I'm pretty sure he's fucking with me."

"I'm not," I said, my eyes on Andi. "It's the truth."

Andi swallowed.

I stuck my leg out and leaned it against hers.

"Wow," Andi said, looking back at me. "She must be pretty special if you like her that much."

"She is," I said. "And if she likes me back even half as much as I like her-"

"I'm sure she likes you back," she said, breaking our eye contact.

"I hope so."

Izzy groaned. "It's so lame to say stuff like that and then not tell us anything, especially when we're both- wait- Andi- how is project rebound going?"

Andi's lips fell apart.

I cocked my head. "Project rebound?"

"Yeah," Izzy said. "I told Andi the fastest way to get over Mike would be to get out there and sleep with someone else asap."

"Is that so?" I asked, trying to keep a straight face.

"Wasn't there some guy in one of your classes that you were going to chat up?" Izzy asked. "What ever happened with that?"

I clenched my jaw.

"Nothing," Andi said. "Nothing at all. But it's fine. I'm over Mike. In fact, he's transferring before the end of the semester, and soon I won't even remember his face."

Izzy shrugged. "I still think it would do you good to get laid."

"I'll keep that in mind," Andi said, lifting her coffee. "And what about you?"

"What about me?" Izzy asked.

"What do we owe this surprise visit to?"

"Oh, right." Izzy shifted in her chair, crossing her legs the other way. "One of my professors is doing a guest lecture thingy here, and I get extra credit for attending."

"Cool," Andi said. "When's that happening?"

"This evening," she said. "I was hoping we could do happy hour, and I could slip away around six thirty and meet up with you guys later."

Andi nodded. "Sounds good to me."

"So what'll it be, Shane?" Izzy asked. "You think you guys can stay out of trouble while I go to this thing?"

My mouth curled into a smile. "I suppose we could try."

"Good," Izzy said. "It's settled then. I'll call you when I get out and see where you guys are-"

"We'll worry about it later," I said. "We've got loads of time until then."

"You want to stay at mine tonight?" Andi asked.

"Of course," Izzy said. "Unless I meet some dashing young suitor who wants to make sweet love to me all night."

Andi smiled. "In which case you'll have to go back to his cause Steph has been cramming like a maniac."

"Deal."

When the waitress arrived with our meals, I stole a glance at the clock and started counting down the minutes until I'd have Andi all to myself again.

There were only four hundred and fifty to go.

FORTY FIVE
- Andi -

Izzy checked her watch. "Okay, guys. I'm gonna head off." She slammed the rest of her Margarita and pushed it towards the edge of the table. "Think you can manage the rest of that without me?"

Shane and I eyed the half empty pitcher between us.

"I think we can handle it," I said. "But I might need to break for food after."

"Me too," Shane said.

Izzy scooted off her barstool. "Just text me wherever you end up, and I'll come find you."

We nodded.

"Have fun," I said. "See you later."

She sauntered towards the exit and disappeared under the flashing Corona sign.

I exhaled as soon as she was out of sight. When I turned to look at Shane, his eyes were already on me.

"Do you think she knows?" I asked.

He shook his head. "No. No way she'd be able to act that normal if she did."

"How is she not getting The Ink about this?" I squinted at him. "I figured she'd be able to pick up on our pathetic acting in a second considering the company she normally keeps."

"I think I was particularly convincing, actually."

I shook my head. "You weren't. And your obsession with trying to get me to play footsie with you was untimely and juvenile."

"You know you can't resist playing footsie with me."

"I can think of other parts of you I'd rather play with."

He raised an eyebrow. "Why don't we go back to the house and you can tell me more about that?"

"After this," I said, tapping the pitcher.

"By all means make it easy for me to-"

"We can't." I craned my neck forward. "Not when she's here. It'll be written all over my face if we-"

"It'll be worse if we don't relieve some of the tension, don't you think?"

I sighed. "Maybe."

He refilled our glasses and slid the empty pitcher beside Izzy's abandoned glass.

"When are you going to tell her?"

He shrugged. "It's weird trying to figure out how to tell her how I feel about you when I haven't even figured out how to tell you."

I dragged a fingertip along the salty edge of my glass. "That's okay. I already know how you feel."

He shook his head. "You don't know the half of it."

I drained half my glass in one go, relishing the way the tequila ignited my throat and sloshed in my empty stomach. "Do you want me to tell her?"

"After."

"After what?" I asked, watching a tray of loaded nachos go by.

"After I do," he said. "I'll tell her this weekend before she leaves. But I'm sure she'll want to hear it from you, too."

I nodded. "She deserves that much."

"I just wish I had some idea how she's going to take it."

I raised my eyebrows.

"She already gave me shit about how insensitive it was for me to get serious about someone when there's no one even on her radar."

"Everyone is on her radar."

"You know what I mean," he said. "So the fact that we've both-"

"Maybe it'll be fine. Even if it takes some getting used to, eventually she'll understand. She's not losing anything."

"Sure she is. And we're the ones gaining." He drained half his glass and licked his lips. "But I guess there's no sense in worrying about it because I'm not going to stop seeing you regardless."

"Really?"

"Really. You're like online poker to me."

I laughed. "I'm flattered."

"You should be," he said. "Though it sounded more romantic in my head."

"I believe that."

"What I mean is, there's nothing I enjoy more."

"Thanks."

"And nothing I'm less likely to give up on."

"Aww."

"And nothing that gets me as high, that gives me such a rush."

"See," I said. "Now that's sweet."

"And nothing I'm more likely to sneak off in the middle of the night to do or wake up early in the morning to do or do on my lunch break or-"

"You guys want another pitcher?" a bright eyed sorority girl asked as she collected our empties.

"No," I said. "Just an order of loaded nachos."

"Yeah," Shane said. "To go."

A few minutes later, Shane picked up the tab, and I picked up the bag with the nachos.

They were sort of an impulse buy, but I already had an appetite, and if the next half hour went the way I expected it would, we were going to be in desperate need of a snack very soon.

I let the bag dangle from my fingertips and strolled along next to him. "Fun day so far," I said, keeping my eyes on the edge of the sidewalk.

"Something about your slightly slurred speech tells me it's only going to get better."

"I'm not slurring."

He grabbed my free hand and held it loosely, making my whole body feel alive.

I looked down at where we were connected. "I don't think we've ever held hands before."

He laughed. "Maybe we did things in the wrong order."

I smiled. "It's nice."

"You should see what I can do with two hands," he said, glancing at me out of the corner of his eye.

"So what do you say we pop in a movie when we get back to yours?"

"I thought we'd pop something in alright, but it wasn't a film I had in mind," he said, pulling me down an alleyway.

"Where are we going?"

"To the fire exit."

"Cause you don't want to be seen?"

"No," he said as we entered the parking lot. "Because I'm in a hurry to get you alone."

I smiled and weaved through the sparsely populated lot after him, the butterflies in my chest crashing into each other the whole time.

When we reached the back door, he opened it and stepped to the side, letting me through first.

I started up the steps ahead of him, stopping when I reached the second floor.

He opened the door and took my hand again on his way by, leading me to his room, his grip on my hand noticeably stronger than before.

And as soon as I followed him inside, he pushed me back against his bedroom door and kissed my salt laced tongue.

I reached the nachos out to the side and lowered them until they hit the desk.

He slid his hands around my hips, the warmth and pressure off them making my insides clench.

"I hate to rush this," he growled in my ear before he pulled my soft sweater over my head. "But it's been far too long since I had you."

I arched my back and tilted my hips against him. "It hasn't even been a day."

"Like I said-" He kissed me as he unbuttoned my jeans and dragged them down over my ass. "Far too long."

FORTY SIX
- Shane -

I felt like a fucking sex addict, like if I couldn't have her in that moment I might die.

It was crazy.

I wanted her more than I wanted my next breath.

I picked her up and carried her over to the end of the bed, sucking the delicate skin of her neck as she lowered her legs again and found her footing.

"Shane," she whispered, letting her head fall to the side so the scent of her hair flooded my nose.

I took her bra off and laid my hands on her hips while she fumbled with my belt, causing a surge of desire to pulse through me.

She pulled my cock out and held the tip against her stomach, stroking it with her other hand.

A growl escaped my throat. "Turn around," I said, twisting her hips.

I pinned my dick against her ass and slid my hands up her stomach, nibbling her ear as I groped her breasts and pinched her nipples between my fingers.

She lifted her arms around my neck and pressed her ass to me, causing a bead of precum to smear across her lower back.

I slid a hand down between her legs, my palm cupping her warm snatch. "Fuck," I breathed when I discovered how wet she was.

I worked my fingers against her until I felt her tension drain into the floor. Then I slid my fingers inside her, causing her body to wilt against me.

She gasped as I scooped her out, her tightness choking my fingers as my other hand crushed her breasts against her chest.

"Bend over," I said, pushing her down until she was resting on her elbows, her perfect ass suspended in front of me.

I pulled her pants a little farther down her thighs and grabbed my dick, pushing it against her wet entrance and watching as I sank into her tight center.

She groaned when I disappeared inside her. "Oh god that feels good."

I dug my fingers into her hips and pulled back before rocking into her again.

She moaned every time, unable to hide her pleasure.

And she was so tight with her knees locked together like that, her shaking thighs sucking me balls deep again and again.

"Don't stop," she pleaded.

I bent over and laid a hand flat against her belly, pressing it towards her spine so every inch of her insides pulsed around me. With the other hand, I flicked her clit in time with the slow rhythm of my thrusts.

"You're going to make me come," she said, arching her back.

And then I felt the temperature rise in my gut like a brewing volcano.

I pulled out of her and slapped my dick against her ass-not just to buy myself time, but because I liked the sound of it, the look of it, the feel.

Then I curled my fingers around her waistband and pulled her pants down to her ankles.

She stepped out of them, and I slapped her ass, causing her to fall forwards and crawl onto the bed.

She rolled onto her back just in time to see me stepping out of my pants, my wet dick standing at attention between us.

"You feel too good, Andi," I said, crawling on the bed after her.

She was propped up on her elbows, and I moved forwards until my face was over hers. Then I lowered my lips to kiss her, realizing every kiss only got better and that I would never stop looking for the next opportunity to taste her.

I lifted my head, locked my eyes on her, and reached for one of her legs, keeping my eyes on her as I slung it over my shoulder.

Then I found her opening again and slid inside, watching the light in her eyes flicker until I hit her so deep they watered.

"Are you okay?" I asked, thrusting inside her as far as I could.

She nodded and bit her lip.

I kept moving and reached a hand down to her heat, touching her swollen clit so her lips fell apart.

She reached one hand up and ran it down my chest so gently it surprised me. "Come with me," she said, her eyes fixed on mine.

I shrugged her leg off my shoulder and picked up the pace, my balls slapping against her.

"Yeah," she whispered, wrapping her legs around me. "Right there."

I sped up again, my upper body rigid as I focused on splashing against her warm center.

A moment later, she gasped and threw her hands over her head, squeezing the pillows in her fists.

When her eyelids fell to half mast, I felt the first wave of her orgasm choke my cock, and I drove inside her, emptying my desire in her belly and letting her see the need in my eyes.

She lifted her head and kissed me.

I collapsed on top of her and closed my eyes. The room was dark then except for the burst of bright, throbbing color I could feel between us where she kept squeezing me as hard as I was stretching her.

"And I thought we had fun at Six Flags," she panted.

I smiled. "Think of the money we could've saved."

She laughed.

I felt it in my dick.

"You were right," she said. "This was definitely the right call."

"So were those nachos. I'm getting stuck into those as soon as I catch my breath." I slipped out of her and laid my head between her breasts.

She dragged her nails through my hair in little swirls as her voice dropped to a whisper. "You were worth the wait, Shane Jennings."

"And you're the best thing that ever happened to me."

"Besides online poker?"

I lifted my head. "I love you, Andi."

She blinked.

"I always have."

"I know," she said.

"What do you think it would take for you to feel the same way?"

She smiled. "You could start by bringing me those nachos."

I groaned and rolled onto my side. "If I'd known it was that easy all along, I would've gotten this party started a long time ago."

I grabbed the takeout off the desk and made my way back to the bed, getting under the sheets as she had.

"Thanks," she said, pulling the Styrofoam container out of the paper bag.

"That's really all it took?" I asked. "To win your heart?"

She looked at me out of the corner of her eye. "Well, that other stuff didn't hurt."

I watched her tuck the top of my bedsheet under her armpits, feeling completely struck by her disarming beauty.

Then I popped open the container and angled it towards her, my stomach growling at the intoxicating smell.

She lifted a cheesy chip and popped it in her mouth.

I followed her lead, snatching one with a large piece of chicken and a fresh jalapeno slice on it.

A moment later, my phone rang.

FORTY SEVEN
- Andi -

Shane was about to throw the covers off and get his phone when Izzy walked in with hers next to her ear.

I froze with a loaded nacho chip halfway to my mouth, as if that might keep Izzy from seeing me wearing nothing but the sheet I was sharing with her brother.

She dropped the arm that held her phone and the color drained from her face, her eyes darting from Shane to me to Shane to me.

Then she took a step backwards into the hall and closed the door.

I dropped the chip I was holding into the Styrofoam box and looked at Shane.

At first I felt a wave of anger that the door hadn't been locked while we were fooling around, but I was even more upset about the way we'd been caught in our lie.

They say a picture says a thousand words, but I didn't want to tell Izzy about me and Shane with a picture.

I wanted to tell her one word at a time, conjuring up as few pictures as possible.

Without speaking, we turned away from each other and tried to locate our clothes.

I was about to scoot from under the sheet and make a run for my pants when she opened the door again.

She blinked several times, as if she was convinced she was imagining the scene before her.

"I can explain everything," Shane said, the sheet pooling in his lap.

"Don't worry about it," Izzy said. "I'm pretty sure my sex ed teacher covered this in sixth grade."

"It's not what it looks like," he said.

I wanted to disappear.

Izzy scoffed. "I'm pretty sure it's exactly what it looks like."

Shane lifted his palm like a white flag. "Just give us two minutes to get dressed, and we can talk."

Her lips fell apart, but she didn't say anything more. Instead, she just pulled the door closed again.

Shane laid a hand on my arm. "I'm sorry, Andi. I know this isn't what we had in mind."

I shook my head. "I thought we had more time. I thought she was at a thing-"

"I came back to get a sweater!" Izzy shouted through the door. "But I can see why that wouldn't cross your mind considering how hot it is in there."

Shane groaned and dropped his feet to the floor, cracking the window before he walked over to collect his boxers in a bunch at the end of the bed.

I scrunched my face. "Would you mind-"

He read my mind and picked up my clothes, bringing them in a clump to my side of the bed.

"Do you think I should stay?" I asked, pulling my bra on.

"No!" Izzy yelled. "I want to talk to Shane."

"I said give us two minutes," he said, glaring at the closed door. "Not stand outside and provide commentary."

"If you don't think I get to have an opinion about this you are so wrong," she said, the anger in her voice making me feel three inches tall.

I pulled on my sweater. When my head came out the hole, Shane had his jeans back on.

I let my eyes linger over his muscled chest for a moment before he pulled his shirt over his head. Then I wiggled into my skinny jeans.

Without talking, we put the nachos away and straightened the bed.

Finally, we gathered by the door.

He turned to me and laid a hand on my face. "It's going to be okay," he said. "I promise."

I tried to take comfort in his eyes.

"There's no one I wouldn't fight for you," he whispered. "I'll make her see what a good thing this is."

I nodded and gave him a hug, pressing the length of my body against him. We fit together just right. All we had to do was make her see.

"I'm aging out here," Izzy said.

Shane opened the door. "Don't be so dramatic."

Izzy looked through me like she didn't even know me.

I felt my hands go clammy in response to her obvious disapproval. "I don't know what to say."

"You could say, 'Sorry for lying to you,'" she said. "Or 'sorry for never ever lying to you about anything and then picking this to start with.'"

I swallowed.

She shook her head. "How could you keep a secret like this from me?"

I shrugged. "Because I kept it a secret from me, too. For a long time."

She made a face like she had a bad taste in her mouth. "Don't even pretend you've always had feelings like this for him."

I pursed my lips.

"Oh my god," she said. "You actually think that?"

I glanced at Shane. "I do, yeah."

She dropped her head and stared at the floor between us.

"Why don't I stay?" I suggested. "We can all talk about it togeth-"

"I'm sure my stomach can't handle that," she said, leaning against the doorframe. "I'd rather you go and maybe I'll come by later."

I squinted. "Maybe?"

"We'll see."

I sighed. "I wanted to tell you-"

"But you were busy. I get it."

"I just didn't know how, and I didn't want to mention it before-"

"Before what?" she asked, cocking her head.

"Before we knew if it was serious."

She raised a palm between us. "What don't you understand about the fact that I don't want to talk to you right now."

Shane stepped forward. "Don't be a bitch, Izzy. She hasn't done anything wrong."

Izzy laughed. "Good one. I'm pretty sure she's done everything wrong that a best friend could possibly do, but I can see why you might not be able to-"

"She's my best friend, too," Shane said. "I know you forget that sometimes, but we've all known each other for the same amount of time."

Izzy turned to me. "Why are you still standing there?"

I felt totally defeated apart from the solace I found in Shane's face.

"You should go," he said. "It's Izzy's turn to try and make sense of this. Let's let her do it on her terms."

"Okay," I said, looking back at Izzy. "I just think it kind of sucks that her first term is for me to fuck off."

She raised her eyebrows. "So you're not deaf?"

I clenched my jaw. "Fine. I'll go. But for the record, Izzy, I'm only sorry I wasn't more upfront with you. I'm not sorry about what we've been-" I felt a pinch in my tear ducts. "I still love you, too. Just so you know."

She extended her arm out the door, inviting me to walk through it.

So I did, looking back at Shane one last time as I stepped into the hallway.

I heard the door to his room close when I was halfway to the fire exit and took a deep breath.

It was frustrating that I couldn't even begin to imagine what was going through Izzy's head. I mean, I didn't have any siblings to be protective of, siblings I had to worry about sharing with anyone else.

And I knew Shane's track record was far more varied and experienced than mine. She probably thought I was weak. Or that he'd manipulated me.

And he had. For fifteen years. By being the most handsome, interesting guy I knew.

But at the very least, I knew she and I were on the same page in that we wanted him to be happy.

If only she could believe he might find happiness with me.

FORTY EIGHT
- Shane -

I was familiar with the multitude of Izzy's expressions, but the angry one she was making just then wasn't one of my favorites.

"How could you?" she asked, the thunder gone from her voice.

I sat down on the edge of the bed. "How could I what?"

Her hands went to her head as if she were going to pull her hair out. "How could you take advantage of our best friend like this? When she's never been more vulnerable?! When she trusts you the way she-"

"Hold on a second. You think I'm using her?"

"Yeah, I do." She set her hands on the edge of my desk and hoisted herself up. "I think you got bored and forgot how much her friendship means to us- has always meant- and you stuck your dick where it didn't belong because you're lazy and it was convenient."

I furrowed my brow. "So you blame me for this?"

"I do."

I sighed.

"Should I not?" she asked. "I mean, I suppose there's a smidgeon of a chance that I'm wrong about this, but I seriously doubt it, especially considering your track record."

"What's that supposed to mean?"

"That you don't really respect any of the women you sleep with, which is why it breaks my heart that you would condemn Andi to that category."

I shook my head. "You've got it all wrong."

She cocked her head and looked at me like she'd forgotten I was a full eleven minutes older than she was.

"First of all, it's not that I don't respect the women I sleep with, okay? I just don't love them. There's a difference, and you and I both know those things aren't mutually exclusive."

"What are you saying?" She turned an ear towards me. "That you love her?"

"Yeah," I said with a lack of hesitation that surprised even me. "I do."

Izzy rolled her eyes. "Oh please, Shane. I just caught you in a post coital nacho fest two minutes ago, and now you want to tell me you're in love?"

"Yeah. Head over fucking heels."

She put her feet on my desk chair, her elbows on her knees, and her face in her hands.

"And that's why you shouldn't be mad at me. Because I'm not treating her like all the other girls. I know she's different, and I'm treating her accordingly."

She peeked at me through her fingers. "And where is this going?"

"What?"

"You and Andi."

I shrugged. "I don't know. Far if I have anything to say about it."

She dropped her hands. "Far?"

I nodded. "But I didn't want to say anything to you until I knew that."

"And now you know?"

"In every bone in my body."

"Let's leave your body out of it," she said. "It's probably what got you into this mess."

"Fair enough."

She sighed. "I still don't get how this even started? You never felt this way before."

"Actually, I think I did. I just didn't recognize the feeling for what it was because she'd always been such a big part of our lives."

"So what changed?" she asked. "What made you suddenly see her as a woman and not as a sister?"

"I never really saw her as a sister."

"Sure you did."

I shook my head. "No. I'm pretty sure I realized you guys were different as soon as you hit puberty."

"But you never said anything? Even back then?"

"Because I was a pubescent bundle of horniness who couldn't make sense of myself, much less my relationship to anybody else."

She pursed her lips. "Mmm. I suppose that is pretty much how I remember it."

"Thanks."

"But I still don't get what happened that made you guys get together. After all this time…"

"A few weeks ago, Mike pushed her around- scared the shit out of her. She showed up here bleary eyed with a busted lip."

Her face dropped. "Shit."

"She asked if I would go get her stuff from his place."

"Uh-huh."

"So I did, and when I came back, I wanted to keep an eye on her. Plus, I felt guilty about the fact that I'd basically been avoiding her ever since she started dating Mike-"

"She mentioned that."

"So I asked her to stay the night."

Izzy raised her eyebrows.

"Anyway, at some point she started worrying about her busted lip- that it wouldn't heal, that it looked like shit. So I kissed it. Just where it was cracked. Just to shut her up."

She narrowed her eyes at me.

"And I felt something."

"What?"

"A shift? A craving? I don't know. But I knew I didn't want to let her slide back into the periphery of my life again."

"So you started seeing more of her."

I nodded. "I took her to my barn dance- like you suggested. I figured she needed a reminder about how she deserved to be treated."

"Sure."

"And that's sort of when we started getting to know each other better."

"And all this time you've both been lying to me about it?"

"It's more like we wanted to make sense of our own feelings before we tried to articulate them to the only person we care about as much as we care about each other."

She groaned. "You are such a jerk. I can't even stay mad at you."

One corner of my mouth curled up.

"I suppose I had The Ink on some level that there was chemistry between you."

I raised my eyebrows.

"Like when we used to go to your football games, I always felt like there was something in her eyes that wasn't in mine. Like she was way more worried about you getting hurt or something."

I turned an ear towards her.

"And sometimes when you guys used to pick me up after theater practice, there would be this weird energy in the car, this tension."

I hooked my thumbs in my pockets.

"And of course the way you treated Steven after he asked her to the spring dance senior year was highly suspicious."

"That's because he asked her before I did."

"You asked her?"

"Casually. But also completely seriously."

"And now you're in love with her, huh? Just like that. Like so much that you genuinely don't want to be with other people?"

I leaned back on straight arms. "Like so much I don't even notice other people."

She smiled.

"It's like brain drain or something. I swear I've never felt so stupid and happy at the same time."

"Sounds like love alright."

"It's not anything I've felt before anyway, but it definitely feels like a good thing. Like a lasting thing."

She crossed her legs. "Does she know how strongly you feel?"

"I've mentioned it," I said. "So I think she knows."

"Uh-huh."

"Plus, my new favorite hobby is thinking of ways to show her how crazy she makes me so-"

"And where does she stand?"

"That's harder to say. She doesn't exactly wear her heart on her sleeve quite as much as I'm willing to."

"I'll talk to her," she said. "And get to the bottom of it."

I sighed. "Sounds good. Because if she doesn't feel the same way, I really need to reel it in."

FORTY NINE
- Andi -

I'd finally accepted the fact that I'd be spending the night alone when I heard a knock at the door.

I hopped towards it while pulling on a pair of thick chenille socks. "Coming!"

Izzy's face looked spoon shaped in the peephole.

"Hi," I said, opening the door.

"I'm sorry about the way I spoke to you earlier." She shifted her overnight bag on her shoulder and lifted the hand that held a wine shaped brown bag. "Can I come in?"

"Of course." I took a step back, relieved that I hadn't quite given up and put my pajamas on considering how put together she always looked. "I'll get some cups."

She closed the door and set her stuff down while I went to retrieve the last two clean wine glasses from the kitchen cupboard.

"Is it a twist off?" I asked, opening the cutlery drawer with my free hand.

"You know it."

I closed the drawer with my hip and met her by the couch.

She waited until I was in the room to sit down.

Then she opened the wine and poured two generous glasses before sliding one towards me.

"So." I lifted the glass and put a bent leg on the couch between us. "Your thing got out early?"

"Yeah." She took a quick sip and set her glass down again. "I think my professor thought he would be playing a bigger role in the pre-screening commentary. He blatantly got cut off. I imagine he's pretty embarrassed."

"Mmm."

"I think he'll probably still give me extra credit, though, for not telling anyone how totally underwhelming his speech was."

I nodded. "And then you got cold?"

"Yeah. I figured I'd swing by the house and grab a sweater from my bag before I met up with you guys again."

I swallowed.

"So." She pursued her red lips. "I guess you're fucking my brother."

My throat solidified.

"Sorry." She scrunched her face. "I didn't mean for that to sound so accusatory. I'm just still trying to get used to the idea."

I took a sip of wine.

"Which I guess is the only thing to do since Shane pretty much told me in no uncertain terms that he's completely smitten and doesn't really care whether or not I give you guys my blessing."

"I do," I said. "I care."

"No you don't. Or you would've mentioned it before you passed go and collected two hundred dollars."

"I still care, Izzy." I took a deep breath. "I spent the last fifteen years trying to convince myself there was nothing more between us than friendship because I didn't want to mess up what the three of us had, what we still have-"

"So what changed?"

397

I shrugged. "I think it has something to do with the completely crap string of relationships I've gotten myself into over the last few years."

She slipped her flats off and pulled her feet up on the couch. "Go on."

"I mean, take Mike for example."

"Sure."

"I was physically afraid of him."

Her face drooped, and I saw real pain in her eyes, pain that told me she still cared.

"And that fear turned me into someone I didn't recognize, someone who told lies and acted like a doormat. I started apologizing for everything until I was blue in the face."

"I noticed that last habit for sure. It was pretty annoying."

"It all sort of came to a head one night in his stairwell. I nearly knocked my teeth out trying to get away from him. And I went to Shane for help because I didn't know where else to go, and I knew I could trust him."

"Of course."

"Not that I can't trust you, but he was here and-"

"I understand. Please continue."

"Anyway, I felt safe with him, and knowing I could trust him was like finding water in the desert or something- like way after I'd forgotten how to drink, if that makes sense."

She narrowed her eyes at me over her glass.

"And then he kissed my busted lip really gently, and not only did I feel for the first time in ages like there was light at the end of the dark tunnel of shit I was in, but I felt pretty and feminine and desirable in a way I hadn't felt in years."

"Uh-huh."

"And the next time he kissed me wasn't that gentle, but it was just as wond-"

"Moving on," she said. "Was the lying to me about it just a reflex then since you'd been telling so many lies recently?"

I cast my eyes into my glass before looking back at her.

She raised her eyebrows. "Well?"

"No. It was because when he kissed me, it opened the flood gates on all these feelings that I'd been trying to suppress for so long, and even I didn't know what to make of them, what to label them, what to do with them-"

"Besides investigate?"

I nodded.

"And now that you've thoroughly-" She cleared her throat. "Investigated, what conclusions have you drawn?"

"I want to be with him, Izzy."

She didn't blink.

"And I think he wants to be with me, too."

"He does."

I raised my eyebrows.

"He's crazy about you."

One side of my mouth curled up.

"He always has been."

I took a sip of wine.

"And I should've known. Or not been in denial. I just didn't want things to change, ya know?"

"I wouldn't say he's always been crazy about me."

"No. He has. I just refused to acknowledge it despite my inklings. But now it seems so obvious."

I shook my head. "I don't think there was anything to pick up on before-"

"There was." She leaned forward, grabbed the bottle, and topped up both our glasses. "He used to treat you differently, talk about you differently. I thought it was just because we'd all been so close for so long, but it was more than that."

"I'm not sure what you mean."

"Like in fourth grade, for example. You know how he used to let you almost beat him at tetherball because he liked playing with you more than anyone else?"

"He didn't almost let me anything. I was good."

"Oh please. No one in the school could even give him a run for his money. You think you were ever really close?"

I bit the inside of my cheek.

"And when you busted your face falling off that skateboard-"

"Because of your shitty bike riding."

She nodded. "I accept that."

"Good."

"Anyway, the way his face fell when he saw how badly you'd been hurt-" She shook her head. "I should've realized that day something was up."

My lips fell apart.

"He'd get more upset when you got hurt than he ever got about anything."

"He didn't like when you got hurt either."

"True," she said. "But that was more a sense of obligation than anything. With you there was something else. He'd be, like, physically sick and unable to eat when you were hurt- or even upset."

"But both of you guys were like that."

She shook her head. "No. Don't get me wrong, I love you like a sister-"

I felt my chest loosen.

"But he's the one that used to bring extra socks when we went sledding because he knew your feet always got cold. And he's the one that used to save the blue and pink sour gummy worms cause he knew they were your favorite. He's even the one that called the dentist to find out how soon you'd be able to enjoy a milkshake after you got your wisdom teeth pulled."

I stared at her.

"It was always him. He was always thinking about you, conscious of you, borderline obsessed with your wellbeing."

I swallowed.

"I thought he was just a nice guy, but it was you all along."

"We were just kids then, Izzy."

"Maybe in the beginning. Until your Tiger Lily bikini came into the picture."

I laughed.

"Seriously, though. I mean, he stopped talking to Steven altogether after he asked you to that dance."

"He did?"

"And he never even told me he asked you."

I pursed my lips.

"Until an hour ago. And neither did you."

"Maybe we did know," I said. "Maybe all three of us were in denial."

"Perhaps. But I should've picked up on it years before that. I should've known as soon as he made up that game."

I furrowed my brow. "What game?"

"That Oreo thing you guys do."

"Oh please. We were seven. Besides, I thought you guys picked that up at your old school?"

"No," she said. "Shane made it up."

"He did?"

"Probably so he could get to know you better."

"When?"

She smiled. "The day he found out Oreos were your favorite."

F I F T Y
- Shane -

I'd lost track of how many times I'd forced myself to stop shaking my leg.

"Here, honey," Brittney said, setting a beer down next to Kevin before draping a hand over his shoulder. "You sure you guys don't need anything?"

I was the only one that lifted my eyes from the card table. "I'm good, thanks."

She bent down and gave Kevin a kiss on the cheek. "I'll call you when I'm done with my thing."

"Sure, babe. Sounds good," he said, glancing away from his cards for a moment to offer her a quick smile.

"Things seem to be going well with Brittney," I said after she left.

Kevin nodded and played a card. "No shit. She wants me to meet her family over Thanksgiving break."

I raised my eyebrows. "That was quick."

He shrugged. "That was my first reaction, too. And then I realized what a lucky bastard I am that a girl like her would even give me the time of day."

I laughed. "Oh c'mon. You don't smell that bad."

"Very funny," he said, glancing at me out of the corner of his eye. "What about Andi?"

"What about her?"

"How's it going?"

I glanced up at the other two guys. Fortunately, they were as cool as they were introverted so I knew I could trust them. "I don't know."

"What do you mean you don't know?"

I pulled my phone out and checked it, but neither Izzy nor Andi had sent me anything. All I had was a message about wheelchair basketball being moved a half hour earlier the next day.

"Shane," Kevin said, dragging me back to the task at hand. "Put your fucking phone away when we're playing cards."

"Sorry, fuck." I laid my hand down. "I fold anyway."

"Answer the damn question, too," he said, leaning back in his chair. "I thought things were going well with you guys."

"They were," I said. "Until this morning."

"What happened?"

"Izzy came to town."

He looked at me. "Have you told her what's going on?"

"She sort of discovered it for herself."

He wrapped a hand around his forehead and groaned.

"I know."

"You're an idiot."

"The biggest, yeah."

"Where is she now?" he asked, laying his cards down and gesturing for the other guys to play on.

"At Andi's. Talking."

He shook his head.

"And it's kind of fucked up because Andi and I have barely made sense of things ourselves- at least out loud."

"It's hard to do that with your mouth full."

I rolled my eyes.

"What do you think will happen?"

I shrugged. "I don't know. All I know is that it's the first time losing her has crossed my mind since we first got together and it feels really bad."

He nodded.

"Like as bad as you felt last year when you got food poisoning at the Sig's cookout."

He clenched his jaw. "I'm still convinced that was a planned attack."

"I think it was just a bad burger, buddy."

He shuddered at the memory. "That is the sickest I've ever been by far."

"My point exactly."

"What are you going to do?" he asked.

"Give them more time to talk it out, I guess."

"Right."

"Then maybe show up with food."

"Can't hurt."

"But I want to do something more," I said. "Assuming Izzy doesn't totally fuck everything up."

"More?"

"I want to do something to show Andi how serious I am about her."

"You mean something to prove you're not the serial dating womanizer you were before she came along."

"I wasn't that bad."

He laughed. "You're the only guy who's hooked up with the Camden twins at the same time, and you still can't tell them apart."

"That's not true. One of them has a tattoo on her hip."

He narrowed his eyes at me. "Which one?"

I scrunched my face. "Chloe?"

He shook his head. "You're an idiot."

"Claire?"

"If you weren't my friend, I would hate your guts, you know that?"

"And I wouldn't put up with your disgraceful beer pong skills," I said. "But my point is, I'm not that guy anymore. And I want Andi to know that I like the version of myself that I am with her, that I want us to go-"

"What is this?" Brandon asked from across the table. "Dr. Fucking Phil? Do you guys want to play cards or can you not concentrate when you're on your periods?"

"Don't be a prick," I said, pushing my cards and chips across the table.

Kevin did the same. "You guys can see that I'm obviously Dr. Phil in this case, right? Not the head case on the couch?"

"All I see is two soppy tampons," Brandon said, looking back and forth between us.

I tilted my head to the couch across the room, and we carried our beers over.

"Sorry to gush," I said, sinking into the ancient three seater.

"You aren't gushing," he said. "Trust me. I'd cut you off if you were gushing."

"So you think you'll go meet Brittney's family?"

He nodded. "I'd wear thong underwear and blush if it would make that girl happy."

I laughed. "Looks like we left the table just in time."

"Whatever. Brandon's just bitter because he's in love with Claire Camden."

"Oh shit. I didn't realize."

410

"She's the one with the tat, by the way."

"Right." I scrunched my face and wished I felt guiltier for not giving a fuck.

"Anyway, I guess Izzy didn't take the news well?"

I took a sip of beer. "She nearly walked in on us, Kev. I don't know how I could even let that happen. It's like love's made me stupi-"

"Whoa whoa whoa."

"What?"

"Did you say love?"

"Yeah."

"Now you're gushing."

I sighed. "I know. And I don't even care. It's like that scene in Elf when-"

"Elf?"

"Yeah, the Christmas movie."

"Let me guess," Kevin said. "That's Andi's favorite?"

"Actually, she prefers the one with the Island of Misfit Toys."

He smacked his forehead with his palm. "There is only one best Christmas movie."

I raised my eyebrows and tipped my beer against my lips.

"Home Alone."

"What are you five?"

"It's a fact."

"Whatever," I said. "All I was going to say was that I like that part where Buddy the Elf is jumping around being like, 'I'm in love I'm in love and I don't care who knows it!'"

"Of course he's in love. Who wouldn't fall for Zooey Deschanel? She's ridiculously hot."

"You're missing the point."

"No, I'm not. I get it. I do. I get that we only had to make it one more year to graduate as free men, and we've fucked it all up."

"Yeah. That's about the size of it." And yet, I was looking forward to the future more than ever now that I believed Andi might play a big part in it.

"Does Andi know you've gone soft in the head?"

"I don't think so," I said. "But only cause I've distracted her by being so hard everywhere else."

Kevin dropped his head on the back of the couch. "You're so lame."

"You would know," I said. "I saw you across the Quad last week."

He lifted his head and furrowed his brow. "When?"

"Wednesday," I said. "Right after Brittney asked you to hold her purse."

He groaned.

"But don't worry. I think you successfully managed to hold it far enough away from your body that no one would've mistaken it for your bag."

"You're a dick."

"I don't think it's that black and white myself, but-"

And then it hit me.

FIFTY ONE
- Andi -

I furrowed my brow. "Are you for real?"

She nodded. "To be honest, he made up lots of games when we were little, but that one was different because he didn't play it with anyone else."

"He played it with you."

"Yeah. If you were around."

"Not only then-"

"Yes," she said. "Only then."

"I don't know what to make of that information."

"You don't have to make anything out of it. I'm only telling you because I spent the hour before I showed up here walking around campus, trying to figure out how I could've failed to realize there was something between you guys."

"Especially considering how accurate your inklings usually are."

"Don't be a smart ass," she said. "I was right about The Rapture."

I laughed. "You mean about it not happening?"

"Yeah. And I picked up on Ashton Kutcher's genuine love for Mila Kunis even before he married Demi Moore."

"True. You did totally call that one."

"And I don't even know them," she said. "Meanwhile, the two people I love most in the world loved each other for fifteen years right in front of me, and I failed to see the signs."

"It's not like the signs were obvious."

"Are you kidding? Didn't you hear me say that he literally never spoke to Steven again after he found out he felt you up at that dance."

I shrugged. "I had to throw him a bone. He was such an attentive date."

She rolled her eyes.

"I didn't do it to hurt Shane."

Hazel Kelly

"I know," she said. "And he knows. But, like, I remember the look on his face at the dinner table when I told my family you got accepted here-"

"Is that Izzy I hear?" Steph asked as she came around the corner.

"Steph!" Izzy stood up and went to give her a hug. "I didn't realize you were home."

I rose to my feet. "I didn't know if you were taking visitors this evening in light of all the studying you've been doing, but seeing as how you're all decked out, I sincerely apologize. Can I get you a glass of-?"

"Did you know about Shane and Andi?" Izzy asked, still hugging her.

"I did," Steph said, making a face at me that gave away the fact that Andi was squeezing her a bit hard. "And I've never seen either of them so happy. I think they're ridiculously cute together."

Izzy loosened her grip and stepped back. "Because I agree- or would like to as soon as possible- I'm not going to kill you for not telling me."

Steph smiled. "That is so awesome of you because I actually have to be somewhere."

I cocked my head. "I'm guessing it's not the library since I can smell your soft curls from here?"

Steph raised her shoulders. "I have a date."

"Lord knows you've earned it," I said. "Who's the lucky guy?"

"I met him at the retreat. He's a grad student."

"Medicine?" I asked.

She nodded.

"He's taking me to Tortellini's," she said, smoothing down the red dress that had successfully survived the dry cleaners.

I smiled. "Wow. So he either really likes you, he's rich, or you're about to meet his parents."

Her eyes sparkled. "I'm pretty sure it's the first one, but obviously I'll keep you posted."

"You look gorgeous," Izzy said.

I nodded. "No kidding. I almost forgot how well you clean up since you've been such a monk lately."

"Yeah, well. It's been a while and-" She bent over and set her high heels on the floor. "All this being around you and Shane lately has made me think I might need to make time for-"

"Little Steph?" Izzy asked.

Steph flinched.

"Please excuse her," I said. "She's been drinking all day."

Izzy shrugged. "It's true."

"I was going to say other interests, but you're not wrong," Steph said.

I turned an ear towards her. "Will you be coming home tonight or-"

"Obviously," she said. "Who do you think you're talking to?"

I lifted my palms towards the ceiling. "I don't know. The fanciest thing I've seen you in lately is pajamas that actually match, and now you're here with your legs shaved above the knee so I didn't want to be presumptuous."

Steph pursued her lips and suppressed a smile. "I suppose I do appreciate you pretending that I'm capable of slutting it up a bit."

"Of course you are," Izzy said. "Besides, at the end of the day we're all just Julia Roberts in Pretty Woman on the inside."

Steph laughed. "Glad to see you're not too drunk to make film references."

"Never," Izzy said. "If anything, drink makes it worse."

A moment later, "Ain't No Mountain High Enough" started playing in Steph's purse. "That's him," she said. "I better go."

"Have fun," I said. "We won't wait up."

Steph rolled her eyes and grabbed her purse, giving Izzy another cheek press on the way out.

"Damn," Izzy said after she closed the door. "She was decked the fuck out."

"I know," I said, topping up our glasses and holding the bottle up to the light to see how much was left. "I'm kind of thrilled for her. She's literally been behaving like a vampire to keep up with her coursework."

Izzy shook her head. "Becoming a doctor is too much trouble. I couldn't do it."

"At least she knows what she wants to do," I said. "Like you do. And Shane. Sometimes I feel like I'm just drifting."

"It's okay to drift. Look at Forrest Gump. He's, like, the happiest guy ever."

"Are you actually comparing me to Forrest Gump? Is that supposed to make me feel better?"

"Yeah. I'm saying you're a legend and that no matter what you end up doing, you'll bring your own special Andi-ness to it and that will be enough."

I sighed. "Want to hear something even lamer than that?"

"Sure."

"The only thing I know for sure about my future is that I want you and Shane to be in it."

She smiled. "I think that's a given considering the fact that we're The Three Musketeers. I mean, we can always take someone else on- like when I find my very own Dartanian- but no one is going to break us up."

I raised my eyebrows. "So you're cool with it?"

She shrugged. "If you guys are happy, why shouldn't I be, too? After all, my happiness is all tangled up in yours anyway, always has been."

A bright warmth swelled in my chest.

"Sure, it might take me some time to get used to the idea, but as long as I keep my imagination from considering the actual implications of your attraction to each other, I suppose I can keep my gag reflex at bay."

"Well that's a relief."

"Plus, I heard this quote the other day I really liked."

"Go on."

"It said the key to a lasting friendship is to have the same taste in alcohol and different taste in men."

"I like that."

"Me, too," she said. "And we fit that description perfectly."

"True. So now what?"

She cocked her head. "Besides opening another bottle?"

I nodded.

"Now you guys do whatever it takes to keep each other happy so you don't spoil my plans for a happily ever after."

I smiled. "Deal."

FIFTY TWO
- Shane -

I switched the bag of warm bagels to my other hand and ran my fingers through my wet hair, noticing a slight twinge in my arm where it had been crushed against a fast moving wheelchair at that morning's game.

"Shane?"

I turned away from the door and looked down the hall.

Steph was approaching in a red dress that I recognized instantly with her heels in her hand. Gently smudged eyeliner framed her eyes, which looked like they were still getting used to the light.

"Late night at the library?" I asked, my mouth curling into a smile.

"Not exactly," she said, glancing down so quickly I almost didn't see the flush sweep across her cheeks.

"Did you have a good time?" I asked, stepping away from the door.

"Yeah," she said. "Too good, in fact. I think I might celebrate by spending the day in bed."

"From what I hear you don't do that enough."

She pulled her key out of her bag and slid it in the door. "Those smell good."

"There are plenty for everyone so don't be shy."

She paused before pushing the door open. "Here for the final verdict, are you?"

"Let's put it this way, you're not the only one who didn't sleep much last night."

She opened the door, and I followed her inside. The curtains were drawn and the only sound I could hear was the kitchen clock ticking over.

"Looks like your damsels in distress didn't have any problems sleeping."

I furrowed my brow. "Did they seem distressed?"

She laid a hand on my shoulder. "I think it's going to be fine."

I swallowed.

"And for what it's worth-" She leaned over and tossed her shoes under the entryway table. "I made a point of telling Izzy that I think you guys are great together."

"You did?"

She nodded. "I did. And I meant it, too."

"Thanks, I owe you one. They both in Andi's room?"

"Most likely," she said. "But it doesn't sound like they're up so I'd take the bagels in with you if you value your life."

I smiled and stepped backwards down the hall. "You're a good friend, Steph."

"Try and save one for me," she said, nodding towards the bag.

"Sure thing."

I walked to Andi's door and knocked lightly before pushing it open. Izzy was curled up and facing the wall while Andi's face was crushed against the pillow closest to the door.

I moved to the side of the bed, squatted down beside her, and ran a few fingers over her temple.

She opened her eyes and smiled as she closed them again, taking my hand in hers and curling it against her warm chest.

"Morning sleeping beauty."

She sighed.

"How did last night go?" I whispered as I scooted the bag of bagels to the side.

She opened one eye. "Sleeping beauty can only be awakened with a kiss."

"Oh right." I leaned forward and laid my lips so gently on hers it made my whole body burn.

She opened her sleepy eyes- which looked darker than usual when framed by her messy bedhead- and scooted over to the middle of the bed, patting the empty space she'd vacated.

I sat down and leaned back against the pillows, marveling at how much more interesting a woman's personal space seems when you're consumed by her.

Her closet was closed, but a few colorful shirt sleeves were jammed in the door, and her desk was covered in a stack of books, each of which seemed to have a highlighter as their bookmark.

Above her desk there was a small speaker and a few pictures, including the one Izzy took of us the day Andi nearly died from heat exhaustion trying to perfect her layup. My heart swelled at the memory.

I was so proud of her for not giving up. And the smile that lit up her face when I gave her the picture for Secret Santa, well, it kept me awake for days.

She scooted towards me and laid her head and a hand on my chest.

I lifted an arm and wrapped it around her.

"Did you have basketball this morning?" she asked.

"Yeah. We got whooped," I said. "Our second best guy couldn't make it, and they showed up with a bunch of new plays."

"Sorry."

"It's cool. It's the only time I actually don't mind losing. The kids were so pumped you'd think they won the lottery."

She gave me a little squeeze.

"So how did things go last night?"

"Fine. Izzy was… surprisingly understanding."

"Surprisingly?!" Izzy said, rolling onto her back and propping herself up on her elbows. "Am I usually not?"

Andi laughed. "No you are," she said, rolling away from me. "I was just nervous is all."

"I told her I knew all along," Izzy said, her eyes on me. "In fact, my only regret is that I didn't think to set you guys up in the first place, in which case I could've taken credit for your sickening happiness."

"So we have your blessing?" I asked, raising my eyebrows.

"Yeah." She sat up against the wall. "Seems like she's just as crazy about you as you are about her, so who the hell am I to get in the way? I'd only lose you both if I tried."

Andi shot me a look that said she knew as well as I did that Izzy would need time to get used to the idea.

Then she rolled over and pulled Izzy into a hug. "We wouldn't be The Three Musketeers without you."

"So true," she said, pushing Andi away with a groan. "Besides, I suppose the only real change is that I used to sleep in the middle."

"We also used to fit in a bed a lot better than this," Andi said.

"Yeah." Izzy cocked her head. "We'd never fit on the pullout now."

"No shame in trying," I said, elbowing Andi.

Izzy rolled her eyes.

I smiled.

"What is that divine smell?" Izzy asked, taking a big sniff.

"I got bagels," I said, leaning down to grab them. "Fresh from Newton's."

Andi raised her eyebrows. "Please tell me you remembered the tubs of cream cheese this time."

"As if I'd ever make that mistake again," I said, remembering her horror at my previous oversight.

"Thanks," Andi said, pulling the bag close. "Did they have any of the ones I like with the-"

"Blueberries?" I asked, raising my eyebrows.

She glanced at me through smiling eyes. "You're the best."

"Thanks," I said.

"Make sure you remember to tell him again in five minutes," Izzy said. "He never tires of hearing that."

"Noted," Andi said.

"Do you guys want me to get you some plates or a knife or something?" I asked.

They looked at each other, each poised with a bagel in one hand and an open tub in the other.

"I think we're good," Andi said. "But if you need one-"

I raised my palms. "No. I'm good if you are."

Izzy clutched her bagel to her chest. "Awww. I want that."

I rolled my eyes. She didn't know what the hell she wanted.

But I did.

I wanted the gorgeous brunette beside me with the smudge of blueberry cream cheese on her cheek.

And that was never going to change.

FIFTY THREE
- Andi -

Shane and I were chilling on the couch when Izzy came down the hall looking fresh faced with her overnight bag packed and ready. She sat down in the chair by the end of the couch and looked back and forth between us.

"What?" I asked, looking at Shane beside me and then back at her.

She shrugged. "You guys are kind of cute together-"

I smiled.

"If I let myself forget who you are for a second."

I rolled my eyes.

"You better get used to it," Shane said.

Izzy clasped her hands. "I'm trying. Trust me."

"When do you have to be back at school?" I asked.

Izzy glanced at the clock on the wall. "I'm giving a girl from one of my classes a ride back at noon," she said. "She's meeting me back at the frat house so I probably shouldn't keep her waiting."

"We should leave now then," I said, rising to my feet.

Izzy shook her head. "You guys are good. I'll say good bye here and text you when I get home."

I furrowed my brow. "Are you sure? We're happy to walk you-"

"Really, it's fine. As amusing as it is for me to watch you guys try and keep your hands to yourselves, I think I'll leave you to it."

I pursed my lips.

"I'm too young to be an aunt, though, so please use protection."

I cocked a hip. "Jeez, we're not that bad."

"Preferably two types," she added.

"Well-" Shane set his hands on his knees and stood up. "Now that you've spoken your mind, I'd like to request that you never ever reference that aspect of our relationship again. Otherwise, I'll consider it an invitation to speak freely and in great detail about the exact-"

I squeezed my eyes shut.

Izzy clamped her hands down over her ears and starting humming "The Song That Never Ends."

I laughed. "I don't know if it's a good thing or a bad thing that we all still turn into children around each other."

Izzy craned her neck forward. "Further proof that we aren't ready to have them, don't you think?"

Shane raised a finger at her. "This is your final warning, Iz."

"Okay, okay," she said, lifting her palms in concession. "The topic of whatever you guys do behind closed doors is officially off the table."

Shane folded his arms. "Good."

"Assuming you lock said doors going forward."

I felt my cheeks burn. "Sorry about that again."

"It's fine," she said. "Two minutes earlier and I'd probably be in therapy right now, but as long as we've all learned from the close call-"

"We have," I said.

"Excellent." She stood up. "In that case, I only have a few more requests."

I raised my eyebrows.

"I want you both to promise me three things," she said, pointing a finger back and forth between us.

"Go on," I said, stepping beside Shane so we were shoulder to shoulder.

"Promise you won't hurt each other."

"I promise," we said in unison.

She bent over and pulled her shoes on without taking her eyes off us. "Promise you'll never take each other for granted."

I glanced at him. "You have my word."

"And lastly-" She yanked her high ponytail with both hands so it tightened against her head. "Promise that we'll always be best friends first, above all."

Shane nodded. "You got it."

"Good," she said. "I think those things- along with my agreeing to remain ignorant about the finer points of your relationship- will go a long way to making sure this never gets weird."

"That's very thoughtful of you," I said, pulling her into a hug.

She squeezed me tight.

"It really means a lot to me that you're okay with this."

"Me too," Shane said, his arms closing around both of us.

We stood there like that for a moment, and I swear I felt so cocooned by warmth and love I thought tears might spill down my cheeks.

"Are you sure we can't walk you back?" I asked when we'd all taken a step back.

"Positive," Izzy said. "I'll see you guys at Thanksgiving break."

"We'll pick you up," Shane said, opening the door. "If your schedule gets out at the same time."

"Sounds good," she said. "Give my love to Steph."

Izzy hugged Shane one more time and then disappeared down the hall.

As soon as she was out of sight, I closed the door and turned towards Shane. "I'm glad that's over," I said, dropping my shoulders.

"Over?" He raised his eyebrows and slipped his hands around my waist. "I'm pretty sure this is only the beginning." He pulled me to him.

"Thank you," I said, laying a hand on his chest.

"For what?"

"For whatever you said to her before she came over."

He leaned his face down and rested his forehead against mine. "You don't need to thank me. But if you insist, I have a few good ideas for how you might try."

I tilted my head back and pressed my lips to his.

"And don't forget the blueberry bagels," he said, leaning his hips against mine. "There must be a reward I can collect for remembering those."

A coil of warmth tightened inside me. "I'll do just about anything for those blueberry bagels."

"Careful now. I'll hold you to that."

"Did you see Steph this morning?" I asked. "Do you know if she's gone out or-"

"She's going to be sleeping all day."

I furrowed my brow. "Really? Did she say that?"

"She did, yeah. When she got home this morning."

"This morning?"

"Around the time I arrived," he said. "In a little red dress that- if I recall correctly- looked really good on the chair in my room."

"Damn," I said, running a hand through my hair. "She must've had the night of her life."

"Let's go have the day of ours," he said, lifting me by the waist.

I wrapped my arms around his neck and my legs around his hips.

"Before I collect my thank yous right here on your welcome mat."

I smiled into his neck as he carried me to my room and locked the door behind us without setting me down.

Then he sat on the edge of the bed and held my waist so I could lean back and look at him, my body temperature rising as I felt him swell beneath me.

"God there are so many ways I want you," I whispered. "I don't even know where to start."

"Then let me," he said, laying me on my back. He lowered himself over me and opened my mouth with his, swirling his tongue around mine.

My feet dangled off the edge of the bed, and I felt like I was floating as he slid his big hands up under my loose tank top and dropped his lips to my neck.

I grabbed the bottom of his shirt and dragged it up so I could admire the way his muscles moved over me, and he stopped touching my body just long enough to pull it off over his head.

A moment later, I felt his warm breath on my chest, and my nipples puckered for his attention.

By the time his thick fingers found the zipper on my pants, my insides were already flooded with anticipation.

I lifted my head just in time to see him sink to his knees at the side of the bed, dragging my shorts and underwear down with him.

And when he draped my thighs over his shoulders and licked my wet heat, I dropped my head back and dug my fingers into the comforter beneath me.

FIFTY FOUR
- Shane -

Her body was going crazy for me.

Each curl of my tongue seemed to work her into a deeper frenzy, and from time to time, I'd feel her thighs come together around my head, locking my face between them as she writhed with pleasure.

And she tasted like candy- like those big bags she used to get at the movie theatre that always cost a fortune because even the most disciplined moviegoer gets greedy in their presence.

And in this case, I was no different.

I couldn't get enough, and I was determined to give her one of those slow build orgasms, one that would sneak up on her for ages until she felt like she'd been dangling over the brink for an eternity.

Then I'd let her come forever, right down my throat while I savored the taste of her on my tongue.

I swear the only thing I wanted more than making her full of me was to be full of her pleasure.

And as her hot little hips squirmed against my face, I became increasingly confident that we were both going to get exactly what we wanted.

"Oh god Shane," she breathed. "I'm going to come."

I suppressed my smile and kept licking her swollen bud. She'd been telling me she was going to come for five minutes and from the amount of silk dripping down my throat, she'd already started.

She groaned and tilted her hips up, as if her body was trying to give her a break.

But I had other plans.

"It's too much," she said. "I can't stop coming."

I sank my fingers into her hips and held her still.

"Shane-" my name was a whispered secret on her lips.

And then her body shook like someone had a given her a shock, and she let out a moan that never seemed to end.

I fucked her orgasm with my tongue, splashing against her desire as she pulsed.

When her clenching began to slow, I reached down, undid my pants, and stood straight up so her legs stayed flat against my chest.

"I want in on this," I said, guiding the tip of my aching dick to her wet slit.

She inhaled sharply through parted lips, and I sank inside her tight heat.

She moaned as I drove against her center, causing vibrations in my dick that traveled up to the back of my neck.

"You feel so good," she said, looking at me through half closed eyes.

I grabbed her ankles and tried to control my speed, but between fucking her and having her taste on my lips, I was so worked up a firehose couldn't have held me off.

Her hips were off the bed as I pounded her, the slap of my balls the only sound in the room besides her panting.

Meanwhile, as I stared at her gorgeous body on the bed, I forgot how to breathe.

I kept thrusting into her, though, looking between her parted lips, her bouncing tits, and my slick cock disappearing inside her.

"Don't stop," she pleaded.

I lost the feeling in my legs.

She craned her head up to watch for a second, and I swear I got even harder.

I bent over and slid my hands under her lower back, lifting her just enough that I could slide her farther onto the bed. Then I rolled onto my side and pinned one of her legs under my top arm.

She looked at me, her eyes searching mine.

The pressure in my dick was so great I started to worry I might pass out before I released my charge inside her.

Andi lifted a hand and laid it against my jaw, her shiny eyes still on me.

I came that second, deep and hard, watching her face as I pumped her hot center full of everything I had.

And when my aching need was finally relieved- my craving for release finally satisfied- I stopped moving and tried to catch my breath.

She dropped her eyes and dragged a finger across my bottom lip. "I didn't know I could come that long."

One side of my mouth curled up, making me aware of how serious and focused my expression must've been before.

She squeezed her raised leg around me and pulled me close. "Don't pull out yet," she whispered. "I can still feel you throbbing."

"Your wish is my command."

She laughed. "I could get used to this."

"Me too." I ran a hand over her smooth thigh, pulled her against me, and admired the pink flush on her cheeks.

"What?" she asked.

"Nothing."

She furrowed her brow. "You just made a face. I saw it."

"No I didn't."

She craned her neck up. "Shane."

I sighed.

"Tell me."

"I just… I've never felt like this about someone, and I don't know what the fuck I'm doing."

Little creases sprang up around her eyes.

"Which is an odd sensation for me. I guess I feel out of my depth."

"Probably because you're so deep inside me."

"An interesting theory," I said. "But if that were the case, the feeling would go away when I eventually pull out of you, and something tells me that isn't going to happen."

She grabbed a pillow from the top of the bed and placed it where we could both lay our heads on it.

"Can I tell you something?" she asked.

"Of course."

"I don't know what the fuck I'm doing either," she said, her voice soft. "All I know is that I've never been happier and that I can't concentrate on anything."

I was relieved it wasn't just me.

"I've been keeping your picture in a drawer."

I raised my eyebrows. "What?"

"Because I can't breathe when I feel your eyes on me."

"Breathing is overrated."

Half her mouth curled into a smile. "So I'm beginning to realize."

"I guess we'll have to figure it out together," I said. "Like we've figured out everything else."

"Like foursquare and snowmen and slow dancing and the egg drop and college apps?"

I nodded. "Exactly. I'm sure this relationship thing will be no different. Someday we'll wonder what we were ever worried about."

She licked her lips. "Can I ask you something else?"

"Sure."

"In fourth grade, were you going easy on me in tetherball?"

I smiled. "Of course not. You had mad skills."

"You are so full of it."

"Actually," I said, glancing down at where we were joined. "I'm pretty sure you're the one that's full of it."

"Touché," she said. "In which case, how do you feel about making this official?"

"You're seriously asking me now? When we're conjoined?"

"Would you rather I release you first and-"

"No," I said, pulling her close. "It's fine. Of course it's official. Whatever. I don't need labels. I just need you."

She smiled.

"Though I suppose the peace of mind might make it easier for me to concentrate. Craving you has been doing my head in."

"I know the feeling," she said. "Like I said, your picture's been in a drawer."

I lifted my head towards the shelf over her desk. "That one?"

"I only put it back up so Izzy wouldn't suspect anything."

"That was a great day," I said, laying my head back down.

"They've all been great," she said, her eyes sparkling.

I rocked my hips against her again, my dick nearly ready to spring back into action. "Let's see if we can make this one our best yet."

She laughed and gave me a kiss. "I can't think of anything I'd rather do."

Epilogue
Andi

I made my way across the icy sidewalk outside my building, holding my bursting duffel bag just off the ground.

Shane grabbed it before I'd even reached the curb. "What the heck is in here?"

"Laundry."

"I hope that's not the only thing you got your mom for Christmas," he said, shoving the bag in the trunk of his jeep.

"It won't be," I said. "I just haven't had a chance to do my shopping yet with finals and-"

"Being so busy with me?" He slammed the trunk and beat me to the front passenger door.

I'd told him a thousand times he didn't need to keep opening the door for me, but he kept doing it anyway.

"Great idea," I said, knocking my boots on the side of the jeep before getting in. I watched him walk around the hood and didn't dare pinch myself. Even after all these months, the fact that we were a thing still thrilled and delighted me.

Even Steph agreed that, clearly, I'd been a doctor in a past life and saved tons of lives or invented penicillin or something because regular girls like me didn't normally get to go around with Adonises like Shane Jennings in real life.

It was obviously a dream.

And I never wanted to wake up.

"What do you mean great idea?" he asked, pressing the window defog button and checking his mirrors.

"I mean, I'll just tell my mom we're dating, and she'll be so happy she won't even notice the laundry."

He laughed. "That sounds like the perfect plan."

"Right? If only I hadn't already told her over Thanksgiving."

"If only."

He pulled into the street, which busy with other students packing their cars to go home for Christmas.

"Are you warm enough?" he asked, pulling his navy beanie off to reveal a deliciously disheveled pile of bedhead.

"Yeah," I said, unzipping my coat. "But I couldn't find my hat anywhere-"

"Glovebox," he said, pausing at a stop sign.

I popped it open and pulled out my favorite winter hat. "Where did you find it?"

"On the ground next to the car."

My face dropped.

"Don't worry. I washed it."

"You're the best," I said, shoving it back in the glove box.

"Hey what happened with that job thing?"

"Oh!" I clapped my hands and turned to face him. "I meant to tell you! My supervisor wants to keep me on for our final semester."

"That's great news."

"I know. I'm so pleased. If things keep going well, I'm pretty sure I can get a letter of recommendation from her that would at least secure an interview for me after we graduate."

"Congratulations," Shane said. "You deserve it. You've been killing yourself for those kids."

"I know," I dropped my head against the headrest. "To be honest, though, sometimes I think I'm not cut out for this counseling thing because I care too much an-"

"That's exactly why you are cut out for it, Andi."

"But what if I don't like it once I'm doing it full time?"

He shrugged. "Then you'll try something else. No biggie. All you can do is try it out and do your best."

I squinted. "And if I fail?"

"There's no shame in failing," he said. "Only in not trying."

"And they say you're just a pretty face."

He furrowed his brow. "Who says that?"

I laughed. "No one. Jeez. I'm just saying I liked your little thought nugget."

"Me, too," he said. "In fact, it reminds me of something I've been meaning to say to you-"

"What?"

"But I haven't found the perfect time."

"Well, you know what they say-" I loosened my seat belt and angled my knees towards him. "No time like the present."

He tightened his grip on the steering wheel and pulled over to the side of the road in front of the local playground.

My pulse rate quickened. "Oh my god is it serious?"

He opened the console between us, pulled out an Oreo, and held it up.

I smiled. "Double stuff for a change, huh?"

"Yeah."

"You realize it's nine o'clock in the morning?"

He smiled. "There's a first time for everything."

"You know you can just tell me whatever it is, right? You don't have to use an Oreo to-"

"Yes I do."

"Okay," I said, placing my fingers on the cookie opposite the one he was holding. "Ready?"

He nodded.

I gave the cookie a gentle twist and came away with the icing side. "Hope that wasn't your last one because I get to pick truth or-" I looked down at my half of the cookie and froze.

A circle of icing had been removed from the center and there was a small, shining ring in the middle of the cookie, the bottom of which was stuck in the icing just enough to keep it from falling out.

I looked up at Shane.

He didn't seem surprised that it was there.

My lips fell apart.

"A few months ago, we both made a lot of promises to Izzy."

I swallowed.

He took the Oreo half from my hands and carefully removed the thin ring. "But I want to make a promise to you, from me."

He held up my left hand and sucked the leftover icing off the ring, which sparkled as the small diamonds in the band caught the crisp winter sunshine.

And as he held the ring at the end of my finger, I swear time stood as still as my breath.

"I promise that I'll always be your best friend," he said, fixing his eyes on me. "And I promise that someday, when the time is right-" He slipped the ring on and slid it down my finger. "I promise I'll be a whole lot more."

I exhaled and glanced down to admire the beautiful ring. "I love it, Shane," I said, looking back at him through watery eyes. "And I love you."

He leaned across the console and kissed me. "You'd be a fool not to."

I laughed and laid a hand on his cheek. "Even then I'd still be your fool."

"And don't you forget it," he said, letting his forehead rest against mine.

"I won't," I said. "I promise."

Other books in the Soulmates Series

———————————————————

Roommates
A Stepbrother Romance

The Boy Next Door
A Small Town Romance

First Love
A Second Chance Romance

Made in the USA
Las Vegas, NV
07 January 2023